THE SPITFIRE GIRL IN THE SKIES

FENELLA J MILLER was born in the Isle of Man. Her father was a Yorkshire man and her mother the daughter of a Rajah. She has worked as a nanny, cleaner, field worker, hotelier, chef, secondary and primary teacher and is now a full time writer. She has over thirty eight Regency romantic adventures published plus four Jane Austen variations, three Victorian sagas and seven WW2 family sagas. She lives in a pretty, riverside village in Essex with her husband and British Shorthair cat. She has two adult children and three grandchildren.

THE SPITFIRE GIRL IN THE SKIES

Fenella J Miller

First published in the United Kingdom in 2019 by Aria, an imprint of
Head of Zeus Ltd

9 7 5 3 1 2 4 6 8

A CIP catalogue record for this book is available from the British Library.

ISBN 9781788548403

Aria
an imprint of Head of Zeus
First Floor East
5–8 Hardwick Street
London EC1R 4RG

www.ariafiction.com
www.headofzeus.com

To my beloved husband.

One

Glebe Farm didn't seem like home any more now that her brother Neil was buried. Ellie wished she didn't have to stay the full week of her compassionate leave but it would be unfair on her dad and Mabel to leave early.

'Ellie, love, you've not eaten anything today. You'll fade away if you don't have something.' Mabel was more than cook-housekeeper here now, she was the future Mrs Simpson and Ellie wasn't sure she was ready for more changes in her life.

'I'm sorry, every time I try and swallow my throat sort of closes up. I had some cocoa and a bit of the Victoria sandwich when I got up, so I'm fine.'

'Why don't you take the dogs for a walk, clear your head. Fred will be back from the bottom field for his lunch soon. He'll not want to see you moping about.'

Ellie bit her lip, somehow keeping back a sharp reply. Neil's funeral had only been two days ago, for heaven's sake, why was she expected to be rushing about the place so soon? It was none of Mabel's business anyway, she wasn't a member of the family yet.

'I'll do that. I'll be back in time for lunch.' Jack and Jasper, the two dogs they'd rescued from Battersea, were delighted to be taken for an extra stroll – not that they needed any exercise as they were always racing about the place catching rats, chasing rabbits and generally enjoying themselves.

Every time she called Jack it made her think of the other Jack in the family. He was a fighter pilot as Neil had been, but he was flying a Hurricane not a Spitfire. Everyone believed the Germans were about to invade and he was going to be at the forefront of the fighting.

George, her one remaining brother, was also a fighter pilot. However, he had severed the link between Glebe Farm and himself and was now firmly in the same camp as her obnoxious fascist grandfather, Sir Reginald Humphrey, and her estranged mother. She no longer considered either of them as part of her life and would probably never know if George was killed in the line of duty.

Jack Reynolds was like her brother now – the only one she'd got. If anything happened to him she wouldn't be able to cope. Pushing that miserable thought aside she whistled to the dogs and walked briskly down the lane towards the farmhouse. She'd seen the tractor with Dad and the two remaining ancient labourers returning to the farm. They were about to retire, were in fact already too old to be working, but Dad was keeping them on until they wanted to go.

She waved to the team of land girls busy clearing the ditches. They didn't work every day here, they were in teams and lived in a hostel in the village and were sent out in rotation to the farms in the area. Dad owned three of them so they tended to be working for him most of the time.

There was always a hot meal at lunchtime and it was served outside on a trestle table. She didn't go out and join them as she wasn't in the mood for small talk. She hadn't been hungry since that awful call to the CO's office a few days ago when she was told that her beloved brother was dead. The fact that he had bailed out over Dover when his Spitfire had been hit should have meant he survived. He was machine gunned by a passing Messerschmitt and had been dead when he hit the ground.

Somehow being killed like this made it even worse. His death had been an unnecessary act of cruelty – he should have been safe over his own home soil and dangling from a parachute. She wished she could join Jack fighting the Germans and killing those that had murdered her brother in cold blood. She was certain no British pilot would do such a thing.

The kitchen was unpleasantly hot so she continued into the sitting room which was cooler. She wandered about picking up and reading an occasional sympathy card from those scattered along the windowsill and mantelpiece.

Did one reply to these? She didn't know the addresses of half of them. The parish magazine was no longer printed because of the paper shortage or they could have put a notice in that. Maybe the vicar would make an announcement? Anyway, she wasn't going to do it.

She couldn't even write to her friends Daisy and Mary, as by the time her letter had been sent to a central postbox and then delivered secretly to the radar station they were posted at, she would be back. Telephone calls were also banned. Even her parents and fiancé, Greg, didn't know what she was actually doing. They just thought she was involved with something to do with radio operations. It was all very hush-hush.

She would leave tomorrow. She couldn't stay here with nothing to do and too much time to think of what she'd lost. Keeping busy was the answer. Unable to settle, she made her way to her bedroom. Her eyes filled when she passed what used to be Neil's room, next to it George's room, neither of them would ever be used by her brothers again.

Perhaps there was something of Neil's left in his wardrobe she could have as a memento and take back with her. Of course, she had a photograph but something more personal would help with her grief. There was a war on, three families in the village had lost loved ones as well, she had to get a grip and stop wallowing in her misery. Dad and Mabel were quieter than usual but they were getting on with their lives.

She put her hand on the door of Neil's room but couldn't bring herself to open it. Too soon. Instead she went into her own bedroom and stretched out on the bed. She could hear the murmur of voices coming through the open window.

'Fred, love, I'm that worried about Ellie. She's taken this hard. I don't like to bring up the subject of her wedding, not when she's so down.'

'She was close to Neil, it'll take her a while to get used to the idea. Greg said he was going to contact the vicar and get the banns read so they could be married as soon as they can coordinate home leave. With that bastard Hitler about to invade us I don't see either of them getting time off in the next few months – so there's no rush, love. Let things settle a bit.'

Ellie was now sitting up on her bed listening. She couldn't remember the last time she'd heard her father say so much. He was a quiet man, not given to talking unless he had something pertinent to say.

He was right. The likelihood of there being a wedding in the next few weeks was zero. She wouldn't even think about the possibility that the man she loved, the man she was going to marry as soon as she could, might lose his life in the forthcoming battle. Nevertheless, planning her big day with her father and Mabel would give them something positive to think about.

What she needed was some paper and a pencil to start making notes. It would have to be simple – with rationing there was no getting enough dried fruit and sugar to make a wedding cake. At least being a farm meant they had plenty of dairy products, eggs and meat. They were only supposed to keep back what would be theirs under the rationing rules but who could possibly know if they didn't send it all to the designated shops? As long as they fulfilled their quota she was certain no one would come out and check.

As she was rummaging through the debris on her dressing table she came across the information Jack had given her about the ATA. So many pilots had been killed or injured when the BEF was evacuated from the beaches of Dunkirk they now needed every able-bodied trained flyer on active service. This meant that the RAF pilots being used to ferry aircraft, mail and personnel from base to base had been withdrawn from the Air Transport Auxiliary. Although the bigwigs in the RAF were obviously not trying to actively recruit women pilots, the form was aimed at men.

After scanning the paper, she found her fountain pen and quickly filled it in. Some details she had to leave whilst she found her logbook and copied out the hours she had spent instructing or solo flying and which aircraft she was familiar with.

Surely, they would jump at the chance of having someone with so much experience, someone who had trained dozens of young pilots for the RAF? The only downside was that she was so young – they might think her too immature to take on such a responsibility.

After blotting the form, she carefully folded it and pushed it into an envelope. There was little point in sending it to the main office, she would send it to Hatfield where she knew there were already a dozen or so women pilots. There were still three stamps left in her stationery wallet. This must be an omen. One for the application, one for a letter to Jack and one to use on the letter to Greg.

By the time the lorry had returned to his base at Hornchurch after Neil's funeral it was as if nothing untoward had taken place. The men were smoking, joking and talking eagerly about getting to the mess for a few beers and a knees-up that evening.

Greg wanted to mourn his best friend for longer than a few hours but his wasn't the only squadron to lose members and the last thing that was needed was for the base to fall into a sombre mood. To win this war they had to stay focused, positive, push the negative things aside and get on with it.

He was about to head for the Officers' Mess on his multicoloured bike – a Christmas present from his darling girl – when someone from his squadron yelled at him.

'There's a party somewhere – hop in – we'll give you a lift.'

Why not? He might as well get legless, drown his sorrows, and what better place to do it than at a party? Neil had been his best friend. His loss was going to be hard to adjust to. Obviously the chaps in this squadron would miss him, but they hadn't trained with him, known him since long before this bloody war started. Stiff upper lip and all that.

The vehicle they were travelling in had been requisitioned – at least he hoped it had – for the evening and was crammed full of young men just like him, all eager to forget they might be next to go for a Burton.

'Do we have to take any booze?' Greg asked the man he was crushed against.

'No, just drop a couple of quid in a kitty on the way in.'

'Who's holding this shindig?'

'No idea. Open invitation to all the bods here.'

The conversation was cut short as the driver spun the wheel and the vehicle lurched sickeningly, throwing him against the man sitting next to him. By the time they'd untangled themselves they screeched to a halt outside an impressive building.

'Here we are, lads,' the driver yelled. 'Not sure when your transport will be returning – hope you've got permission to be out all night.'

The CO had told the squadron to go out and get drunk but hadn't specified when they should return. He hoped to God there wouldn't be a German raid tonight as there'd be no one sober enough to fly.

He followed the noisy group up the stone steps, under the portico, and into an entrance hall that reminded him sharply of his own ancestral home. But the resemblance was superficial as this place was in urgent need of repair – whoever lived here must be land rich and cash poor, unlike his own unpleasant family.

There was a dozen or so partygoers milling about in the space but the sound of jollity and revelry was coming through the open double doors of the drawing room. No sign of a bar so he couldn't find himself a much needed drink before he entered the fray.

The drawing room, like the hall, was vast, elegantly furnished, but definitely run down. Two sets of French doors stood wide open onto a terrace. This was where the party was. The last thing he wanted was to smile and be sociable but that was how it was done in the RAF. Onwards and upwards – think about tomorrow not yesterday.

As he was making his reluctant way towards the terrace a familiar voice hailed him. 'Greg, how wonderful to see you. I hoped you would be here.' The honourable Elizabeth Hamilton rushed forward and threw her arms around his neck. She was a deb he'd had a brief affair with a couple of years ago. He'd met up with her again at a village social just after he'd been transferred to the squadron and had spent an enjoyable day catching up over a picnic. She wouldn't ask him how he was feeling, want to talk about his grief; she was exactly the distraction he desperately needed.

'Elizabeth, I might have known you would be anywhere there was a party going on.' He extricated himself from her arms without reciprocating her kiss but she seemed unbothered by his rejection.

'I'm sorry about your friend, I know you have just returned from his funeral. The night is for forgetting, for having a jolly good time and I'll help you do that.'

The next few hours passed in a haze of loud music, too much alcohol and wild dancing. By the time it got dark he'd forgotten everything apart from the pleasure of holding a beautiful girl in his arms and twirling her around the ballroom. His misery at the death of his friend had been numbed by drink. Live in the moment is what they were advised to do and he was doing that with a vengeance.

'I'm bushed, I need some fresh air and another drink.'

'So do I, Greg, let's get one and have a stroll around the garden. Now it's dark, it's lovely out there.'

When she kissed him he responded and what happened next was inevitable. If they'd still been inside, in full view of his comrades, things would have been different.

He tumbled her to the ground behind a concealing shrub and she was as eager as he to make love. For a few minutes he forgot Neil, Ellie, everything that mattered to him as his baser instincts took over. It had been too long since he'd slept with a woman and not even a bomb dropping could have prevented him from being unfaithful.

Jack got back to base by the skin of his teeth, just avoiding jankers for being AWOL. He'd been given a twelve hour pass to attend Neil's funeral and that should have been plenty. The trains were running late, overcrowded, bloody hot, and you'd have thought he was travelling to the other side of the world, not a few miles to Croydon – or Kenley as this part of the base was known.

No one from his squadron had bought it so they were on duty tonight. On his way to the dispersal hut he stopped to speak to the ground crew. They were totally loyal to the guy who flew their aircraft – they were both cheerful and uncomplaining too.

'Everything at readiness, guys?'

'All tickety-boo, sir.'

'See you later, probably.'

They didn't salute, nobody bothered with that nonsense. Everyone got on together and worked as a team which was better than the rigid discipline you got in the other services. He half smiled when he thought of Ellie – they'd not had time to talk today but he'd managed to hand over the form he'd got from the ATA bloke. If she managed to get released from the WAAF he might see her occasionally if she flew into his base.

He paused to put on his Mae West and nodded to the telephone orderly at his blanket covered table. He was there to take any calls and tell them when to scramble. The other bods ignored him and he made his way to the last vacant camp bed and settled down. He could do with a bit of kip and with luck nothing would happen until dawn.

He put his hands behind his head and tried to relax. They were all different – some read a book or newspaper, some managed to sleep, others just lay there waiting for the inevitable call on the telephone telling them to scramble.

His task was to attack any bombers – not that there had been many so far, thank God. Hurricanes were the workhorses, reliable, dogged but not fast enough to catch a Messerschmitt. The Spitfires were the racehorses of the fighter planes and their job was to intercept the German fighters that flew above the bombers to protect them.

He must have dozed off because when the telephone rang he jerked awake, his heart pounding, palms sweaty. All the guys were sitting up but no one had moved.

The telephone orderly shook his head and smiled. 'Nothing to report, sir, all clear. The NAAFI van will be here at 07.15.'

'Another hour and we can go for a cuppa,' one of them said.

'I'm going to the bog,' he announced. You couldn't go anywhere without letting someone know where you were just in case the balloon went up.

During the Dunkirk evacuation they'd flown sorties non-stop and everyone was still knackered. The bloody Huns would be gathering on the other side of the drink waiting to invade. The army couldn't stop them if they were this side of the Channel. It would be up to the boys in blue to keep them at bay. He hoped there were enough of them and that they were strong enough to do it.

When he returned the dispersal hut was awake, guys wandering about exchanging small talk and cigarettes. He heard the next crew arriving and along with the others he replaced his Mae West on its peg, clambered out of his flight suit, and headed for the NAAFI truck.

He was proud of the way he'd acquitted himself over Dunkirk. Despite the fact that a Hurry was a sitting duck if attacked by a Messerschmitt he'd managed to shoot down two German bombers single-handedly whilst taking several tracer bullets in the fuselage of his plane. His ground crew had repaired it, but he'd not flown it since.

He was astride his brightly painted bicycle when the telephone orderly poked his head out of the dispersal hut and yelled for him to come over.

'Call for you, Sergeant Pilot Reynolds.'

Jack took the receiver. 'Reynolds speaking.'

'Good show, old chap. I need to speak to you pronto. Come straight to my office.'

'Yes, sir. Be with you in ten minutes.'

As he was pedalling furiously across the base he wondered what the Win Co wanted with him.

He walked into the Officers' Mess a non-commissioned bod and walked out a flying officer. He hadn't been bothered about not having a commission, but the best gen was found in this place, although the best beer was in the Sergeants' Mess.

Officers had better accommodation, had the services of a batman to take care of their personal laundry and keep them up to scratch. They could have made him a warrant officer which was the next in rank to a flight sergeant. They could have just moved him up to be a pilot officer – the rank below flying officer.

The first thing he wanted to do was tell Ellie. He'd give her a ring at Glebe Farm when he got the chance. His move to the Officers' Mess and all that entailed kept him busy for the next two days and his conversation with Ellie was forgotten.

Two

Ellie went down to the airfield to check on her one remaining aircraft, safely stored in the hangar. She pottered about down there unwilling to return to the farmhouse and be dragged into conversations about wedding dresses and honeymoons.

Mabel meant well but a girl's wedding should be organised by her mother not the housekeeper who happened to be involved with her father. Not that she wanted Mum to do it – she never wanted to see her again. Her parents were divorced – the connection to her mother was over.

When she had suggested to Greg that they got married as soon as they could she had been knocked sideways after Neil's funeral – but now she wasn't so sure she was ready to commit the rest of her life to anyone, even a man she loved as much as she did him.

Marriage often meant babies and she certainly didn't want one of those. She wanted to join the ATA and ferry aircraft all over the country, not stay at home changing nappies. Perhaps it wouldn't matter to have things planned though, with both of them in the services the chance of them getting leave at the same time was pretty remote.

When she got back she saw an official looking brown envelope addressed to her waiting on the telephone table. She opened it and her hands clenched. She was being posted to a radar station somewhere in Suffolk. She was to report there when her compassionate leave was up at the end of the week and not return to Kent. She examined the travel docket which had been included and saw she was to catch the eight o'clock train from Romford to Colchester where she would have to change to catch the Norwich train. Presumably she would be collected from Felixstowe as she didn't have the exact location of the radar station she was posted to.

Her eyes filled – if she'd known she wouldn't be going back there she would have made a point of saying goodbye to the two girls she'd made such good friends with over the past few months – Mary Smith and Daisy Jenkins. Fortunately, she'd brought everything she owned with her in her kitbag. This is what people did just in case something happened in their absence.

She wondered if this would make it easier for her to be released to join the growing band of female ferry pilots, or more difficult. When she'd first arrived to be trained she'd had no idea what she was doing for the first few weeks as it was all very secret. The RAF men at her posting had been working round the clock to man the radar screens and hadn't had any time off for months. By the time she'd left, there were two dozen more trained WAAF and the men had been released for duties elsewhere.

It was customary for anyone who'd been promoted to be moved on but she had only moved up from an ACW1 to ACW2 – which hardly merited being posted elsewhere. There was something else in the envelope and she tipped it out. In her palm was the stripe that indicated she had been promoted again. She looked at the opening of the letter a second time and saw they had decided to bump her up to leading aircraftwoman in one step without being in the intermediate rank. Now that was more like it – definitely worth bragging about.

'There you are, love, I've been looking for you all day. Fred and I have come up with a few ideas for your wedding.' Mabel smiled tentatively and Ellie felt a twinge of remorse for her less than charitable thoughts earlier.

'I'm sorry, I'm here now. There are one or two things I want to say about that as well, but before we discuss a possible wedding, I've got some good news to share with you.'

Over tea she told them about her promotion and transfer and they were suitably impressed.

'Will they make you an officer?' Dad asked hopefully.

'Actually, I don't think I'll be in the WAAF long enough to be an officer. I've applied to join the ATA and I'm hopeful they'll take me.'

It took a bit of explaining but both of them were thrilled at the thought she could be flying again.

'Well I never did,' Mabel exclaimed. 'There can't be more than a hundred young ladies in the country able to fly an aeroplane and my Fred's daughter is one of them. You'll be doing a lot more good for the war effort doing that than you are fiddling about with the wireless, or whatever it is you're doing.'

'This leads me onto the subject of my wedding. I don't want to get married until the end of the war whatever I said before. It doesn't mean I won't marry Greg eventually, but not at the moment.'

They exchanged glances and Dad smiled. 'That's good then, Ellie love. Not that I don't like your young man, I do, but no need to rush into things, not when there's a war on.'

From nowhere she found herself saying something quite unexpected. 'Why don't you plan your own wedding? You don't want people talking about you living in sin, now do you?'

Mabel flushed painfully but her dad nodded. 'We didn't like to tell you, love, but I asked Mabel to be my wife a while ago – when the decree absolute came through. I'm not having any gossip about the woman I love so we'll go ahead and arrange the ceremony.'

'It's quite possible that I won't be able to come, I doubt I'll get any more leave in the next few months. Make sure your friends take plenty of photographs then I can share them with you when I do get home. I'll speak to the vicar about Greg and I on Sunday before I leave.'

'I'm ever so pleased you don't mind, Ellie, I don't want to do anything to upset you.'

'You've been more of a mother to me in the past few months, Mabel, than my own ever was. I can get on with doing my bit knowing Dad's happy and being looked after.'

Later that evening she was outside with the dogs when Dad strolled out to join her. 'Don't you worry about talking to the vicar, I know you don't hold with all this church business. Not sure that I do, neither. I'll tell him when I ask him to call the banns for Mabel and I.'

She hugged him. 'Thank you, I'm going to write to Greg tonight, tell him about the ATA and the postponement of our wedding. If he really loves me he'll be happy with that – he's going to be far too busy flying his Spitfire to think about anything else.'

The phone could be heard ringing in the passageway and she hurried in to answer it. Mabel had gone to collect the eggs and was the other side of the farmyard.

'Glebe Farm.'

'Ellie, sorry to ring so late. How are you doing?'

'Jack, I'm so glad you called. I've got something to tell you.'

'And I you. Shall I go first?'

It was an extraordinary coincidence that they'd both been promoted. 'Congratulations, Flying Officer Reynolds. I'm heading for Suffolk on Monday. To tell you the truth I'll be glad to leave here, it no longer seems like home. With Mabel and my dad getting married soon I'll just be in the way.'

'Have you told Greg you've changed your mind?'

'I'll post a letter to him tomorrow. I can't give you the address of the place I'm going to be, it's still very hush-hush, but I can write to you. I'll let you know if I get into the ATA.'

Greg had just returned from a sortie – which had turned out to be a false alarm – and dumped his flying gear in the dispersal hut before pedalling back to his quarters. His batman met him with a jolly grin.

'Right, sir, couple of letters for you on your bureau. Anything else you need me to do?'

'No, thanks, no ribbons or bars to sew on today.'

This was a standing joke with them as he'd received another ribbon after Dunkirk.

He recognised the writing on the top one and swallowed a sour taste in his mouth. Since having sex with Elizabeth the other night he'd been tormented with guilt. It had meant nothing to either of them – just a bit of fun – a spur of the moment sort of thing fuelled by too much alcohol. It wasn't as if he hadn't slept with her before. She was a modern sort of girl, not like Ellie, who wouldn't dream of doing such a thing before she was married. He bitterly regretted what had happened and felt deeply ashamed.

His fingers were slick with sweat as he tore open the letter. Good God! She'd been promoted and applied to join the ATA. Then he read the last paragraph and his stomach knotted. She didn't want to get married immediately after all, wanted to wait until the war had ended and God knows when that would be.

He leaned against the bureau not sure if he was relieved or horrified by this new development. He didn't want her in the ATA, it would be far more dangerous than being a wireless operator somewhere. She should have discussed this with him before she sent in her application. Then he half smiled. His Ellie was an independent young lady, didn't need his permission to do anything and certainly wouldn't expect him to interfere in her decisions.

His head cleared. In the circumstances, the longer it was before he married her the better – at the moment he was so consumed with guilt he would feel obligated to tell her about his disgraceful lapse of judgement. If she ever knew she would break off the engagement and that he couldn't bear.

There was a briefing in an hour which gave him ample time to write a response. Even if he posted it right away it wouldn't reach her before she left so it made more sense to send it to the address of the anonymous postbox provided in the letter and let the authorities forward it.

That night, as he sat staring morosely into his warm beer in the mess, there was an announcement from Winston Churchill.

The Battle of France is over. I expect that the Battle of Britain is about to begin. Upon this battle depends the survival of Christian civilisation. Let us therefore brace ourselves to our duties, and so bear ourselves that if the British Empire and its Commonwealth last for a thousand years, men will say: 'This was their finest hour'.

'Crikey, sounds like the balloon's about to go up,' Freddie said loudly.

'Let's hope we get another week or two before it starts,' another bod said.

The Win Co, Cecil Boucher, had been sitting further down the bar, drinking whisky not beer. 'The PM managed to convince the population that the evacuation of the BEF wasn't a defeat but a victory. He's talking about us, chaps, we're the buggers who must prevent that bastard Hitler invading.'

There was a murmur of agreement but nobody spoke, the old man obviously had more to say. He was respected by everyone and they would all take note of anything he told them.

'It's going to be bloody grim. The Luftwaffe are preparing as I speak. They have a bigger air force than us, their fighters are faster than ours, but they don't have one thing that we do.' He paused and looked around, making sure every officer in the room was listening. 'We are all volunteers. We are fighting to keep fascism from this country. We might not have the fastest planes but we are better pilots. We won't give in until we win.'

This speech was even better than the one Churchill had just given. The place erupted into cheers and spontaneous applause. It put his personal problems into perspective. What the hell did it matter that he'd slept with one girl whilst being engaged to another if the bloody Germans invaded?

When the room settled down again Win Co had more to say. 'We are setting up a satellite airstrip, it will be known as Rochford, you'll be flying from there in rotation. I warn you the conditions will be primitive, under canvas, but it means the Huns won't find all our kites in the same place when they come.'

Tuesday, 18th of June was a day he'd never forget. It was the moment that he and the other chaps in the mess became fully committed to defeating Hitler whatever the cost to themselves. He was now in 54 Squadron, his squadron leader was James Lethart, not a chap given to long speeches but he was always first into the fray and they followed him willingly.

On Monday Ellie was dropped at the station to catch the designated train and, as always, most of the passengers were in uniform. She was proud of the new stripe on her sleeve.

An officer in the same grey-blue as her made room for her kitbag in the corner of the space where the two doors were.

'I should squeeze in here, there's no room anywhere else. You going far?'

She perched herself on top of her bag, rather too close to the speaker and the soldier on the other side. 'Somewhere near Felixstowe. Where are you based?' She recalled Greg telling her most of the bomber bases were in East Anglia somewhere, the fighter bases were mostly in Essex, Kent and Sussex. 'My fiancé used to fly a Blenheim. He's now in a Spitfire.'

'Horrible jobbies, Blenheims. I bet he's glad to be away from them.' The young man didn't introduce himself, neither did he say where he was based or what he flew. Too late she understood she had been most indiscreet and shouldn't have mentioned any specific details even though he seemed to be a genuine RAF officer.

Only the other day she'd read a poster saying:

Keep It Under Your Hat! Careless Talk Costs Lives.

Embarrassed at her *faux pas* she scrunched into her tiny space and pretended to fall asleep. The soldier disembarked at Colchester where she knew there was a big barracks – a dozen or more in khaki uniform followed him and she was glad she'd had the foresight to stand up as her toes would have been trodden on several times in the crush of the narrow space.

After picking up her kitbag she shuffled along the passageway until she spotted an empty seat. This time she didn't make the mistake of speaking to anyone. It was a good thing she'd been backwards and forwards to Ipswich many times last autumn to meet Greg or she might not have known when she reached the correct station.

Removing the station names was supposed to put off enemies, but she reckoned it caused more trouble for anyone trying to travel than it ever would for a German spy. The train steamed in and out of anonymous stations before puffing to a halt.

A helpful soldier grinned at her. 'Felixstowe, miss.'

'Thank you.'

She was glad to get out of the smoke filled compartment as even with the narrow window open it had been unpleasant. Perhaps she should take up smoking and then she wouldn't find it so nasty. Neither Greg nor Jack smoked and she was glad of it.

She slung her kitbag over her shoulder and marched briskly to the exit. The ticket collector didn't even ask to see her travel docket, he just waved her through with a smile.

Immediately she spotted a huddle of other WAAFs. As she hurried towards them an ancient bus, painted in sky blue, trundled into the forecourt and rocked to a noisy halt. The girls piled in.

Ellie scrambled after them to be greeted by a chorus of cheerful voices. 'Anyone for the skylark? Off we bleedin' well go,' yelled a girl about her age with peroxide blonde hair and violent red lipstick as the vehicle lurched away over the cobbles.

The bus driver talked constantly but his Suffolk accent was so strong she had no idea what he was saying. The bus screeched to a rolling halt and there was a collective sigh of relief.

'Thank the good Lord for that. I ain't never felt so sick in me life,' the peroxide blonde said loudly. 'Would you Adam and Eve it? We're getting on a bleedin' boat.'

Sure enough they had arrived at a jetty. One by one they clambered into the RAF ferry boat that was to take them across the Deben. Ellie's feet were soaked – there had to be a better way to get in and out of this bobbing ferry.

As far as she could see she was the highest ranked amongst the group but nobody took any notice of this. They all piled in together and she was surrounded by chattering, laughing girls who seemed already to be the best of friends.

Peggy, the blonde, dug her in the ribs with her elbow. 'That bus driver was a bit of laugh, weren't he? Only thing I got was that we're going to Bawdsey.'

'That's news to me too. Seems nice enough around here.'

The boat rocked gently on the river, the sun was shining, and one could almost believe there wasn't a war on and that they were on a pleasure trip. When they arrived on the sandy beach they jumped out, dragging their overfull kitbags after them. After checking in at a small guardroom they were told to make their way to a large manor house about half a mile away along the bank.

The building reminded her of the place she'd trained and she was looking forward to investigating further. By the time they arrived at the manor house the others were complaining, red faced and exhausted. Ellie was glad her kitbag didn't seem as full as theirs – then she worried she'd forgotten something. She did a quick mental review. Her small canvas bag of cutlery – her irons – was there, her two shirts, five collars, underwear (known as 'passion-killers'), stockings, spare black-laced shoes, and two pairs of winceyette pyjamas. Her greatcoat was over her arm, her gas mask on her shoulder. Tin hat! She'd left that hanging on the door of her last billet. Too bad – she'd requisition another and blame her recent bereavement for her omission. You could be put on a charge for not being correctly dressed.

They straggled towards the building, she in the lead, pleased with her new posting. This was a not a large concern, smaller than her previous one. There were a series of towers in the distance – presumably they were aerials of some sort to receive the radar signals.

There were men in uniform as well as women. She couldn't wait to discover what her role was to be.

Her travelling companions were directed elsewhere and she was told to report to the CO. This office was to the rear, possibly a room once occupied by a butler or housekeeper. She didn't have to wait long outside the office under the scrutiny of the snooty admin girl.

The officer sitting behind the desk had grey hair scraped back in a no-nonsense fashion but had a pleasant smile. 'Come in, Simpson, we've been eagerly awaiting your arrival. I'm sorry for your loss. You will be working alongside newly trained operatives. There to give guidance and direction if needed. I don't have to tell you that we're expecting the Luftwaffe to arrive in their hundreds any day. You come highly recommended. If you make a success of this posting you will be given the opportunity to become commissioned.'

Ellie saluted. 'Thank you, ma'am. It is a privilege to be here.'

'Your duties will commence at 08.00 tomorrow. Dismissed.'

Ellie saluted a second time and marched smartly out. She was puzzled as to why she had been singled out for such rapid promotion. Although she had acquitted herself well she wasn't aware that she had been any better than those she worked with – certainly no more deserving.

Having a supervisory role as well as using the radar itself was going to be interesting. It wouldn't be easy but she was eager to take on a more responsible position. Her recent promotion meant she no longer had to share a dormitory with nine other girls but was to share with another LACW, already in residence, that she had yet to meet. She was unpacking her belongings in the box room that had been allocated to them when she realised it wasn't all good news.

The more valuable she was to this radar station the less likely the CO was to release her to join the ATA. This was a civilian organisation and not part of the services.

Three

By the time Ellie had finished hanging up her spare uniform, folding her underwear and other items into the locker, she had been joined by the person she was to share with.

'Good morning, or rather good afternoon. I'm Joan Smith.' The tall, dark haired girl stuck out a hand and she took it. Her accent was upper crust. Ellie wondered why Joan wasn't an officer.

'Ellie Simpson. I expected to be bunking in with the other girls – I only thought corporals and above had separate accommodation.'

'This is an excellent posting as far as our billet is concerned. However, I give you fair warning that the food is appalling. Barely edible and I suggest you fill up on toast and marmalade at breakfast as that's the only thing they can't ruin.'

'Is there just one canteen?'

'Only around one hundred here so don't think we qualify for a trained cook.' She sat on the edge of her bed, careful not to disturb the carefully folded blankets, sheets and pillow. 'I'm not sure that we will see much of each other as we've been allocated different teams. We've both got newly trained girls – I've been doing this for a while but I believe this is your first attempt at supervision?'

'It is. I only got my promotion a couple of days ago.' She looked away and swallowed the lump in her throat, not wanting to mention how she'd got this news.

'Good show. I'm on A watch and on duty at 23.00 tonight. You're B watch, following me, and start at 08.00 tomorrow. Plenty of time for me to show you the ropes.'

Joan gestured towards the noisy room on the left. 'That's where our girls are accommodated. The three I've been working with for the past few weeks have been split up and can now work unsupervised so I'm starting with a new trio tonight. I hope the arrivals in my watch get some sleep.'

Ellie was well used to these watch rotations – she supposed they were the norm everywhere you went. She would be working four watches in a row and then have a day and a half free after each rotation.

She was shown various buildings and the grounds where the men were housed. Some shared cottages by the ferry while others lived in a variety of estate houses. There were also the usual service huts amongst the trees somewhere.

'We grab something to eat on the way to the operations block and another on the way back to the manor at the end of our watch,' Joan said as she pointed to the cookhouse, a converted stable situated halfway between the manor and operations.

'Is there time to go to Felixstowe when we have time off? Do the ferries run all the time?'

'They do indeed. You can obtain a sleeping-out pass from admin but woe betide you if you're late back.'

'How far is Bawdsey from Norwich, do you know? I've never been there but heard it's got a castle and a theatre.'

'It's close enough to hitchhike, so is Ipswich. I've done it a couple of times. There's a Sunday evening dance in the ballroom and also the NAAFI where you can get a decent cup of tea.'

They completed their tour and Joan retired to their quarters to get a few hours' sleep before she did her overnight watch. This didn't mean Ellie couldn't go into the shared room, she just thought she would wander about on her own for a bit before she went up.

Tea wasn't as awful as she'd expected, but then even a bad cook couldn't do much harm to a ham salad and tinned fruit. With so few living on this base it wouldn't take long for her to know all the faces and names. The list of the girls in her watch was in her pocket. April Curtis, Faye Jones and Rebecca Solomon – she had no idea what they looked like but intended to search them out before tomorrow morning.

The first place to look was the crew room and sure enough there were three girls sitting on their own. She marched up to them confidently. 'I think we're in the same watch. I'm Ellie Simpson – I'm going to help you settle in. This is your first posting after training and you might well encounter situations you've not met before.'

The girls shuffled their chairs round so she could join them. 'The girls we came with have gone to bed as they're on duty at 23.00,' said a small pretty WAAF with startling red hair. 'I'm April, by the way.' She pointed at the girl on her left. 'This is Faye and that's Rebecca.'

Introductions over, Ellie put them at their ease with anecdotes about her training and subsequent experience at her previous posting. Within the hour they were happy in each other's company but she rather thought that Rebecca might become a real friend. When Faye and April said they were going for a walk she remained behind.

'I didn't see you at tea, Rebecca, was it the fact that the salad was ham?'

'It was. I'm the only Jewish person on the base and they've not had to make allowances for someone with my dietary needs before. I was allowed to make myself a cheese sandwich and took it outside to eat.'

'I don't know a lot about Judaism, but I did know you don't eat pig in any form. There won't be a synagogue close by so what are you going to do about your sabbath prayers?'

'There's a war on, so like anyone else I'll just have to do my best. They hold a morning service here, so I'm told, but that's for Christians. I won't be attending.'

'I only go to church occasionally, I'm not very religious. However, I expect attendance will be compulsory for me.' She grinned. 'Seems strange that they hold a dance on Sunday evening – I thought Christians were supposed to do nothing apart from read the Bible and think good thoughts.'

The conversation moved on to more personal matters. Rebecca, who was twenty-three, was married to a captain in the army. When she expressed her reservations about marrying Greg before the end of the war her new friend agreed.

'I can't tell you how difficult it is being parted from my husband. We were married just before war broke out – if I'd known what was to happen I'd have said no too. I've married outside my faith which means I'm cut off from my family now – as far as they're concerned I might as well be dead.'

'I'm estranged from my mother and my one remaining brother, but at least I've got my dad and future stepmother. Whilst we're here, we can support each other.'

Although they remained together until they could fetch a mug of cocoa from the NAAFI, Ellie didn't mention anything about her application to join the ATA; neither – for some reason – did she mention her friendship with Jack. Strangely, she was more comfortable talking about her nasty grandfather and his fascist beliefs than she was about the other things.

When they went up at nine thirty the girls in A Watch were about to go and find themselves something to eat before they started their long shift. During the nine hours one of the four would be designated to make tea for the others to keep them awake.

Her room mate was also about to depart. 'I'll see you tomorrow morning when we change over.'

She settled down in her little room and wondered what Greg had thought about her letter saying she didn't want to get married until the end of the war. It would be some time before she received a reply as the letters had to be rerouted via an anonymous PO box. Maybe she could meet him in Felixstowe if he could get a twenty-four pass. This seemed unlikely but she decided to write him a quick note with the suggestion and get it into the postbox before she turned in.

Jack was pleased to see a letter from Ellie waiting for him in his new billet at the Aerodrome Hotel, once used for overnight passengers when the place had been a civilian airport. The batman he shared with the other three pilot officers was a cheerful guy, but his northern accent was so thick he was hard to understand. He was sharing with a guy called Chalky White.

He scanned the contents and was pleased to see Ellie had decided to postpone the wedding indefinitely. She was too young to get married in his opinion and he thought Greg, although a stand-up guy, wasn't right for her. Their social differences didn't matter at the moment, but when the war was over and she had to become a lady of the manor her lack of class would show. No – sod it – she was a classy broad if ever he met one. It was the fact that she came from an ordinary family that would make her uncomfortable in such grand surroundings.

Look what had happened between Fred and Ellie's mom – they were divorced now and it was all because they'd married out of their social class.

The door to his room crashed open and Chalky poked his head in. 'Win Co wants to talk to us before it all kicks off.'

After a mad dash across the concrete to the crew room he was pleased to find he wasn't by any means last. He found himself a bit of empty wall to lean against and watched as dozens of other guys piled in. Even with the windows open the place was soon too hot and filled with cigarette smoke.

Win Co stood on the raised dais at the end of the room and raised his hand. The room quickly settled into alert silence.

'Once the balloon goes up there'll be no respite. You'll be flying over the Channel and are to land to refuel and rearm at Hawkinge if necessary. Any questions?'

There were none, and as the blokes wandered out no one was talking about what was to come. Everyone knew they could die next time they flew, but you didn't dwell on this. If Hitler was to invade, first he would have to defeat the RAF and that wasn't going to happen – not whilst he and the other guys were flying.

The Luftwaffe had flown non-stop during the evacuation of the BEF from Dunkirk and were no doubt taking a break for a week or two before beginning an all-out attack on Britain. New aircraft and pilots were arriving all the time and he was sure their defences were adequate whatever came across the Channel.

Spitfires, with their fast Merlin engines, engaged the Messerschmitts who flew above the German bombers. Hurricanes attacked the bombers. He was happy with the division of labour and would continue to do his bit.

He stood for a moment looking around the airfield, which used to be the main airport for London before the war started, and thought the place was well protected from aerial bombardment. There were pillboxes around the perimeter manned by the army twenty-four hours a day and all contained suitable weaponry for shooting down German planes. What used to be the terminal building was now an administration block and fuel and oil was housed in the existing tanks. An ammunition store had been built, but apart from that the place was more or less as it had always been.

During the evacuation at Dunkirk they'd been flying non-stop and all the squadrons were grateful for the respite before it started again. Two of the squadrons had been posted elsewhere but his remained where it was and had been joined by 111 Squadron who also flew Hurricanes. There was also room for a squadron of Gladiators, Blenheims and Beaufighters – the smaller bombers – when they arrived. The big jobbies were in East Anglia, Lincolnshire and up north.

His lot were on call tonight so he would spend a couple of hours in the Officers' Mess before cycling to the dispersal hut where they had to wait to be given the call to scramble. They were rarely called out in darkness but it got light around four o'clock and that was when the recce planes flew over the Channel.

He heard the distinct chug of a Tiger Moth approaching and it made him think of his time at Glebe Farm. He hoped Ellie had sent in her application to join the ATA as then there would be the slight chance of seeing her occasionally.

The Moth circled and then landed on the far side of the airfield, too far away for him to see if the pilot who jumped out was male or female. No – that wasn't right – the female flyers had to wear skirts. Bloody ridiculous making girls fly in a skirt and not pants. If they were going to do a guy's job then they should be allowed to wear the same uniform. The pilot was obviously male and was busy unloading parcels from the Moth.

He and the other blokes put on their flight suits and Mae Wests and then lounged about outside chatting and smoking. Some read, some played cards, others chess and there was even one bloke who knitted. Naturally enough he was known as Needles.

When it got dark they drifted in ones and twos inside and stretched out on the camp beds. They'd not been scrambled for two nights now – their luck couldn't hold. He dozed fitfully and was awake when the orderly answered the strident demands of the telephone.

He listened intently and was already on his feet when Chalky took the call. 'Right, Jack, Ops say there's been a plot seen over Calais and it's heading our way.'

Jack held his breath waiting for the order to move but it wasn't his turn yet. He went to the bog whilst he had time. One of the guys had to piss in his pants over Dunkirk because he'd failed to go before they took off. Not something he wanted to experience himself.

Another couple of hours dragged by and the two bods who'd gone in search of the recce kite had just returned. They'd seen nothing. A wasted journey.

From outside he heard the telephone ring a second time. The orderly yelled, 'Squadron scramble. Base angels ten.'

He was on his feet and first through the door leaving the others to swear and curse as they got in each other's way.

He tore across the grass to his waiting Hurry. The ground crew had already started the engine and he grabbed his parachute from the wing tip as he arrived.

Once his chute was on, one of the ground crew who had been balancing on the wing by the cockpit put his hand under his arm and heaved him into the aircraft. As always, within seconds he was safely strapped in, door closed, helmet on, mask fixed and radio ready.

He waved 'chocks away', released the brakes and eased open the throttle. The entire Squadron was on the move. Everyone taxiing at once. Chalky was leading today. Jack took his position behind the leading three and waited until he could take off. Within a few minutes the entire squadron was airborne. Ten Hurricanes soaring into the air where they belonged.

Four

After the first shift Ellie was able to relax. The three girls she was working with were all competent, if inexperienced, and she doubted they would need much help from her. Having started their rotation in mid-cycle, so to speak, she wouldn't get her thirty-six hour pass until she'd completed four watches.

She rarely saw her room mate and spent her free time with Rebecca. Joan had shown her the basic electric heater that had been supplied by the radar mechanics. It consisted of an element inside a jam tin – on this you could boil a kettle or make toast. This was strictly forbidden, naturally, but no one took any notice of this. If the food had been better then perhaps the girls wouldn't have taken the risk of being put on a charge.

After completing their fourth watch, the one that ran from one o'clock until six o'clock, she had joined the other two girls in the larger room to make tea and toast and marmalade.

'How many slices, Ellie?' April asked as she waved a slice of bread impaled on a fork.

'Two, please, I'm starving.'

Rebecca was in charge of making the tea and was busy on the far side of the room straining it into the mugs. The room smelt delicious, there was nothing better than the aroma of hot toast when you were hungry.

Not only had they pinched mugs from the canteen, they'd also got plates. As they carried their own irons they'd no need to take cutlery as well.

April dropped a piece of toast onto a waiting plate and passed it to her. Soon they were all busy munching and slurping tea. The heater that had been used for the tea had cooled enough to be put back under the bed, but the one that had been used for toasting was still in the centre of the room as it was too hot to move.

Suddenly the door opened and Sergeant Frost appeared. This was a spot inspection. They were instantly on their feet and Ellie automatically stepped in front of the heater, hoping to prevent it from being seen.

Rebecca had had the presence of mind to toss a cardigan over it. There was a pungent smell of burning wool but Frost didn't seem to notice.

She pointed to the offending object. 'Not good enough, items of clothing should be put away, not left lying about on the floor.'

'Yes, Sergeant Frost,' they chorused.

Ellie was sure the woolly would catch fire at any moment and if it didn't actually burst into flames the smell would still be so strong they would be found out and put on a charge.

'As you were.' Frost nodded and vanished as quickly as she had arrived.

Rebecca snatched the garment from the heater and flapped it overhead, laughing. 'Golly, that was close.' She sniffed the wool. 'April, it's a bit singed on the inside but perfectly wearable. Sorry, it was the nearest thing I could find.'

'Heavens, I thought we'd had it then. I don't understand why she couldn't smell it.'

Ellie pushed the offending heater across the room with her shoe – it was still too hot to pick up – until it could be put under the sink where it was hidden by a draped towel. The room had its own sink which the six girls shared. She and Joan were obliged to use the bathroom down the corridor along with another roomful of WAAFs.

'I think the smell of toast and marmalade was even stronger than the burning cardigan. I think Frost just had to do the inspection but didn't want to find anything. I bet she does the same as we've just done. No one can be happy eating only the horrible food we get from the cookhouse.'

'Good point. I'm sure the mechanics made these makeshift cooker/heaters for that very reason,' Faye said. 'By the way, we've only got one more shift and then we get our pass. I want to go into Felixstowe. I gather we can book into a hostel – most of the girls do this.'

'We need to get an overnight pass,' Ellie said. 'It's too late to get one from admin now and we won't have time before we go on our watch at eight o'clock tomorrow morning.'

'According to the other girls it's just a formality – doesn't take more than a few minutes to fill in the form.

The ferry runs back and forth all day and so do the buses,' Rebecca added.

'That's good. I'm going to bring back a packet of biscuits if I can find any.'

'We don't have ration books and we might not get anything decent without coupons, April,' Faye told her friend.

'What a swizz! I think if you're in uniform you can buy anything so we might be lucky. If not, we'll just have to do with stolen toast, butter and marmalade to keep us going. At least we can eat out when we're in Felixstowe and you never know, they might have spotted dick or roly-poly pudding for afters,' April said.

Ellie remained with her team and they played a lively game of Whist until she decided to call it a night. 'I'm going to turn in. Thank you for allowing me to spend the evening in here – I actually would prefer to be billeted with you and not on my own with Joan.'

She said her good nights, nipped downstairs to use the bathroom and turned in.

The next watch was relatively uneventful although there were several blips on the screen. She swallowed a lump in her throat when one of them disappeared – at first she couldn't see if it was a hostile or one of theirs that had gone down. If it was a friendly aircraft they transmitted an extra blip. It was one of their boys and the plane crossed the coast flying barely higher than the treetops and the aerials.

At the end of their watch, as they were hurrying to the admin office to get their sleeping-out passes, she mentioned the damaged aircraft that she'd plotted earlier. 'It was such a relief when he didn't ditch in the drink. I do hope he managed to get back to his base.'

'I'm dreading watching one of ours crash,' Rebecca said. 'It's strange that we've already had half a dozen stagger past in the short time we've been here.'

Ellie didn't want to talk about it any more as it just reminded her that Neil hadn't made it, and that Greg and Jack were still flying sorties every day and putting their lives at risk.

They'd already agreed not to go to the cookhouse. They were looking forward to finding something more palatable to eat in Felixstowe when they got there.

Greg had had little sleep the past few nights as his squadron was on call. They'd been scrambled every morning but hadn't seen a dicky bird. The chaps seemed relaxed enough, no one talked about those that had died only a few weeks ago, it was as if they had never existed.

He was surprised to see an envelope with Ellie's familiar handwriting waiting for him on his return to get some kip. He opened it and smiled. She'd get a thirty-four hour pass every four days and suggested they might be able to meet in Felixstowe if he could get a twenty-four hour pass.

If the bloody Germans stayed in France for a bit longer it was just possible he could get a few hours free. His squadron had done a week of nights and they should get the day off before they started days. He wouldn't get leave overnight, but he might get time to go to Felixstowe and meet up with his darling girl for a few hours.

He checked exactly when she would be in Felixstowe and it coincided with the end of his night shifts. When he spoke to the adjutant he was happy to sign a chit giving him twelve hours off base. 'Make bloody sure you're back, Dunlop, or we'll both be for the high jump. Not supposed to allow any of you chaps out of my sight just in case the balloon goes up.'

'Scout's honour, Sarge. You can rely on me.'

He cadged a lift to Romford and was fortunate a train steamed in just as he arrived. He didn't need to buy a ticket so dodged past the guard and leapt onto the train as it was pulling out again. In his effort to get on he managed to step on several brown jobbies and if there'd been a bit more room no doubt there would have been fists thrown.

When he disembarked at Ipswich it occurred to him that he hadn't told Ellie he was coming and he had no idea how big this town of Felixstowe was or if he'd be able to locate her. He hadn't come all this way to fail. He wasn't going to leave without spending time with her, however short it might be.

When he explained to a friendly guard that he'd travelled without a ticket or travel docket and needed to pay he was waved away. 'No need, you boys in blue are going to save us from the Huns. You can travel anywhere you like for nothing as far as I'm concerned. There's a train to Felixstowe in half an hour, it comes into the same platform so stay where you are.'

Greg felt a bit guilty travelling for nothing, especially as there was a war on, but he thanked the guard and didn't argue. Wearing a uniform did give one some privileges after all. He'd left the base at eight thirty – it was now nearly eleven o'clock. With any luck he would be in Felixstowe before Ellie arrived. She would be coming on a bright blue bus so it shouldn't be hard to spot her transport. Her watch didn't finish until one and it must take at least an hour, if not longer, to get across the river on the ferry and into the town. Before he left the station, he must ask about trains back as he wasn't going to risk being AWOL.

The town was small enough for him to walk to the ferry terminal from the station. There was a decent café and he parked himself at a window seat so he could watch who clambered out on the hard. He'd barely taken a few mouthfuls of his tea when the small boat chugged across filled with uniformed RAF and WAAF personnel. Ellie was the first to scramble out and he smiled as one of her shoes got wet.

'I'll be back in a minute,' he called across to the ancient waitress. 'I need another cup of tea, please, for my fiancée.'

The sun was shining, making the river water sparkle. It was hard to be depressed on a day like this. He pushed his guilt aside and strode towards the woman he loved.

'Ellie, I can't tell you how good it is to see you.'

His sudden appearance caused her to stop so suddenly the girl behind cannoned into her back and if he hadn't jumped forward they would both have ended up on the ground.

44

'Greg! I didn't expect to see you today. I can't believe you're here.' Without hesitation she flung herself forward and to a chorus of whistles and cheers he kissed her.

She pressed his chest and immediately he released her. 'I want to introduce you to my team…'

With his arm still around her waist he turned, but the three girls had already clambered onto the waiting bus along with the half a dozen RAF chaps.

'Oh no! We must catch the bus too. I don't know where the girls will be staying.' She started to move towards the vehicle but he grabbed her arm.

'I can't run off, I've not paid for my tea in that café over there. From what I've seen Felixstowe isn't all that big, it should be easy enough to find them later. I've got to catch the four fifteen train, so we've not got long.'

'Then I'll spend every second with you and find the others afterwards. I've got so much I'd like to tell you about my job but I'm not allowed to talk about it.'

'I don't want to talk about your current job. I want to know if you've heard anything from the ATA.'

Hand in hand they walked back to the café and two steaming mugs of tea were waiting for them.

'As all letters have to go in a roundabout route, I don't suppose I'll hear for a few weeks. I suppose I should have told you before I applied but it's what I want to do and why I don't want to get married until the war's over.' She looked earnestly at him. 'If I'm flying myself I won't have time to worry about you or Jack and I know just how dangerous things are going to be for all aircrew.'

The last thing he wanted to do was talk about the chance he was going to go for a Burton. Why had she mentioned Jack in the same sentence as him? Was there something going on between them he didn't know about? He was about to enquire further when his stomach clenched. He had no right to ask. She was not going to betray him the way he'd done to her.

'Have you heard from him lately?'

'Actually, we spoke on the phone just before I came here. He's been promoted – he's a pilot officer now.' She pointed to the insignia that indicated he was a flight lieutenant. 'You did tell me you'd been promoted too. I'm an LACW now which doesn't seem to make much difference, apart from a few extra shillings in my wage packet at the end of the month.'

They were silent for a bit as they sipped their tea. He looked over his shoulder and beckoned the waitress across. 'Can you make us something to eat? I don't see a menu anywhere.'

'I can do you cheese on toast, egg on toast or, if you're prepared to wait a bit, a nice plateful of fish and chips. My Stanley fetched me some lovely fresh cod from the market this morning.'

Ellie's eyes lit up as if she'd been offered a banquet. 'Fish and chips would be absolutely perfect. Would you mind if we went for a walk along the river whilst you prepared it for us?'

'You go along, lovey, it'll take me half an hour.' The old lady hurried off muttering to herself.

46

'I wish I could take you somewhere special, you deserve a treat.'

'Believe me, darling, freshly cooked fish and chips will be perfect. The food at Bawdsey Manor is horrible.'

They finished their tea and walked down to the riverbank. Occasionally they heard the drone of an aircraft, but nothing flew close enough for him to identify it. He had a pretty good idea what her job was, she was a radar operator, but he knew better than to say so.

The meal was surprisingly delicious and was washed down with a second mug of tea. By the time they'd finished and he'd settled the bill he only had an hour before his train left.

'I really mustn't miss my train.'

She gestured to the waiting bus. 'That will leave as soon as the next ferry comes in. Haven't you noticed there's a shuttle service running especially for us.'

To be honest he'd not noticed anything apart from how beautiful she was, how much he loved her, and how much he bitterly regretted his drunken evening with Elizabeth.

'I'm not from Bawdsey, will I be allowed to go on it?'

'He never asks for identification – as long as you're in blue you'll be okay. Look, the ferry's just coming now.'

There were only a couple of passengers as well as the two of them but the bus driver didn't complain. He crunched his gears, the ancient vehicle wheezed and groaned, and they rattled directly to the station.

'I've still got three quarters of an hour – shall we go in search of your friends?' He didn't want her to be wandering about on her own in case she was accosted by someone. She didn't realise just how lovely she was but he'd been well aware of the appreciative looks from all the men they'd passed.

On enquiring they were directed to a hostel and he was pleased to see her friends had booked in here for the night. Ellie added her name to the reservation book.

'I've just realised you don't have an overnight bag with you.'

'I've got my toothbrush in my pocket. That's all I need really. I'll wash and change when we get back. It's what everyone does.'

She politely enquired where her friends might have gone and was told they'd gone to look at the pier, which was in the process of being demolished in case there was an invasion.

There wasn't time for him to escort her there. If he didn't get moving he wouldn't be back at the station on time.

'Darling girl, I've got to dash. I doubt I'll get a pass again until things settle down a bit. Take care of yourself, I love you.' His eyes were moist and there were tears on her cheeks as he kissed her goodbye.

'I love you too. I'll write to you every week as always. You never know, the next time I see you it might be when I fly into Hornchurch as an ATA girl.'

He kissed her one last time and strode off too choked up to say anything else. She deserved better than him. When this bloody business was over he would tell her what had happened and just pray she could forgive him. He wasn't sure he could marry her with this secret between them.

He slept from Ipswich to Romford. He didn't want to consider the future and sleeping kept his dark thoughts to himself.

Five

After an enjoyable break Ellie returned to Bawdsey determined to repeat the experience after the next four day rota. They had to miss the weekly Sunday dance this time as they were on duty. After the third watch she and Rebecca spent the evening chatting and reading. The other two had gone out somewhere.

'I noticed that both of them were done up to the nines, Ellie, do you think they're meeting gentlemen friends?'

'I don't see how they could be. The men here are segregated from us – they're not even allowed inside the manor except for the Sunday dance.'

'I didn't think either Faye or April were like that.' Rebecca shrugged. 'I suppose when there's a chance we could all be blown up by a bomb when the invasion starts your perceptions change. Anyway, there are plenty of men to choose from and some of them are quite attractive.'

'Are they? I must say I've not noticed. I've only got eyes for Greg. I've had ample opportunity to sleep with him but wanted to wait until we're married.'

Her friend looked horrified. 'You can't leave it that long. What if he was killed? Wouldn't you regret not having been his lover? After all, you are engaged.'

This was a strange conversation but then Rebecca was a married woman so had a different outlook. 'I must say I did consider it. If he had stayed overnight after my brother's funeral I would definitely have gone to him. In fact, if he gets any leave again I'll do it. I just don't want to be an unmarried mother.'

'No danger of that nowadays. He'll have something – all servicemen do.'

Ellie didn't like to ask exactly what the 'something', to which her friend referred, was. The very thought made her feel hot all over. She might be an experienced flyer, an excellent radar operator, but when it came to worldly matters she was sadly lacking.

'It's nearly eleven o'clock. I'm going to turn in. I hope the other two don't arrive after midnight as I'll have to report them.'

The only time they were allowed to be off the premises later than that was when they had an overnight pass. The limited facilities on the base meant there was only the NAAFI, the cookhouse or the crew room. They must have gone across on the ferry and spent the evening at the Ferry Boat Inn.

Just before midnight a racket on the stairs alerted her to the arrival of the missing girls. The noise they were making echoed up the stairwell.

'Shush, you two, you'll wake the whole building,' she hissed over the banisters.

Then, to her horror, she saw they were not alone. Two sheepish chaps were assisting Alice and Faye up the stairs. The girls were both inebriated and scarcely able to stand.

Rebecca joined her in the passageway and they exchanged worried glances. Not only were the two girls drunk, their uniforms were incorrectly buttoned and neither of them were wearing the regulation stockings.

'You two men, remove yourself from our quarters immediately if you don't want to be reported and put on a charge.'

The jolly smiles of the escorts vanished, as did they.

'Come along, girls, Rebecca and I will get you into bed. We'll talk about this in the morning.'

Between them they got their friends undressed and into bed. If she'd been shocked by the state of their uniforms she was even more horrified to discover neither of them were wearing knickers. Shocked to the core she pulled Faye's nightie over her head, put a clean chamber pot beside the bed in case she was sick and scuttled off to her own billet.

It wouldn't have been so bad if the girls had been going out with the men concerned – but to have sex with men they couldn't possibly know was another thing altogether. Maybe she was a prude, but she was certain both girls would regret their behaviour when they were sober.

The two of them barely made it on time for their watch. They both looked peaky and wouldn't meet her eyes. The matter was never discussed. They worked together well enough but no longer socialised. She and Rebecca remained firm friends and this was some consolation.

The expected massive attack from the Luftwaffe had so far not materialised but there were enough blips to report every watch to make her feel she was doing her bit. One day seemed very much like the last and it wasn't until she happened to look at the calendar hanging in the recreation room that she realised it would be Greg's birthday the following week.

'Rebecca, I need to go into Felixstowe and buy a gift and card for my fiancé. Will you come with me? We don't have to book into the hostel if you don't want to.'

'We can go in for the afternoon and evening. It doesn't get dark until after ten so as long as we get back before then we won't need to worry about the blackout.'

Ellie hadn't asked April and Faye to accompany them.

Although she knew it was highly unlikely he would be there, she couldn't help but look out for Greg when she disembarked from the ferry. Of course, he wasn't there. Although most things were rationed she wouldn't need coupons to buy a birthday card or a small gift. The difficulty was finding either item. There was a national paper shortage and in the end she abandoned her search.

'At least I've got a letter written just in case. I'll post it now.'

This left them the remainder of the day and the evening before they had to return. 'Shall we find ourselves something to eat before we go back?' Rebecca suggested.

She was about to answer when she spotted a poster in a shop window. 'Look at that – there's going to be a film show in the church hall. Shall we go to that? It will be finished in good time to catch the last ferry.'

This left at eleven thirty and the film show finished at ten o'clock. The last bus left at eleven fifteen. The film show was cartoons and newsreels but enjoyable nonetheless. Afterwards tea and biscuits were served and it would have been rude to refuse.

The fact that the film projector had broken down twice during the performance had meant the show didn't finish on time – but neither she nor Rebecca factored that into their timetable. It wasn't until she glanced at her watch she realised how late it was.

'We have to run – it's after eleven – we mustn't miss the bus.'

Her heart was pounding, her face perspiration-covered, but still they were too late. 'What are we going to do? If we don't get to the ferry before the last one we won't be back before midnight and we'll be put on a charge.'

Rebecca was equally distressed. 'How much money have you got left? Do you have enough to pay for a taxi?'

'I do. What a good thing I didn't buy Greg a birthday present after all.'

It took them a while to find a taxi driver and when he dropped them at the ferry the last boat was already chugging across the Deben.

'We could swim across,' her friend suggested.

'I think we'd be in even more trouble if we turned up dripping wet. Shall we try and wake up one of the fishermen and ask him to row us?'

Eventually they persuaded a fisherman to help them. They had to wait outside whilst he got dressed. The minutes were ticking by. If he didn't get a move on they would have spent a fortune and still have missed their midnight deadline.

He'd obviously taken longer to row across than it took to travel in the RAF motorised boat and by the time they docked they were already ten minutes late. She was obliged to give the man half a crown. Not satisfied with this as a reward, and it was more than generous, he grabbed hold of Rebecca and kissed her soundly on the cheek.

'That was an expensive day out,' she whispered as they crept furtively up the stairs.

'But good fun, though.'

'How can you say that? We're both on a charge.'

The following morning they had to appear before the WAAF CO. After explaining their efforts to get back on time they received the lightest of reprimands but she now had a blemish on her record.

'We should have got a sleep-out pass and not a late pass then it wouldn't have mattered what time we got back,' Rebecca said with a sigh.

'Never mind, it's the dance tonight and we've not been yet. I'm not all that fond of dancing but from what I've heard it's a jolly affair and not to be missed.'

'I suppose we ought to go, but to be honest I find it too difficult seeing other people enjoying themselves when my Derek is so far away.'

'I miss Greg too, but neither of them would want us to be sad. I bet they both go out for a drink or three whenever they get the opportunity.'

Jack got to know the other guys on his floor and soon they were good chums. Usually he was too knackered to do more than gobble down his breakfast and tumble into bed. Nothing much was happening and even though they were scrambled most nights there'd been no sorties and no sign of any bombers.

The high point of his week was the arrival of a letter from Ellie. Her letters were amusing – she seemed to be having a better time than he was. Maybe he would try and see her himself one of these days. If Greg could get a twelve hour pass then maybe he could too.

On second thoughts, he would do better finding his own girlfriend and not hankering after Ellie who belonged to someone else. There were plenty of pretty girls working on the base, most in uniform, and the other guys seemed to take advantage of this. He hadn't slept with a girl for months. In fact, not since he'd met Ellie.

He and Chalky became best buddies. His friend was happy to listen for hours to his tales of his acrobatic flying in America.

'I wondered why you sometimes sound like a Yank – now I understand. No wonder you're such a damn good fighter pilot.'

'I don't want to make a career out of flying when the war's over. What about you?'

'Not bloody likely. Both feet firmly on the ground for me when I'm demobbed. I'll go back to working in thecity.'

'I'd like to go to university and become a civil engineer or architect. Somehow, I guess, the idea of putting buildings up rather than knocking them down appeals to me.'

'Shall we go to London tomorrow? Could do with a night out.'

They were sitting outside in their flying gear enjoying the early evening sunshine. The other guys in the squadron were similarly sprawled about waiting to see if they would be scrambled this afternoon. The telephone rang. Seconds later he and Chalky were given orders to patrol over London.

This wasn't a scramble, just a routine sortie. He took off first, closely followed by Chalky. After buzzing about for almost an hour and seeing absolutely bugger all he requested from ops that they be allowed to land. Permission was refused and they continued to circle around the city at seven thousand feet. He was now in the rear with his friend taking the lead.

He saw an aircraft dive into the layer of cloud a mile away and contacted Chalky on the RT.

'Enemy aircraft. Did you see them?'

'Tally-ho! Follow me.'

Seconds later two more Huns shot through the clouds. They were Junkers 87 dive-bombers. He switched on his reflector sights and turned his gun button to fire and raced towards the enemy aircraft. These were easy meat and he couldn't wait to shoot one down. He was flying at high speed behind the other Hurry, approaching the enemy, when he glanced behind and to his horror saw half a dozen Messerschmitt 110s a couple of thousand feet above them.

They were already starting to dive and rapidly overtaking. If they didn't take immediate action they would be shot down. Frantically he called his friend.

'Look out behind. Messerschmitt behind you approaching fast.' Despite his constant shouting Chalky appeared oblivious and continued to pursue the bombers which were almost in range. The enemy aircraft were right behind them and the leading German fighter opened fire. The tracer bullets and shells screamed past above his head. Too bloody close.

He spun his aircraft sideways and dived through a layer of cloud just below. Bloody hell! Just in front of him was one of the Junkers. He opened fire but missed and the enemy aircraft vanished into the clouds.

Where the hell was Chalky? He was about to call him again when he spotted a kite flying parallel to him through the cloud. When they both emerged into clear sky he saw it was one of the dive-bombers.

This time he wouldn't miss. He opened fire and sent the remainder of his ammunition smashing into the plane. Pieces of fuselage and cockpit covering shattered. A stream of smoke poured from the enemy engine and seconds later the Junkers was engulfed in flame. This was his first kill of the war. Sickened by the sight he turned away and tried to call his mate on the RT. Again – no response.

He returned to base and almost turned his Hurry on its nose after an appalling landing. His hands were shaking as he scrambled out and was glad of the assistance of his ground crew. Bill Preston, his squadron leader, was waiting to speak to him. Jack quickly explained what had taken place and Bill nodded.

'We can't contact Chalky. As soon as you're refuelled we're going up to look for him. We're hoping he ditched in the sea.'

The search proved fruitless. Not even a sign of a wrecked Hurricane. Bloody war! Couldn't even be a funeral if there wasn't a body to bury.

When he returned to his room everything was the same as it had been when he'd left. Chalky's belongings were scattered about the place – he wasn't a tidy bloke – but his friend would never be back. He didn't want to sleep in here tonight. The guy next door was on duty. Jack collected his things and moved next door. His head was full of thoughts of Chalky, how they'd been sitting, laughing, planning a day out in the Smoke together. Now his buddy was dead in the cockpit of his plane somewhere under the water of the English Channel.

The next morning he had to put it aside. There wasn't time to mourn lost comrades. Raise a glass in the mess to whoever had bought it and then put on a brave face. This was the only way anyone could cope with the death of so many. He'd lost friends before and no doubt would do so again and just had to get on with it like everyone else. He desperately wanted to speak to Ellie. She'd understand how he felt.

After eating a late breakfast, he went to make his combat report and received yet more bad news. The bloke whose bed he'd borrowed last night had gone for a Burton. Not even fighting the enemy, but misjudging his landing and crashing into a building at the far end of the runway. What a sodding awful way to die.

Six

'There's a very official looking letter for you, Ellie,' Rebecca said. 'I thought I'd bring it up.'

Ellie had been washing her hair at the communal sink in the girls' room. It was far easier to do it during the day when the demand was less. Quickly snatching up a towel she wrapped her hair in it wishing she'd kept it short the way she'd had it when she was flying. It took far too long to dry now it was below her shoulders.

'Thanks, I've been expecting to hear...' She stopped, realising she hadn't told her friend about the application. As it had been more than five weeks since she'd posted it she'd begun to think her application might have been tossed in the wastepaper basket as totally unsuitable.

Her friend was waiting expectantly for her to finish the sentence. She decided to open the letter before telling Rebecca anything else, after all there might be no reason to mention the ATA at all.

She read the letter with growing excitement. They wanted her – in fact they were eager for her to join as soon as possible. A letter had been sent to WAAF headquarters already asking for her to be released from the service.

'I'm going to join the ATA. I didn't mention it before because I didn't know if I'd be accepted.'

'When do you leave?'

'They want me to report to Hatfield as soon as possible.'

Within ten minutes her hair was put up in a chignon and she was ready to visit the CO. Rebecca had congratulated her, given her a quick hug and then hurried off on an errand of some sort. Satisfied she looked smart, Ellie clattered downstairs, through the house, and only slowed her pace as she approached the admin offices.

For once the sniffy admin girl who guarded the CO's privacy smiled at her. 'I was about to send for you – how did you know the queen bee wants to see you?'

Ellie waved her letter. 'I just got this – I expect she's had something similar. Do I go in?'

'Of course, no need to knock, the door's open.'

She marched smartly to the desk and saluted.

'Goodness, that was quick. It seems I am to release you to join the ATA. I'll give you a forty-eight hour pass – that should be ample to get to Hatfield and take their test. Don't get your hopes up, Simpson, it's some time since you flew.'

It hadn't mentioned anything about having to take a test in her letter. 'Not that long, ma'am, about nine months. It's like riding a bicycle, you don't forget.'

She left the office in a rush and collected her pass before dashing upstairs and flinging the bits and pieces she would need for two nights away into a bag. Thank goodness she still had her dad's canvas haversack, a relic from the first war, so she didn't need to take a half empty kitbag. Then she reconsidered – would she need her flying kit and dungarees? She had no intention of taking her flying test in a skirt and stockings.

Emptying her overnight things into the bottom of the kitbag she then added the goggles, scarf, gauntlets, and helmet that she'd had with her ever since she'd left Glebe Farm. It seemed like a lifetime ago but it had only been six months.

So eager was she to leave she neglected to say her farewells to the girls she'd been working with for the past few weeks and ran down the path that led to the ferry without a second thought. Fortunately, the small vehicle was already chugging back towards her so she didn't have to wait long to board.

Only herself, three other girls and two RAF jumped in the boat. Albert – the bus driver – greeted them with his usual garrulous monologue and the bus lurched and creaked its way into town. The next train didn't leave for an hour and a half and she wasn't prepared to wait that long.

She would hitchhike into Ipswich – everybody did it – although not usually on their own. Being in uniform meant that vehicles, and they were mostly nothing but service vans, cars and lorries, always stopped for you.

She'd barely positioned herself with her thumb out before a large lorry containing a dozen noisy soldiers rumbled to a halt beside her. The driver, a smiling young man with a mop of black curls, beckoned her over.

'You'd better come in with me, miss, I'll not let a pretty girl like you travel with them blokes in the back.' This remark was greeted by a raucous cheer and several unseemly remarks.

Blushing furiously, she climbed in through the door he'd been leaning out of and settled in beside him. The third time he attempted to put his hand up her skirt she wished she'd gone in the back.

'If you try that again, soldier, you'll regret it. I have noted down your number and will write a formal complaint to your commanding officer.'

His cheeky grin vanished. He slammed on the brakes, almost causing her to go head first into the windscreen. The swearing and crashing coming from the back meant those travelling there had been equally mistreated.

'Stuck up mare, get out of me cab. I ain't taking you nowhere.'

She didn't need telling twice and had the door open and was on the ground before he'd finished speaking. Her intention had been to rush round to the back and ask to be taken in there but she wasn't given the opportunity. The door slammed and the lorry shot off covering her with dirt.

The road was empty in both directions. He'd dumped her somewhere in the middle of the countryside and she had no option but to start walking. An ominous rumble of thunder made her look up. Heavy black clouds were rolling in from the sea and she hadn't brought her mac with her. Part of the regulation uniform issue had included a strange garment that was half macintosh and half groundsheet.

Even her passion killers were soaked before a smart black car pulled up beside her. The kindly old gentleman turned out to be a local doctor, which explained why he still had petrol for his vehicle.

'You poor child, I hope you have a change of clothes wherever you're going.'

'Unfortunately, sir, I haven't. But I'm sure I'll dry off as soon as it stops raining. I apologise for making your seat wet.' In fact she did have her flying kit but she had no intention of telling him that.

'Don't worry about it, my dear, far worse happens at sea. Do you want me to drop you at the station?'

She wiped her dripping hair from her cheeks. 'Yes please. That would be wonderful.' This time she didn't make the mistake of discussing her destination.

Her driver was finding it difficult to see as his rudimentary windscreen wipers scarcely cleared the torrential rain. This didn't deter him and they arrived safely at Ipswich station just in time for her to leap onto the train to London. She was lucky and found a seat next to an equally wet and shivering ATS girl. They exchanged commiserative smiles but were both too wretched to talk.

The train stopped at every station, sometimes for barely a minute, sometimes longer, and the journey to Liverpool Street took almost three hours. One would have thought that in the warmth of the carriage her garments would have dried out but that wasn't the case. If she had time she would find the ladies' waiting room and change before she caught the train to Hatfield.

The thunderstorm had been local and the weather was warm and sunny from Colchester onwards and she and the girl next to her received several strange looks from those getting on the train. With her once smart uniform sticking uncomfortably to her, she eventually found her way to King's Cross. A helpful guard told her the correct platform and that she had an hour to wait. Plenty of time to change, but even more importantly to find a hot drink and something to eat.

Members of the armed forces were supposed to remain in uniform at all times – she could be put on a charge if she was seen dressed as she was. The chances of that were minuscule and anyway to her it didn't seem to make much difference whether she changed now or when she got there. The wet uniform had been rolled as carefully as she could and put in her kitbag. She prayed she would have a billet that would allow her to dry and press it before she returned to Bawdsey.

What she hadn't reckoned with was the fact that to get onto the aerodrome she would have to get past the security guards. They would be expecting a smartly dressed WAAF not a girl in dungarees.

She prayed her ID and the letter from Mrs Pauline Gower would be enough to get her in to take her flight test. It didn't specify on the letter exactly when she would be flying – it could be today or tomorrow – but she was determined to get there as soon as possible. With this in mind she paid an exorbitant sum to a taxi driver to take her from the station to the airfield.

As they approached her pulse accelerated. Crisscrossing the sky were the familiar outlines of Tiger Moths as they did circuits and bumps. She guessed these were other potential candidates for the ATA, that she wasn't the only one being tested today. What she hadn't expected was for huge Harvards and Battles to be doing circuits and bumps at much higher speeds around them.

When she explained why she wasn't in uniform to the security guard and police guarding the gates she was asked to show her soaked uniform. Once they'd seen this they let her in.

'Miss Simpson, you will be escorted to the office,' the senior policeman said with a smile.

The offices for the Air Transport Auxiliary, Hatfield ferry pool, were behind the de Havilland hangars and workshops. The headquarters were a large wooden hut – not at all what she expected. Overhead she heard the deep throated roar of experimental fighter aircraft which drowned out the little Tiger Moths.

Being on an airfield again after so long, breathing in the old familiar smell of aviation fuel, oil and smoke was enough to calm her nerves and give her the confidence to face whatever came next.

The friendly policeman pointed to the door and abandoned her. Inside there were three closed doors. She knocked on the nearest one. No reply – so she knocked again and was asked to come in.

The woman sitting behind the desk smiled and pointed to a chair. 'Miss Simpson, no doubt you can explain your bizarre appearance.'

Ellie hastily did so and was relieved when the woman laughed. 'Good show. Your logbook please.'

This was ready and was handed over. The woman spent a few minutes perusing the pages before snapping it shut. 'From this I see you haven't flown since last year.'

'That's correct, ma'am, but I'm sure I won't have forgotten.'

'Come along then, let's see what you're made of.'

She followed her from the office, around the hangar to where a Tiger Moth waited on the edge of the apron. The woman climbed into the front seat leaving her to take the one behind – the pilot's seat. Ellie had expected to be nervous, to have forgotten what order to do things in but it all came back to her.

Deftly she fastened the straps and gadgets, did her preflight checks in a steady, clear voice and was ready when she was told to do three circuits and landings.

'Keep a good lookout. This is an RAF base and there will be other aircraft coming in and out.'

The first take off was perfect, the circuit of the aerodrome and landing couldn't have been better. It was as if she'd never been away from her beloved Moths. On the second circuit she was overconfident, forgot to keep a lookout for other planes and narrowly avoided what would have been a fatal collision.

The passenger in the front kept silent. Ellie knew if she messed up the final circuit she would fail. So far the score was one good, one dreadful. She climbed to a thousand feet and throttled back to cruising speed. She was watching the altimeter like a hawk and kept a close eye on the turn and bank indicator. On the crosswind leg everything was going to plan. She checked for any incoming or leaving aircraft before beginning her descent.

She closed the throttle and trimmed the glide – it had to be 60 mph to make a perfect landing. She could see the aerodrome directly below, exactly where it should be. The Tiger Moth flew over the fence and she levelled out. She mustn't pull back too much on the control column. If she had judged correctly they would land smoothly without a bounce and she would be in.

The Moth touched, the grass whizzed beneath the wheels – a perfect landing. She sat for a few seconds before undoing the straps and climbing out of the aircraft.

'Well done, Miss Simpson. You're exactly the sort of pilot we need. We'll go back into the office and complete the paperwork.'

Ellie wanted to turn cartwheels but somehow managed to walk sedately behind the ATA officer. The letter was going to be sent to her CO and if everything went smoothly she was to report to Hatfield as soon as possible.

'Accommodation has been arranged for you tonight. The adjutant will give you details. Report to her when you arrive and she'll give you a list of suitable billets. Unfortunately, we don't have any official digs.'

'Thank you.' She was so overwhelmed by it all she couldn't think of anything sensible to say. If she could have saluted she would have done so, but this was hardly appropriate dressed as she was.

Eventually she found where she was to stay, a B&B a mile away. The landlady greeted her with a smile.

'Come along in, ducks, I expect you'd like a nice hot bath. Give us your wet things I'll get them dry and ready for you to wear when you leave tomorrow morning.'

The bath was the regulation five inches but she felt much better after it. In her flying gear she returned to the kitchen and was fed a delicious steak and kidney pie followed by roly-poly pudding and custard. By far the best meal she'd had since the fish and chips she'd shared with Greg.

No sooner had she thought this than she decided she would go and see him at Hornchurch. She didn't have to be back at Bawdsey Manor until lunchtime the day after tomorrow. If she left first thing in the morning she could easily get to his base and would be able to spend the day with him. Of course, he might very well be on duty, in which case she would go home and see Dad and Mabel.

'Excuse me, could I possibly use your telephone?'

'Go ahead, ducks, put the pennies in the box when you've done.'

Ellie gave the number to the operator and waited to be connected.

Seven

Greg and the rest of the squadron had twenty-four hours off duty – they couldn't leave the base in case there was a flap on – but apart from that they were free to do what they liked. He was heading for the bar when someone yelled his name.

'Hey, Greg, there's a call for you.'

He was beside the phone in seconds, his heart pounding, expecting to hear the worst possible news. Instead it was Ellie.

'How amazing, I didn't think I'd be able to speak to you in person, just leave a message. I wanted you to be the first to know I got into the ATA and if they let me go I'm starting next week.'

'That's fantastic. Are you going to be based at Hatfield?'

'I am, for the moment at least. I don't think there's more than twenty women working for them at present. I can't believe they've taken me on. I don't have to be back at base for another thirty-six hours. I don't suppose you can spend a bit of time with me before I go back?'

'Talk about serendipity, darling, I'm off duty until ten o'clock tomorrow night. If you can come here, I'll meet you at the gate when you arrive. I can't leave the base.'

'That's what I thought. I'm catching the eight o'clock train in the morning and even with having to go from King's Cross to Liverpool Street, catch the train to Romford and then find my way to Hornchurch – I think I could be with you by eleven.'

'I can't tell you how happy I am. I'll let the gate know to expect you and they'll ring me when you arrive. You can't wander about the base unescorted.'

'I should think not. Although I will be in my WAAF uniform and I'm sure there are plenty of those on your base.'

'Actually, not many. They're building accommodation at the moment and I expect we'll be overrun with pretty girls in blue in a month or two.'

'My new uniform is blue, but dark blue. Very smart and with gold buttons. We have to fly in a tight skirt which is quite ridiculous. I hope that changes soon. I've got to go and get measured as soon as I'm officially on their books. I've no idea where I go but no doubt someone will tell me.'

'You do realise, sweetheart, that you'll be a civilian and based about an hour from here by road.'

'As neither of us can get petrol, even if we had a car, that's not much use. I'm hoping I can cadge a lift if I get any free time and there's a Moth coming to your base.'

'You'll just have to fly in your dungarees until then which sounds as if it'll be a lot more comfortable.'

Someone poked him sharply in the back. 'I've got to go, there's a queue forming behind me. See you tomorrow.'

He replaced the receiver and apologised to those waiting. 'My fiancée has joined the ATA,' he told the chap behind him.

'Jolly good. Now, bugger off, I need to make a private call.'

Greg didn't know why he'd blurted out his news to someone he didn't know, but for the first time in weeks he was optimistic about their relationship. Was it possible he could persuade her to change her mind and marry him before the end of the war? If it was anything like the last one, it could go on for years and he didn't want to wait that long. Once he was married he could put the sordid incident behind him. He'd come to the decision that it would be better if Ellie never knew of his indiscretion. He would forget about Elizabeth. He was quite sure she had already moved on to someone else by now.

In the mess he discovered that two from his squadron had also arranged to spend the following day with their partners. One a wife and the other a fiancée like Ellie.

'Why don't we meet up for lunch?' Dickie Forsyth suggested.

'I say, what a top-hole idea,' Giles Hodgson-Smythe bleated.

The last thing Greg wanted was to share any of the precious time he had with Ellie with these two nitwits. They were excellent airmen and came from the same strata of society as himself, but there the resemblance ended.

'If you don't mind, chaps, I'd prefer to have Ellie to myself.'

His refusal was taken in good part and the two began to make enthusiastic plans for their day. He hoped their respective partners would be as pleased as they were. Not his problem. He left them to it and headed for the NAAFI. He couldn't take her to the canteen but hopefully he could arrange something a bit special if he sweet talked one of the girls behind the counter.

When he returned to buy himself a much needed pint of bitter he was pleased with what he'd accomplished. With a bit of bribery, he'd persuaded Iris, the most amenable of the girls working there, to pack him up a picnic which he would collect before he went to meet Ellie. The weather had been decidedly dodgy these past few weeks, not at all summery. The low cloud and frequent showers were probably what was keeping the Huns away.

The base was huge, there were plenty of places they could go where they wouldn't be disturbed to eat their lunch as long as it didn't rain. He could put the picnic basket on the rack behind his saddle and she could sit on the crossbar. He would then pedal them around the perimeter. This way he could show her his Spit and if the coast was clear he would let her sit in the cockpit. It was possible that in the future she might be flying one of these herself.

The room he shared with Johnny was quiet, his friend would be downing as much alcohol as he could tonight and would then, if things followed in the normal pattern, play the piano and lead the officers in a selection of filthy songs. Johnny never drank to excess when he was likely to be flying the next day. There was nothing worse than being in the claustrophobic cockpit of a Spitfire with a crashing hangover. You only made that mistake the once.

He picked up the book he was reading, a crime story by Margery Allingham with a detective fellow called Albert Campion. Writing a damn good book was another thing women could do as well as men. He made sure he turned out his light long before his room mate was likely to be back – he needed to be sound asleep by then unless he wanted to be dragged into a drunken conversation.

When there'd been no call from the gate by eleven o'clock Greg decided to pedal down there. He'd been prowling about in the admin office getting on everyone's nerves. He was chatting to the policeman when a local bus ground to a halt and his beloved girl jumped out.

As he couldn't leave the base he had to wait impatiently inside the gate while she was signed in.

'Ellie, darling, I'm so glad to see you.'

'I'm glad to see you too. I hadn't realised just how huge this place is. There must be dozens of pillboxes around the perimeter and hundreds of soldiers as well as RAF personnel.'

'There are, sweetheart, which is why we're going to find ourselves a quiet spot and have a picnic.' He'd barely finished speaking when a slow, steady drizzle began.

'Never mind, Greg, I'm sure we can find a dry corner in a hangar somewhere. I got soaked to the skin yesterday so I'd prefer not to do it again today. Can we wait here until it stops?'

He shook his head. 'Sorry, we'll have to make a dash for it. The NAAFI's open to visitors so we'll go there.'

With her balanced precariously on the crossbar he cycled furiously back to the main building, much to the amusement of several chaps he passed. He almost catapulted her over the handlebars when he skidded to a halt and they were both laughing.

'Golly, that was fun. I've not ridden on the crossbar since Neil used to bring me back from the village after cricket.'

He was obliged to introduce her to a couple of his friends and didn't much like the way they looked at her. The third person to waylay them was the one person he'd hoped to avoid. Johnny had seen him with Elizabeth and might say something.

'What ho, old fellow. Is this your little popsy then? You're a lucky chap. You don't deserve someone as lovely as this.'

Ellie wasn't fooled for a moment by Johnny's charm. 'Thank you, but I'm nobody's popsy. I'm Greg's fiancée.'

He put his arm firmly around her waist and guided her away before the conversation could continue down dangerous paths. Iris pointed to the rain which had now set in and looked as though it wouldn't stop all day. 'Pity about your picnic, sir, you'll have to eat it in here now.'

'Sadly, I think you're right.' He'd already paid for the food but ordered two mugs of tea and dropped the required pennies on the counter.

They were happily ensconced at a window table when an orderly appeared at the door. The place was fairly full of off duty pilots and they all paused and looked his way.

'General flap on, sirs, everyone to report to the crew room immediately.'

'I'm sorry, Ellie, I've got to go.'

She was already on her feet and into his arms before he finished speaking. 'I know, I love you. Be careful up there.'

Ellie watched him stride out with the others, proud of the way he stood out, taller, more authoritative somehow. Her appetite had gone, she would never eat all this carefully prepared food on her own.

She carried the box over to the counter where the friendly girl was staring anxiously out of the window as if expecting the Luftwaffe to arrive at any minute.

'There hasn't been a siren, if there was an attack coming here we'd know about it.'

The girl nodded and managed a small smile. 'You're right, miss, but everyone's saying this base is going to be a target once it starts.'

Then the hideous wailing of the air raid siren filled the air. Ellie had no idea where the shelter was so would just have to follow someone who did.

She and the girl were the only people in the NAAFI – everyone else had rushed off to their posts.

'Where's the shelter?' Ellie shouted over the racket.

'I don't know. I've forgotten. We was shown, but I can't remember.'

This wasn't good. The siren continued to wail. They needed to get to safety. There must be someone out the back who knew – they couldn't all be as clueless as this girl.

'Quickly, we'll go through the kitchen.' She tucked the picnic box under one arm and grabbed the terrified girl's elbow and half dragged her into the now deserted kitchen.

As they reached the back door Spitfire after Spitfire screamed overhead, racing into the sky at full throttle to protect the airbase and destroy whatever planes were coming. Greg would be one of them. She prayed he would return safely – that all the boys would.

There were uniformed people running desperately for a building fifty yards from where they were. She was about to join them when she was almost lifted from her feet by the whump – whump – whump of a huge anti-aircraft gun. This was followed by the rat-tat-tat of machine gun fire – the soldiers guarding the base must be seeing something she wasn't.

'I think we'll be safer staying here. If we cross the open space we could be gunned down if there are any German fighters close enough.'

The girl had gathered her wits and pointed to the sky. 'Our boys won't let them get through. Look at them, miss, ain't they wonderful?'

Right above their heads, at several thousand feet, half a dozen Spits were shooting at a dive-bomber – she thought it a Junkers. The German didn't have a chance. Smoke poured from his fuselage and then the entire aircraft was engulfed in flames. It spiralled crazily towards the ground.

He was the enemy but she wished he'd been able to bail out. The triumphant British fighters roared off in search of another target. Why were the sirens still howling? Surely they were safe now? Then, as the skies cleared of Spitfires, a low flying bomber roared in scarcely above treetop height, heading straight for the building she was standing in.

The world stood still. Was this it? Was her life going to end before it had hardly begun? She held her breath as it thundered overhead and her eyes widened when she saw quite clearly the bomb hatch open and two, black deadly shapes drop onto a building at the far side of the apron.

She was rocked back on her heels by the sound of the explosion. Then, as the German plane began to climb away the fighters returned and this too, was shot down. A few minutes later the all clear sounded and the airfield was suddenly swarming with rescue vehicles, fire engines and ambulances.

The smoke and dust from the damaged building was clearing and she saw, with relief, that it wasn't as bad as she'd feared. Despite having been dropped from such a low elevation the bombs had missed their target, the building had broken windows and so on but looked relatively unscathed.

'Me name's Iris. That could've been worse. I almost wet me pants.'

'I'm Ellie. I was terrified. I expect they'll be needing a lot of tea. Is there anything I can do to help whilst you wait for the others to come back?'

'No, you're all right, miss. I should go back to your table and eat yer lunch. Your young man will be back safe and sound soon enough, don't you worry.'

Their roles had been reversed and now Iris was doing the comforting. 'I'd hoped they would be back already now the danger has gone. There must be more Germans up there somewhere that we can't see from here.'

'Here, miss, you read the Daily Sketch and I'll make you another cuppa, I reckon that's gone cold by now.'

Ellie took the proffered newspaper and returned to her abandoned mug. She reached for it and was shocked to find it still piping hot. It had seemed like a lifetime but in fact could only have been a few minutes.

'This one is fine, Iris, thanks.'

Within half an hour the place was busy again, the noise as loud as before with as much laughter and jollity. Her hands were still shaking – how could they all be so calm after such a shocking event? She collapsed into her chair and opened the paper. Today was July 12th – her first brush with death. Her stomach curdled as she realised that as an ATA pilot she could be in mortal danger every time she took off.

Eight

Kenley was quieter, Jack thought, in the days following the death of Chalky and the other poor bugger, and the mood depressed. To lose two pilots might seem insignificant against the deaths incurred by the army during a battle – but there are only twelve members of a squadron and they were like a family. It wouldn't have been so bad if they'd shot anything down, had something to show for the loss, but these two guys had died for what seemed like nothing.

Pilots were in short supply and it was a week before the CO was able to stop flying himself as two new blokes arrived. Neither of them had flown in combat, the rest of the squadron knew these raw recruits were likely to get shot down first time out unless they were very lucky.

The days passed and spirits improved. They flew sorties most nights, and often in the days as well, but rarely reported seeing any enemy action. Every time the telephone rang he was on his feet and heading for his kite almost before he knew why they'd been scrambled.

Jack was on call when an order to scramble came through. Ops reported ships were being attacked in the Channel and every fighter was needed to protect them. He was second in command today, the role that Chalky used to have, and he relished the responsibility. They always flew en masse nowadays – nobody was sent up without the rest of the squadron to protect them. They were a far more formidable fighting unit with them all there.

The operations room directed them over the radio. He saw at once they were hopelessly outnumbered. In the distance he saw a small formation of German bombers, with at least two squadrons of enemy fighters flying above to protect them.

'Bandits include many snappers. I say again, many snappers, keep a good lookout. Over.'

He didn't need to be told there were dozens of Messerschmitt 109s. He could see them for himself. He looked around at his courageous Hurricanes and was filled with the determination to do some damage. With any luck, they would be joined in the scrap by other squadrons – he bloody well hoped so – Hurrys weren't built for speed, they needed Spits to knock out the fighters whilst they concentrated on the bombers.

They dived in formation, guns firing, and one of the bombers, a Dornier, nosedived into the sea. One down – three to go.

'Watch that bastard behind you, Yellow Two. He's close, boy, real close. Break Yellow Two.' The RT screamed at him. For a moment Jack didn't react, then he remembered he was Yellow Two today. He took violent evasive action and the Messerschmitt screamed past him, guns firing, and he felt his kite judder and there was a sharp pain in his shoulder. He was hit – but he didn't know how badly.

Then the squadron of Spitfires arrived and everything changed. He returned to the fray knowing these boys would keep the snappers at bay whilst he and his squadron dealt with the bombers. They scored a direct hit on one, exploding it satisfactorily. Then the others vanished into the clouds.

His kite was sluggish, not responding as it should. 'Yellow Two returning to base, Yellow Leader. Took some damage during the scrap.'

He left them to it and turned the kite towards the coast keeping everything crossed that he would make it and not have to ditch in the drink. The rain was obscuring his vision, but the low clouds would help to protect him from marauding fighters.

Hawkinge was the closest airfield and the one they'd been told to use if in trouble. He was flying ever lower, if he didn't see the strip soon he'd have to attempt a crash landing. He was too low to use his parachute.

Then the engine cut out completely. He was gliding. To his delight he saw a runway beneath him and guided his crippled plane towards it. The wheels didn't drop. A belly flop then. He braced himself and his brave little Hurry hit the deck, slithered along before pitching forward. For a hideous moment he thought they would turn turtle but then the tail crashed back.

His breath hissed through his teeth. He was down. He was still alive. He'd barely unfastened his harness when his cockpit was thrown back and frantic arms reached in and grabbed him.

'Out you come, sir, sharpish like.'

He was hauled out by his straps and then thrown bodily to the ground. The two blokes who'd grabbed him landed with a thud on the grass and yanked him to his feet. He was given the bum's-rush away from the kite.

There was an almighty bang and the three of them were flung face forward into the dirt. A wave of heat surged past and there was a strong smell of singeing flying jacket.

It took him a few moments to sort himself out but then he rolled over a few times to put out the sparks and with the help of his two rescuers staggered to his feet.

'Sod me!' That was all he could think of to say as he watched his aircraft burning. A fire truck zoomed past him and soon the flames were doused.

'Come along, sir, you'd better let the medics have a dekko at that shoulder.'

Jack glanced down and saw his battledress was soaked red. The last thing he remembered was thinking that he'd been shot in this arm a few months ago on the same side.

Ellie remained glued to the window and counted the Spitfires in as they began to return. Thirty-six, three squadrons, had taken off but only thirty-four had landed. She couldn't bear to think that Greg was one of those missing.

A hand squeezed her shoulder. 'Sweetheart, I'm here, don't look so stricken.'

Her chair flew backwards with a crash and she buried herself in his arms. His uniform was rough beneath her cheek. He smelt of engine oil and sweat. They didn't kiss, they just held each other. After a few minutes he gently prised her away.

'Is there anything left in that picnic basket? I'm absolutely starving.'

'I've not opened it. In fact, I've not even drunk my tea. I'll get us some more.'

'No need, Iris is bringing some over.'

They munched happily for a while before she could bring herself to ask about the missing aircraft. 'Do you know what happened?'

'One of the chaps bailed out safely, the other ran out of fuel and landed at Hawkinge, it's near Folkestone.'

'I'm so pleased no one was killed or injured from here.' She looked at him more closely. He looked older, exhausted, he should be resting not entertaining her.

'I'm going to leave as soon as we've finished this so you can get some rest. I won't be very far away once I'm settled in Hatfield and I might be allowed to borrow a Tiger Moth and come and see you occasionally.'

He grinned. 'I should think that would be highly unlikely, but one can but ask. I think someone from admin wants to speak to me.' He stood up but the young man shook his head.

'No, sir, it's your fiancée, Miss Simpson, I need to speak to.'

What could an orderly at Hornchurch possibly want with her?

'I beg your pardon, miss, but there's a phone call for you. It's from Hawkinge.'

This was even more puzzling but she trotted along behind him, Greg at her side, curious to know how anyone at this aerodrome could be asking for her.

'Hello, Ellie Simpson here. How can I help?'

'I've got a Jack Reynolds here, critically injured, he's got you down as his next of kin. The chap who landed here a while ago from Hornchurch told us you were visiting your fiancé there. Can't believe our luck. Can you get here as soon as possible?'

'I'll be there as soon as I can. Which hospital is he being transferred to?'

'The Royal Victoria.'

The line went dead. She looked at the receiver, unable to process what she had just heard.

'What is it, Ellie?'

She explained to Greg and he was equally horrified. 'I still can't quite comprehend how our chap was even involved in this. No doubt you'll discover what happened when you get there.'

'I don't have to be back at Bawdsey until my watch at one o'clock. Hopefully, that will give me time to visit and get back without being put on a charge.'

Critically injured – that meant Jack could die. First Neil, now someone she considered as close as a brother to her.

The orderly was speaking to someone on the telephone. 'If you don't mind getting wet and cold, miss, there's an ATA pilot just about to take off and he's going to Hawkinge. I've asked him to wait for you.'

She nipped into the nearest WC and changed back into her flying gear. When she came out Greg handed her an oilskin he'd found somewhere. 'This will keep the worst out, darling. There's a vehicle outside waiting to take you over.'

There was barely time to kiss him goodbye before she was racing around the perimeter and scrambling out with her kitbag to greet the ATA pilot. This was a middle aged man, but he was friendly enough especially when she told him she was about to join the service herself.

'Shove your bag in first. It's going to be a bit nippy, but no doubt you're used to it. You're lucky I'm still here, I had to wait for the worst of the rain to clear. As you know, we mustn't fly in poor visibility.'

It was drizzling, grey, but there were patches of blue sky ahead. She was strapped in and ready before him and enjoyed every minute of the short flight to Kent. She refused to think about the reason she was going.

At the airfield there was transport laid on to take her to the hospital. On the way the driver explained how they'd been able to find her.

'Not often something like this happens, but sometimes luck's on our side. When we rang Kenley to tell them about your friend they told us he had no family and that you were put down as his next of kin. The bloke from Hornchurch was waiting to use the telephone and recognised your name and said he'd spoken to you earlier. So here you are, miss, and hopefully not too late.'

The vehicle lurched to a halt outside the Victorian building. She jumped out, called her thanks, and with her kitbag over her shoulder hurried inside. The place was pristine, but the all-pervasive smell of boiled cabbage and antiseptic one always found in hospitals was still there.

She explained who she'd come to see and was directed to a ward on the first floor. It wasn't official visiting time but the sister in charge greeted her with a smile.

'Miss Simpson, we have been expecting you. Flying Officer Reynolds lost a great deal of blood and is being transfused. The next few hours will be critical. We are hoping having you here might be what he needs to fight for his life.'

Ellie dumped her kitbag in the corner of the sister's office and followed behind the nurse. She could almost hear the starched white apron crackling as they crossed the boards towards a side ward which contained just the one bed.

Her throat closed. Jack was paper white, propped up on the pillows, his auburn hair the only colour in the room. Was she too late?

'He's semi-conscious, Miss Simpson, talk to him. It will be better if he's awake.'

There was already a chair by the bed and she slipped into it. 'Jack, Jack, it's me, Ellie. I've come to see you.'

There was no response. Tentatively she reached out and took his hand, almost recoiling at how cold it was. She chafed it between her own and continued to babble nonsense. Telling him about Greg, about the ATA, about anything she could think of. She looked more closely at his face and there was definitely a little colour in it now. From somewhere came the impulse to kiss him. Perhaps, like the prince kissing Sleeping Beauty, her lips would wake him up. She would see his laughing green eyes staring back at her. It would pay him back for kissing her that time when he said goodbye.

She glanced over her shoulder to see there were no lurking nurses watching, then leaned across the bed and touched her lips to his.

Someone was talking to him, the voice sounded familiar, but it was a long way away and he couldn't understand the words. This person was holding his hand, stroking his arm, calling him back from the darkness.

It was Ellie. What the hell was she doing here? He was coming fully awake, his shoulder hurt like buggery, but he was alive. Before he could open his eyes the bed creaked and Ellie kissed him.

Now, it was almost worth getting injured for that. His eyelids flicked up. Her eyes widened in shock and if he hadn't felt so grim he would have laughed at her expression.

'Jack, I wouldn't have done that if I'd known you were awake.' She flopped back on the chair but didn't release his hand. The longer she held it the better as far as he was concerned.

'How the hell are you here?' This wasn't what he'd intended to say but probably best not to mention the kiss.

When she explained he managed a weak chuckle. 'I should have told you I'd put your name down as my next of kin. Must've been a bit of a shock for you.'

Her smile was radiant. 'I'm glad you did, otherwise I wouldn't have known you were injured.'

They were interrupted by the arrival of the nurse. 'Excellent, Flying Officer Reynolds, you gave us a bit of a scare but I think you'll do now.' She took his pulse, checked his lines and his dressing and sailed away.

'I could do with a drink, is there any water on the table?'

'No, just an empty jug and glass. I'll go and get some.'

Ellie remained with him for the next few hours, feeding him broth, tea and copious amounts of water. He was feeling almost human by the time she told him she had to go. He was visited by the doctors and whilst they were there she went to find herself something to eat and make a couple of phone calls.

'I have to catch the train tonight if I'm going to get back in time tomorrow. I've rung Dad and he said you're to go there to convalesce. I've spoken to the doctor and they think you'll be able to travel unescorted in a week if you continue to improve.'

'That would be great. I'm hoping I'll be fully fit to fly within a fortnight. Things are really hotting up and every pilot is going to be needed to keep the Germans out of Britain.'

'A week's convalescence is what I was told. Take care of yourself, Jack, and don't give me a scare like that again.'

She squeezed his hand but didn't offer to kiss him a second time. He watched her walk out, head high, shoulders back. He'd never known anyone quite like her. His chest squeezed and for moment he couldn't breathe. Sod me! How had this happened? Somehow, he'd fallen in love with her, and she belonged to someone else.

Nine

It was midnight by the time Ellie arrived at Ipswich station and the last train to Felixstowe was long gone. Even if she had got there, neither the bus nor the ferry would be working until eight o'clock the following morning.

The weather had perked up, the rain had gone and it was a perfect summer's evening. There was a long wooden bench in the ladies' waiting room and she would try and get some sleep on that. She gave up after an hour and remained upright until the first train steamed in.

Having ample time before she needed to be on watch she found an early morning café and had a much needed cuppa and several slices of toast. She was becoming used to margarine and when you're hungry anything tastes good.

When she signed in at the little hut by the ferry she still had four hours before starting her watch. Plenty of time to have a strip wash and change into a fresh uniform. It occurred to her that when she left the service she was supposed to hand in all her equipment and uniform. As her civvy clothes had been sent back to Glebe Farm months ago she had nothing to put on. Surely they couldn't expect her to leave in her knickers? She giggled at the thought – after all even her underwear belonged to the WAAF.

The CO was just going into her office so Ellie showed her the letter. 'Well done, Simpson, I knew you could do it. I can't demob you until I have confirmation from head office – but I've recommended that you be allowed to leave as we now have more than enough trained operatives based here.'

'Thank you, ma'am, I appreciate your support. This might seem a strange question, but I haven't got any civilian clothes here so how can I hand in my uniform when I leave?'

'Good Lord, you don't have to give in clothes you're wearing. By the way, this weekend there will be a "stand to". Everyone is confined to base and must participate unless on watch.'

Ellie didn't like to enquire what this exercise was and hoped that one of her team might be better informed than she was. She found Rebecca in the NAAFI when she came down feeling fresher and a little more awake despite having been up most of the night. Quickly she explained where she'd been and the dramas with Jack.

Her friend congratulated her on her success. 'I'm surprised that your Greg didn't mind you dashing off to be at the bedside of another man.'

'Oh, Jack and I are just good friends. He's like a brother, part of the family. Greg's got nothing to worry about on that score. Do you know anything about this "stand to" business?'

'I don't know much more than you do, Ellie, but it's supposed to prepare us for how to deal with an invasion and so on. After all, we're rather vulnerable here, stuck on the side of the cliff like this.'

'What exactly do we have to do? I hope someone puts up a list – I don't want to be in the wrong place and leave under a cloud.'

'Please don't talk about that, it's going to be miserable when you go. I hope whoever replaces you is someone I can get on with. Faye and April are getting a dreadful reputation – I don't want to be associated with them.'

'I'm going to miss you too, Rebecca, we must keep in touch. I'll give you the Hatfield address as I don't know where I'll be billeted until I actually start.'

The following morning they worked their final shift of the rota but instead of being able to go to Felixstowe they had to participate in the exercise.

'Look, we're designated as stretcher-bearers and have got to find the room so labelled. Not sure what we have to do after that,' Rebecca said.

Someone overheard her and laughed. 'That's a cushy number, you just have to sit there until it's over.'

The room was easy enough to find and they settled down with the other two girls with a packet of biscuits she'd brought with her and two flasks of tea. She and Rebecca had books to read, the other two had cards. She thought this was indeed the easiest job in the world.

Then the telephone rang. Ellie picked it up and was told the four of them were to collect a casualty from one of the watch stations.

The casualty was a very large airman who had developed influenza. He was quite capable of walking to sickbay but the powers that be decided it would make the exercise more real if he was transported by the stretcher-bearers.

Each of them took a corner and lifted. Her arm almost came out of its socket. The man weighed a ton. It was a long walk and the further they went the lower the stretcher was to the ground. Then Rebecca dropped her corner and the unfortunate patient rolled into the mud.

They helped him to his feet. 'No harm done, ladies, but I think I'll walk the rest of the way.' He stomped off and the four of them trailed along behind with the empty stretcher.

'I hope he doesn't make a report – we'll be for the high jump,' one of her companions said.

'He wasn't hurt and didn't seem too cross with us.' Ellie couldn't finish her sentence as the air raid siren sounded.

'Come on, girls, we've got to go into the official shelter.'

She and Rebecca ran behind the other two who had been there longer than them and knew the ropes. Their appointed shelter was a huge, man made tunnel. They shuffled to the end leaving the others to chat at the entrance.

'I wonder how long we've got to stand about in here. I desperately need a pee,' she said quietly to Rebecca.

'You could always go in here, I don't suppose anyone would notice.'

Ellie was horrified, but laughed. 'I couldn't – what if any of the airmen turned around and saw me?'

Another half an hour passed and the need became desperate. 'I'm going to risk leaving here. I can go in the bushes where nobody will see me.'

However, when they emerged it was to find they were only a few yards from the manor itself. 'I'm going in, much nicer to use a real WC.'

When she emerged, Rebecca was grinning. 'The NAAFI is open – why don't we get a cup of coffee and a bun before we go back?'

'We might as well, although the all-clear hasn't sounded yet.'

They returned a little while later to see that the last three people sheltering were geared up in their anti-gas clothing, tin hats and gas masks and were running out of the end of the tunnel.

She'd never moved so fast in her life as she put on her gas cape and gas mask. They then raced through the tunnel and down the drive hoping to catch up with the main party who were heading for a gas dugout in the woods.

Running and laughing in a gas mask was ridiculous. When she laughed and gasped for breath the rubber sides of the mask flapped up and down and honked, making hideous noises. The more this happened the more they giggled.

They tumbled into the dugout and collapsed on the floor. She hadn't realised something as boring as an exercise could be such fun.

Her demob papers came through and she said her final farewells to the girls she'd been working with for a few short weeks. She left Bawdsey for the last time with only her canvas haversack. Even her kitbag had been handed in. Of course, her gas mask was still over her shoulder.

There'd been no travel chit, she was no longer in the services and must pay for her own train ticket. Duly, she bought the ticket to Liverpool Street. She was to take up her position at Hatfield even if her uniform wasn't ready, after all she didn't need it to fly. This, once ordered from Austin Reed in London, would take at least ten days. She had been told initially it could take anything up to three months but when she said she was paying for it herself things changed.

Dad was going to pick her up from the station but she decided to walk and save the petrol. When she got home she took off her grey-blue for the last time. It was strange being in civilian clothes after so many months in uniform. What was even stranger was having free time, not being sure what was going to happen next.

The Spitfires from Hornchurch seemed to be flying non-stop but engagement between enemy planes and our boys, if there were any, took place somewhere else. At least Jack was safe in hospital and she only had to worry about Greg.

She had been home for three days when Jack rang.

'Ellie, what are you doing home?' She explained and Jack was delighted. 'I'm being discharged tomorrow morning. Can someone pick me up at Romford at lunchtime?'

'I'd love to but we haven't got any petrol spare at the moment – we're waiting for a government delivery for the tractors.'

'Not up to walking three miles at the moment. Maybe I can get a taxi, or hitch, don't worry about it, I'll get to you somehow.'

'No, I'll be there one way or another. You're a hero, wounded in the service of your country, that has to count for something.'

'I've been given two weeks to recuperate and then have to report to Kenley on 7th August.'

'I'm just waiting for my uniform and then I take up my position with the ATA. I could go before it's ready but want to be correctly dressed when I start.'

'I'm looking forward to spending a few days away from the carnage. Have you heard from Greg?'

'No, but judging by the amount of aircraft going back and forth all day and night he won't have time to call me. If anything happens to him I'm sure I'll be the first to hear.'

She put the phone down not sure if she was pleased Jack was coming or sad that it wasn't Greg. One thing she was quite sure, the next time she spoke to her fiancé she would suggest they got a special licence and got married immediately. She didn't want to wait any more.

Dad and Mabel had been on edge all day and when she told them Jack was coming to convalesce they exchanged glances.

'We thought, Ellie love, that as you're here we would get married. The banns have been called and we don't want a big do. Now our Jack's going to be here too, seems silly not to get it done.'

She ran across to embrace him and then kissed Mabel too. 'Perfect. I thought I'd miss it. Aren't you going to invite any of your friends, Mabel? Even if we can't have a wedding cake, I'm sure we can manage a few sandwiches and things.'

'Bless you, lovey, it's all in hand. My friends and I have been saving our sugar ration. I've already made a cake, not fruit, but a nice Madeira.'

'I can't let Jack walk here, not after he was so ill last week. Surely you can find me enough petrol to get to Romford and back?'

'I'll siphon a bit from one of the tractors. Our Jack deserves a bit of a fuss after what he's been through.'

This was the second time he'd referred to Jack like this and yet he'd not even mentioned Greg. It was a shame that Dad and Mabel preferred Jack – no doubt because he was more down-to-earth like them. She was certain they would come to love Greg as much as she did when they knew him better.

'I'm going to ring Hornchurch and see if there's any possibility Greg can get a few hours from the base.'

'You'll do no such thing, young lady, he's doing his duty and won't have time for such things as weddings. Those blighters have been attacking shipping and ports, our fighters are flying non-stop to protect them.'

Suitably chastened by his reminder, she nodded. 'You're right, Dad, it just doesn't seem right that he won't be here when he's almost part of the family.'

'We'll take plenty of snaps and you can send him a couple. I reckon he'll like seeing a picture of you in a pretty frock again.'

'I'd rather be in my new uniform. It should be ready next week – could you possibly wait until then?'

'Well, as long as you're both here it doesn't make any difference to us.'

'I'll ring Austin Reed tomorrow and see if I can hurry them up a bit. It's not as if they're making hundreds of women's ATA uniforms at the moment. I'm going to be one of about twenty, the rest are men.'

'You're as good as any man, Ellie love, and don't you forget it.' Dad cleared his throat and she was tempted to go over again and give him a hug but he didn't go in for that sort of thing if he could help it.

'I'm going to take the dogs for a quick walk. Do you want me to shut up the birds for you, Mabel?'

'Thank you, that would be grand. I'll start making a list for the wedding next week.'

As she wandered about in the dark she heard the unmistakable sound of heavy aircraft approaching. Immediately searchlights pointed into the sky and the heavy sound of ack-ack coming from the emplacements around Hornchurch drowned out the night time birds.

Moments later the Spitfires were swarming into the sky. She swallowed the lump in her throat and hurried inside. She didn't want to see any of the brave young men from Hornchurch being shot down.

Ten

Ellie was shocked to see how pale and thin Jack looked, but his lopsided smile was still in place and his alarming hair as bright as ever.

'You found some petrol then?'

'Dad got it from one of the tractors. You'll be all right going home as the delivery's coming today.'

She closed her eyes and held her breath as the squadron of Spitfires roared overhead. She could no longer bear to watch them. It was purgatory being so close to the base and not knowing how things were going.

Jack squeezed her arm affectionately. 'You'll hear soon enough if anything happens to Greg. No point in worrying yourself into an early grave, that won't help anyone.'

He was right. As soon as she was working and too busy to think about anything else the better. She hastily changed the subject. 'Dad and Mabel are getting married next week. I've asked them to wait until I get my new uniform as I don't want to be in their photographs in mufti.'

'The navy blue with the gold buttons and badge is very smart. I can't wait to see you in it.'

They chatted of this and that as she drove him back to the farm. He was so easy to talk to, small wonder that Dad already considered him part of the family.

She glanced sideways at her passenger and their eyes met. She returned his smile. If anything, he was more handsome than Greg, certainly more striking. It was strange how things worked out and that she loved Greg and not him. No – she did love him – but not in the same way, the way she had loved her brother Neil.

The dogs were ecstatic to see him and even the cats wound themselves about his ankles with their tails upright like bottle brushes. Mabel had prepared a special lunch in his honour and they ate it outside on the trestle table, covered in a crisp damask cloth. Mabel didn't usually bother with such things at lunchtime as the men came in to eat as well.

Only the four of them sat down to a delicious chicken and ham pie followed by plums and custard. 'Why didn't the men come into eat as they usually do?'

'I forgot to tell you, Ellie love, neither of them are working here any more. I've got a team of land girls coming most days so I didn't need them as well.'

She was shocked by this as both labourers had worked at the farm for years and were too old to find employment elsewhere. This was the sort of thing she expected from someone like her mother, not from her dad.

Mabel had seen her dismay. 'No need to look like that, lovey, they were happy to be retired on a nice little pension. There's plenty of daywork to be had in the village if they want it.'

Ellie's cheeks flushed and she fiddled with her cutlery to hide her embarrassment. Jack poked her in the ribs with his good arm. 'You thought Fred had dumped them, didn't you? Not like you to think the worst of someone.'

'It's not. I'm sorry, Dad, I don't know why I'm so wound up at the moment.'

'No need to apologise, I'm glad you were concerned for them. It's worrying about your young man every time you hear the planes go over. You'll be better when you're away from here, doing your bit for the war effort.'

The meal continued but the mood was spoilt. Jack made his apologies and retired to his room saying he was worn out after travelling.

'Don't you worry about getting up again, I'll bring your supper on a tray,' Mabel told him.

The day before the wedding the phone call from London finally came. 'I'll come up with you, Ellie, I could do with a day out. I'm going back to Kenley when you leave – don't want to be in the way of the honeymoon couple.'

'Please, don't remind me. I know intimate relations are not the prerogative of the young, but the thought of...' She couldn't finish her sentence and he chuckled and changed the subject.

He was looking much better, being outside in the sunshine and having three good meals a day was just what he needed. They'd spent most of the days together, she really enjoyed his company and would miss him when they both returned to duty.

★

'I've just got a couple of errands to run whilst you're getting the final adjustments to your new uniforms done, Ellie, I'll meet you here at midday.'

This gave her a couple of hours. She'd been told there might be some alterations to be made and to allow for that. 'That's fine. Then I'd really love to go to the pictures. I noticed *Gone with the Wind* was on at the cinema we passed. There's a Lyons' Corner House nearby where we can grab a bite before we go in.'

'Okay, sounds like a good idea to me. I've not been to the movies since God knows when.'

'There you are, miss, a perfect fit now. You'll need a taxi to take everything back. Would you like me to call one for you?'

Ellie examined herself from all sides in the long mirror. She'd loved her WAAF uniform but this was a cut above. The design and shape were identical, but the colour and trimmings really set it off. She pinned on her forage cap at a jaunty angle and was ready to go.

'We're going to the cinema before we go home. Would you mind very much if I left everything here and we picked them up on the way back?'

The assistant beamed. 'That will be perfectly acceptable. Your items will be stored behind the counter until you return. I'd no idea young women like you could fly aeroplanes. Good for you, Miss Simpson.'

Jack arrived as she stepped out onto the pavement. His expression said more than any words.

'I'm going to take some photos. Do you think the shop assistant peering through the window at us would take a couple of us together?'

The assistant was only too pleased to oblige. Photo shoot over they headed for the café. 'Where did you get the camera and film?'

He touched the side of his nose and winked. 'Friend of a friend. I promised Fred I would get one from somewhere so I can take photographs tomorrow. I'll print off extra copies so you can send them to Greg.'

She couldn't help but notice she was receiving admiring glances from both men and women. 'I love this uniform.'

'The fact that it's been made to fit makes all the difference. I take it you've got all the rest of the stuff you need? Did you leave it in the shop to collect later?'

'I did. They wanted to put it in tissue paper and large boxes but I've told them to pack them into brown paper parcels tied with string so we can carry them. I got them to make me two pairs of slacks as well. I know we're not allowed to wear them but flying in a tight skirt is ridiculous.'

'When you've got your flight suit and Mae West on no one will know what you've got on underneath.'

'I don't know if we're issued with flight suits. Talking about underneath, it's going to be a joy to wear my own things and not the regulation passion killers.'

'I can't believe I'm discussing panties with you. Better change the subject, don't you think?' He did an excellent imitation of a leer and she giggled.

The remainder of the afternoon was just as enjoyable. The film was as romantic and exciting as she'd been told. Austin Reed called a taxi for them and they bundled into it loaded down with her uniform.

'I hope we can find someone to give us a lift back, Jack, we'll never carry all this ourselves. There isn't a taxi any more as both drivers have been called up.'

'Don't worry about it, something will arrange itself. Maybe you could stand outside the station like a cover girl and hitch us a lift.'

She viewed the five large parcels. 'I've got to transport all this with me when I leave the day after tomorrow. Even if I still had a kitbag I doubt I'd fit it all in. And I've still got my flying gear to add to this, plus things we mustn't mention.'

He stretched out his legs and smiled lazily. 'Problem solved, ma'am, I'll come with you. I can't return to Kenley until Saturday and I've got nothing else to do.'

'That would be amazing, if you're sure? I'll pay for your ticket, of course.'

He smiled again. 'I'm a man of means, Ellie, I can buy my own tickets. Anyway, a man in uniform doesn't have to pay most times.'

Then she remembered that he'd sold two of the aircraft from the flying club they'd run together before the war, so he must still have that money. He certainly hadn't had time to spend it all.

The journey to Romford was short and soon they were on the platform faced with the dilemma of how they were going to get back to Glebe Farm. Under normal circumstances he could have carried three of the parcels, but he only had one good arm at the moment and she certainly couldn't carry four.

As they emerged on the forecourt she laughed. 'Look at that, our transport awaits.' Standing where the taxis used to be was a pony cart driven by one of her dad's tenant farmers.

'I hope you're here for us, Mr Foster?'

The man touched his cap with the whip. 'I am, Miss Simpson. My Bessie will get you home in no time.'

'Thank you so much.'

They tossed the parcels in first and then followed them. Mr Foster snapped his whip in the air and the willing cob leaned into the traces and the vehicle trundled over the cobbles and onto the smooth tarmac.

Although a trifle bumpy, the ride was most enjoyable especially in the early evening sunshine. The dogs went wild with excitement on seeing Bessie – they weren't familiar with equines. The racket brought Mabel out from the kitchen and she was struck dumb when she saw Ellie in her finery.

'I've never seen the like, ever so smart, much better than your WAAF uniform. I'm not surprised you wanted to wear it tomorrow.'

Their driver refused to take any money, bade them a polite goodbye and expertly turned his horse and cart and trotted back up the drive.

Jack looked exhausted and she decided she wouldn't allow him to come with her when she left. She had two perfectly good suitcases, the ones she'd used when she was a weekly boarder, and with the help of a porter she would manage her luggage herself.

The next day they walked to the church for the morning ceremony and she was pleased to find a couple of dozen people waiting in the congregation. Someone had picked bunches of garden flowers and the church looked lovely. The organist had been called up so there were no hymns but the wedding was perfect. She'd never seen her dad looking so happy and was glad for him and Mabel.

There was a delicious buffet luncheon ready in the pantry and it only took a few minutes to take it out and place it on the trestles. There was even champagne for the toast.

Jack retired early which gave her time to talk to her dad about her departure the next day.

'I don't want him to come with me, he's not strong enough yet, in fact, I doubt he'll be ready to fly again by the weekend either.'

'He's made up his mind, Ellie love, you'll not persuade him to stay behind.'

'I'm going to leave now, whilst he's asleep. I've already packed my cases. Would you mind very much using some of your precious petrol and driving me to the station?'

His smile was sad. 'You've changed so much over the past year, Ellie love, I scarcely know you now. I'll take care of Jack, he's part of the family. Go and get your cases and I'll bring the car round.'

She hugged Mabel and congratulated her for the umpteenth time. 'I can go away now confident that Dad's happy and being well looked after. If I can get leave I'll come and see you both, but at least I can ring whenever I like and you can write to me. I don't have an actual address yet, so send any letters to Hatfield.'

'You're a good girl, I think of you like my daughter now. We're ever so proud of you, lovey, not many young ladies could do what you do. Take care of yourself.'

Until the car was actually turning onto the lane Ellie was worried Jack might suddenly reappear and demand to accompany her. Things would be different now. She was starting a new life as were her father and Mabel. She thought it unlikely she would ever live permanently at Glebe Farm again.

When the war was over and she was Greg's wife she supposed she would have to live in one of his family's grand houses. If the house she'd visited in Mayfair was anything to go by, then the country estate would probably be a stately home. Her mouth curved – she didn't want to be a lady of the manor but as long as she was with Greg she didn't care where she lived or what she had to do.

Eleven

One day merged into the next and Greg had no idea what the date was, or even the day of the week. Being stuck at the Rochford satellite aerodrome just made things worse. Living under canvas had never been something he enjoyed even in pre-war days.

He was either in the air, waiting to fly, or dead to the world on one of the camp beds. The NAAFI van provided them with decent hot food, but he hadn't been able to change his clothes or have a bath for God knows how long. Another disadvantage of being stuck out here was that he had no access to a telephone so couldn't receive or make calls even if he wanted to.

For all he knew Jack could have died from his injuries. When Ellie had last spoken to him, the night she'd gone to Folkestone, she'd said their friend was expected to make a full recovery. Since then he'd heard nothing.

At least the weather was better – being in a tent would be bloody horrible if it was raining. He was sprawled on the grass in his flying gear waiting for the next scramble.

Digger Jones, an Aussie pilot, had joined their squadron a few days ago to replace one of the chaps who'd bought it.

'Hey, Digger, do you have any idea what the date is? I'm damned if I know.'

'Don't you read the paper, mate? It's printed on the front you know.'

Greg didn't have the energy to respond physically. 'Ha, bloody ha. I'm waiting – what day is it?'

'It's Wednesday, 24th July, 1940.'

'That means we've been on duty ten days on the trot – no wonder I'm bloody knackered.'

The chap on the end of the row flapped his hand in Greg's general direction. 'Don't forget, old fellow, we only had a few hours respite before we were scrambled again. Therefore, by my calculations, we've flown every day for double what you said.'

There was no time to respond as the order to scramble was yelled. They were so efficient now, that despite their exhaustion, they could be in the air less than two minutes after the call. Once he was airborne, and in his usual position as Yellow Two, he waited to be told why they were up.

They cleared the afternoon haze and below him, like a chequerboard, he could see the fields of Kent. They continued to climb, engines roaring, the cockpit so noisy it was hard to hear the RT. You had to be 20,000 feet up before getting into a dogfight.

He'd learned the golden rule for staying alive. His only chance of survival was never to fly in a straight line or stay level for more than a few seconds. Do that and you're dead. If you've a snapper on your tail you have to push your Spit to the limit. Risk stalling, feel the kite juddering from end to end as you turn as tightly as you can. He was good at it now and hoped to God his luck remained as he had everything to live for.

On the port side he spied a squadron of Hurricanes, probably from Biggin Hill or Kenley. He reported his sighting to Yellow Leader just in case he was wrong and they were Huns. This was going to be massive – the biggest battle so far.

The controller yelped into his RT telling them more Germans were grouping over Gris Nez but he didn't know exactly how many.

A black blanket of German aeroplanes approached. The chatter on the RT stopped. Nobody needed telling what to do – it was bloody obvious.

Seconds later he was in the middle of it. He fought his own battle. He'd never seen so many German kites. It was hard to see which were enemy and which friendly but he focused on those he recognised as snappers and went in machine guns blazing.

He was so close he could see the German in his cockpit, his mouth open in shock as he breathed his last. Greg passed underneath, congratulating himself on his fourth kill. Then three 109s appeared from nowhere. He threw his kite about hoping he was making it impossible for them to get him.

He was out of ammo, had to return to base to refuel and rearm. He taxied into Hornchurch – they didn't do either at the satellite field – and threw back the cockpit cover. His gauntlets were covered in oil. Where had that come from?

The ground crew scrambled onto the wing and helped him out. 'Bleedin' hell, sir, you was lucky to get back in one piece. We'll not be able to fix her here, she'll have to go back.'

What the hell was he talking about? Greg dropped to the ground and turned to look at his beloved Spit. There was oil dripping from the engine and the fuselage was like Swiss cheese. *Bleedin' hell* indeed.

'Sorry about that, but at least I got my kill first. Are there any spare kites for me to take up?'

'Not a bleedin' one, sir. You'll be able to take a break until one arrives.'

Greg tottered to his quarters and fell, still in his flying gear, onto his bed. He should have gone to the dispersal hut, hung things up, but he was too tired. He was woken by the rattle of crockery.

'Here you are, sir, lovely cuppa. I'll just give you a hand out of your things and get them spruced up for next time.'

'How long have I been asleep?'

'You slept the clock round, sir, and you're not the only one neither. We certainly done them in, it were the biggest battle yet and them Huns turned tail.'

'So where is everybody?'

'Still operational, sir, another wave of them bleeders came through a couple of hours ago.'

Greg gulped down his tea, almost gagging at the smell that was wafting up from him. He stripped naked, wrapped a towel around his waist and headed for the bathroom. He couldn't remember the place being so quiet – everybody must be in the air apart from him. Nothing he could do about it. He'd be back for the next sortie as long as he had a kite to fly.

His batman had his clean uniform ready on the bed and his flight suit and Mae West had vanished. Just as he was setting out for the canteen half a dozen Spits roared in to land. His first port of call would be the adjutant – he had to know who'd gone for a Burton, how many kills they'd had, when he'd get another plane to fly.

'You look better than you did yesterday, young man. Get yourself something to eat and then have a few hours off base.'

'Thank you, sir, I'll see if I can borrow a vehicle and drive over to Hatfield. My fiancée is a pilot in the ATA now and I'm pretty sure she started a couple of days ago.'

'Here, take my car. Don't prang it, it's the only one I've got. Make sure you're not incommunicado for more than a few hours.'

After gobbling down a heaped plate of egg and bacon, several slices of toast and two more mugs of tea he was ready for anything. It wasn't until he was pulling up at the gate of Hatfield airfield that he thought he might have been wiser to ring first.

Ellie had arrived at the tiny ATA office at Hatfield expecting to be greeted enthusiastically – but the reverse was true. The CO, Pauline Gower, was absent and the office was manned by a bored young woman. She judged her to be in her mid twenties, immaculate in her smart uniform and with her ash blonde hair carefully arranged so it didn't touch her collar. Her pale blue eyes showed no sign of recognition.

'Ellen Simpson? Sorry, I have nothing here about your arrival. However, as you are wearing the uniform you must be one of us.' Her cut glass diction made Ellie flinch.

'I was told to report as soon as my uniform was ready. I need to know where I'm billeted or is that something else you have no information about?'

'Accommodation is arranged by yourself. As you are not on any list or rota for today you have ample time to find somewhere. Do you have your logbook?'

This was the same as asking her if she was wearing her uniform – a pilot always had their logbook with them. She reached into her haversack and placed it on the desk. She watched with satisfaction as the pages of her logbook were examined. She was pretty sure there would be few female pilots with such an impressive number of hours logged.

The woman looked up with admiration. She stood up and offered her hand. 'Amanda Bradshaw, I'm impressed. I'm astonished that someone as young as you has managed to rack up so many hours – and hold an instructor's licence, too.'

'I started flying when I was fourteen, of course I couldn't get certified until I was seventeen but by then it was just a matter of taking the tests one after the other.' She nodded towards the chair in front of the desk and Amanda smiled.

'Yes, please sit down. I apologise for my less than gracious welcome. Shocking headache, too much champers last night.'

An orderly brought them tea and biscuits and Ellie consumed them with relish having had nothing since the night before. Over the next half an hour she explained that she had given a dozen or more RAF pilots basic training.

'I'd like to put you on the list for tomorrow – we are only flying Moths to Scotland for training purposes at the moment. You have to find your own way back and it's not easy carrying your chute. However, Pauline will want you to do a few shorter hops before she sends you up north.'

'When will she be back, do you know?'

'She's at a meeting with the bigwigs in London. Should be back tomorrow sometime so hopefully you will be flying the day after.' She rummaged through a pile of papers and waved one triumphantly. 'This came in yesterday – it's the address of some digs no more than a mile from here. It would help if you had a bicycle but the locals are good about giving us lifts and any military vehicle always picks us up.'

The thought of trudging a mile lugging her heavy suitcases after spending a sleepless night in the waiting room at Liverpool Street station filled her with dismay.

'Thank you for the tea and information. I'll get out of your way and get myself settled. What time should I report for duty?'

'You won't be flying so come in whenever you're ready. We meet in the crew room, and orders are handed out then. We don't fly if the weather's bad – but you already know that.'

'I would be grateful if you would add me to your list of pilots. It's possible I might have correspondence or telephone calls directed here and I don't want them to be told that nobody's heard of me here.'

'I wasn't lying, we haven't been told about you. I think it must be because Pauline didn't expect your uniform to be ready so soon – you must have paid a fortune to get it done in ten days. However, I've got your details now and you are officially part of Hatfield ATA. There are a couple of dozen men of all shapes and sizes, plus fourteen women – well, fifteen now.'

'I take it the men are delivering and collecting operational aircraft whilst we just ferry Moths to Scotland.'

'That's what the discussion is about in London. Even if we're not allowed to fly fighters or bombers we should be allowed to take passengers, parts and parcels to the RAF bases. The bigwigs aren't happy about us flying at all and don't want us associated with them. Ridiculous – women can fly as well as any man.'

The telephone rang shrilly and Ellie jumped. Her nerves were jangled after being awake for so long. Amanda listened and then laughed. 'Yes, she's just arrived. Send him up.' She put down the receiver with a clatter. 'Believe it or not, your fiancé has just turned up at the gate asking for you.'

'Greg's here? That's wonderful.' She shoved back her chair with such violence it clattered to the floor. She snatched it up and smiled apologetically before making a dash for the door.

A small black car was approaching rapidly, she could see him behind the wheel. She waved frantically and his smile made her heart cartwheel.

He was out of the car and in two strides he snatched her from the doorway. His kiss was passionate and she responded, much to the amusement of the numerous ground crew working in the nearby hangar. Eventually the catcalls and whistles became so deafening they were obliged to step apart.

'I only arrived an hour ago. What are you doing here?'

His answer was drowned out as a Mosquito bomber roared overhead. He waited until he could be heard. 'My kite's too badly damaged to be repaired by the aircrew and there are no spare Spits for me to fly. I've got a few hours off base and the adjutant lent me his car to come and find you.'

'Come into the office and I will collect my suitcases. You can drive me to my digs – I was rather dreading having to carry them all that way.'

'Good God! Gregory Dunlop. I've not seen you for years.'

'Amanda, I might have guessed you would end up in the ATA.' He embraced her briefly. 'Small world. I'm glad Ellie will be with people I know.'

'When are you planning to get married?'

He looked at Ellie and raised an eyebrow. 'As soon as I can persuade my fiancée to do it.'

'I know I said I want to wait, but I've changed my mind. If you get a special licence we can be married as soon as you like.'

His shout of triumph echoed through the building causing several heads to pop out of office doors to investigate.

'Darling girl, I'll organise it immediately. It will mean marrying without your family present – do you mind about that?'

She was incandescent with joy. 'I don't care as long as you're there.'

He snatched up her cases as if they weighed nothing at all and strode to the car and shoved them on the back seat. She was in the passenger seat and ready to leave when she realised she'd left the address on the desk in the office.

'I won't be a minute, you can turn the car around whilst I fetch the paper.'

Amanda handed her the address. 'I didn't know Greg was engaged. He obviously adores you, I'm sure you'll be very happy together. Have you been engaged long?'

'Since last Christmas – we almost got married a few weeks ago but I got cold feet. A dear friend of ours, a Hurricane pilot, almost died the other week and that brought me to my senses.'

'Good show. Make the most of his leave, he's lucky to get any.'

The car was facing in the correct direction and Ellie scrambled in beside him. 'You've lost a lot of weight. Has it been absolutely horrible?'

'I don't want to talk about it. I want these few hours to be about us. We can talk about our future and forget about this bloody war. By the way, how's Jack?'

She told him and about the wedding. His eyes glittered and her heart went out to him. 'I wish I could have been there for you. If I hadn't got shot up I would still be on call like the other poor blighters.'

This was the second time he'd mentioned this and she came to a decision. He could be killed the next time he went on a sortie and she didn't want him to die without having spent the night in his arms.

Twelve

Jack wasn't sure if he was more relieved than disappointed when he got up the next morning and discovered Ellie had gone the previous night.

'She didn't want you to put yourself out for her, Jack, you need to get your strength back so you can return to duty fully fit,' Fred told him over breakfast.

'Typical of her, always putting someone else before her own needs.'

He pottered about the house getting in Mabel's way and was horrified to discover she was still living in her rooms downstairs and hadn't joined Fred in his bedroom. They must be embarrassed because he was there – at least he hoped that was the reason. They might be getting on a bit, but there was no reason why they shouldn't enjoy a healthy sex life.

When she was out collecting eggs, he rang the base and spoke to the adjutant. Although he wasn't fighting fit they agreed he could still make himself useful with admin work if he returned a week earlier than expected.

At lunchtime he told them he was leaving the following morning. 'There's no need to do so on our account, Jack lad, we love having you here.'

'I know that, Fred, but I can make myself useful at Kenley and I can't do anything to help here.'

'But you're safe, there's no sirens going off or bombs being dropped. You boys deserve all the rest you can get,' Mabel said as she sniffed and wiped her eyes.

'I've loved being here, have got better quicker than I would have anywhere else. But I'm fit enough to leave and it wouldn't be right for me to malinger when I could be doing something to help the guys stay safe.'

There was no further argument and he insisted on walking to the station the next morning. He didn't have his kitbag to carry. He caught the first train from Romford and was in Croydon catching a lift to Kenley by mid-morning.

As he checked in at the gate he realised he'd need a new chute, Mae West and flying gear. His chute had been incinerated – God knows what had happened to the rest of his things. Perhaps it would have been better to return to Hawkinge and see if he could find them.

His uniform had been repaired, sponged clean and pressed but he was looking scruffy and returned to his quarters to change before he reported to the adjutant.

His batman greeted him effusively. 'Well done, sir, didn't expect to see you back so soon. Your kit was brought back and it's looking tickety-boo now. You'll find it on your usual peg in the dispersal hut.'

'Great, that makes things a bit easier. I'm not sure if you can do much with this jacket and shirt – but do your best.'

Once more smartly dressed he reported to the adjutant. 'Excellent, excellent, just the chap I need. I've a pile of paperwork just begging for your attention.'

Jack was about to drag up a chair and begin to sort out the overfull in-tray when he was waved away. 'Good God, man, get yourself something to eat first. Remember, you're on sick leave, not officially on duty so you can tell me to bugger off if you want and not do anything at all.'

'I wouldn't dream of doing so, sir, and I'll be back in half an hour.' He paused as half a dozen kites roared past, undercarriages down, coming into refuel and rearm. 'How many?' He didn't need to elaborate, the adjutant understood immediately to what he was referring.

'Too bloody many. Two from your squadron I'm afraid – one of them the new bod. They don't stand a chance unless they survive their first sortie and get some experience.'

Jack didn't want to know who the other one was, they were all mates of his. This would mean the squadron was desperately short of planes and pilots.

'Are there any new Hurrys here to replace those lost?'

'We've got spare kites, not enough bods to fly them.'

'Thanks, that's all I needed to know.'

Instead of going to the dining room he went to sickbay and persuaded the medic to sign him fit for duty. The stitches were removed and this made flexing his shoulder less painful and a lot easier. There were guys in the ATA able to fly with one arm – admittedly they didn't have to shoot anyone – but if they could do it so could he.

There wasn't time to eat, he wanted to go up with those that had come in a few minutes ago. He grabbed the nearest bicycle, there was no sign of his own brightly coloured one, and pedalled furiously to the dispersal hut on the far side of the aerodrome.

The first person he saw was his squadron leader. 'Good show, didn't expect you back until next week. Take that Hurry, Jack old son. Be ready in five minutes.'

Jack was ready in less and raced to the new aircraft and was delighted to find he had the same ground crew as before.

'This one only arrived this morning, sir, no canvas covering, all metal skin and the Merlin mark two engine.'

By the time he'd finished speaking Jack was installed in the cockpit, his harness fastened and waiting to leave. There was no time in a scramble to do the preflight checks, you had to rely on your ground crew to have done everything necessary and that the kite was airworthy.

The engine roared into life, the prop spun, and he taxied across the apron and joined the other six who were preparing to speed down the runway to rejoin whatever battle they'd come from.

His RT crackled into life. 'It's every man for himself. Get into the bastards and shoot them down. Over and out.'

He had no idea what to expect or even where the battle was taking place. Travelling at over three hundred miles an hour meant you could be over the Channel in minutes. He climbed steadily and saw immediately why the instruction had been so vague.

The sky ahead was black with bombers and the sky was full of dogfights. He'd leave these to the Spitfire boys and concentrate on hitting the bombers. He recorded one definite kill and one possible before running out of ammunition and fuel.

His new kite handled beautifully and it was reassuring to know that if he was hit again he was less likely to go up in a ball of flames than before.

He spoke to ops letting them know he was on his way back. When he landed he was pleased with his efforts, but not so much with his shoulder, which hurt like hell. It didn't matter – as long as there were German planes in the sky above Britain he would be up there shooting them down.

It didn't take long to deliver Ellie's suitcases to her new digs. The house was small but adequate, her room clean and the bed comfortable.

'What time do you have to be back at Hornchurch?'

'The adjutant said I could have a few hours – I can stretch that a little but must be there by five at the latest.'

'Then we've got time to go to your London house, haven't we? I just want to spend time alone with you, make plans for the future, pretend everything is as it used to be.'

'It's under covers, sweetheart, but if you don't mind that then I'm game. There won't be anything to eat so we better pick up some supplies on the way.'

'No, let's not waste any time. Do you know where you have to go to obtain a special licence?'

'I've been thinking about that. I'm pretty sure one of the chaps was married the other day by the padre – I think

I just have to get the CO's permission and we don't have to get banns read.'

'Then get permission when you get back. I'm not going to be on active service until I've demonstrated I can find my way across country without getting lost. It's going to be the barrage balloons that will cause me problems once I'm allowed to deliver to the airfields.'

'Are you saying you could marry me tomorrow if I can arrange it?' His voice was husky, he was as moved at the thought as she was.

'I am. I'm sure I'll get permission to leave Hatfield for a few hours tomorrow. I suppose it all depends if you've got a new aircraft by then.'

'If I have then we'll have to postpone, but if we can't be married tomorrow then we can be married as soon as this flap is over.'

She couldn't quite find the courage to tell him she wanted to sleep with him but she was sure when they were alone at his London address it would be easy enough to make her feelings clear.

They chatted about inconsequential things on the short drive and she was sure he'd guessed her reason for wanting to come here. He glanced at her a couple of times; his eyes blazed with something she didn't recognise, but thought must be desire. Her skin prickled with anticipation. What did it matter that she was breaking the rules? They would be married in a few days and wouldn't get a honeymoon so it made sense to pre-empt their marriage vows.

She remembered the archway that led to the courtyard at the rear of the building from the visit she had made not long after she had met Greg. This had been cut short when her father had suffered a stroke. Was it only a year ago? It seemed like a lifetime.

He knew where a key was hidden and let them in. The place smelt disused, damp and neglected. He took her hand and led her upstairs and she couldn't help thinking that it would be rather unpleasant being naked in a damp bed.

A bubble of laughter escaped and his hand tightened on hers. 'What's making you laugh, darling?'

She told him and his expression was priceless. She wasn't sure if he was shocked or amused by her thoughts. Then he smiled and pulled her almost roughly into his arms.

'Are you quite sure you want to do this? We only have to wait another day and then it will be legal.'

'It's perfectly legal now, it's just not considered good form to do it before you're married.'

They were now on the floor with the main reception rooms. The bedrooms were another flight of stairs. Her heart was pounding as they headed towards them. Very soon she would be an experienced woman, no longer a naïve young girl.

He took her to his own bedroom and pushed open the door. His exclamation of disgust was followed by hers. They staggered backwards, gagging, hands over their mouths trying to keep out the noxious smell.

She didn't release her breath until he slammed the door. 'How did all those dead birds get in there?'

'God knows! I think they could have been nesting in the chimney and couldn't get out because the house was shut up.'

'We can use another room, but I'll let you look in first, if you don't mind.'

He shook his head. 'No, darling girl, I've changed my mind. When I make love to you for the first time I want it to be perfect, no regrets and no risk of an unwanted pregnancy.'

Until he mentioned this she hadn't even considered the possibility. She did want to have his children, but not now, not whilst this beastly war was on and they both had a job to do.

'I definitely don't want a baby. I didn't know if there was any way to prevent this happening.'

He put his arm around her waist and guided her back downstairs. 'There's something called a prophylactic, I won't go into details, but it's something I must use and I don't have one about my person at the moment.'

She giggled. 'I should think not. A gentleman wouldn't carry such a thing about on the expectation of jumping into bed with someone.'

Instead of spending the afternoon making love they went to a restaurant and shared a bottle of wine and a delicious meal before driving back to her digs in Hatfield.

'I can't hang about, sweetheart, I'm pushing it for time as it is. I'll speak to Win Co as soon as I'm back and will give you a call. If you don't hear from me, don't worry, it will be because I'm back on duty again.'

They kissed and he folded his long length into the small car and drove away at high speed. It was a good thing she'd eaten as she'd missed the evening meal. Her landlady offered to make her a sandwich but she refused.

'Thank you, Mrs Cooper, I had an enormous lunch not long ago. I should love a cocoa if there is any going later.'

'Of course there is, Miss Simpson. You just tell me what you like and I'll do my best to get it for you. I can't tell you what a godsend it is having a lodger, what with my Charlie being away and having three children to feed and clothe on the pittance I get from the government.'

'I want you to use my rations for the children first, I can get a good meal in the dining room at work.'

'Bless you, I wouldn't dream of it. The nippers are with me mum tonight to allow you to settle in. They'll be back tomorrow.'

'You didn't have them evacuated?'

'Not on your life, I've got an Anderson shelter in the garden and that'll do us fine. I'm not having my children brought up by strangers, bombs or no bombs.'

Ellie thought this a dangerous decision. The house was no more than two miles from the place where Mosquito bombers were being built as well as being the base for the ATA. It was bound to be a target and this house was too close for comfort.

Next morning she set off briskly to walk to the base and was unsurprised when an RAF vehicle stopped to offer her a lift after she'd been walking no more than five minutes. She'd hoped this would be the case as it was drizzling, the sky grey and unsummery.

'Hop in, miss, you don't want to walk if you can get a ride,' the driver said.

She did as he suggested and reported for duty half an hour before the allotted time. Her day began at nine o'clock and she was to work thirteen days on and two off. After filling in several other forms she was directed to the room in which all the ATA pilots waited until they were given the slips of paper, detailing their journey, through a hatch which opened into the operations room next door.

Most of them were friendly, but after an initial greeting they ignored her, getting on with what they had been doing before she walked in. Someone was cutting out a frock on the floor in the corner, four men were playing bridge at a table, two others were reading the paper and the other two girls – well, they were women really as they were considerably older than herself – were knitting.

One of these introduced herself. 'I'm Prunella Culley. You have to get used to hanging about in here as we don't fly unless the weather's good.'

'I won't be going up until I've done a couple of cross country flights to prove I'm competent.'

'Go to the quartermaster for anything you need. I expect the office could ring him and make sure he's got something in your size. Hope you've got large feet, flying boots don't come in small sizes we've discovered. Of course, if you've got your own you don't have to worry.'

'I've brought my own goggles, helmet, gauntlets, dungarees, flying jacket and boots. I gather once I'm on the rota I'll be ferrying Tiger Moths to Scotland.'

'Then all you need is your Sidcot suit and parachute.' Prunella told her. 'It's not getting there that's the problem, it's getting back. You have to catch the train lugging your chute and other stuff. Damned nuisance, if you ask me.'

Thirteen

As expected, Greg was back with his squadron that night – and to make matters worse they were driven out to the satellite aerodrome at Rochford where they would be rostered for the next few days at least.

He was grateful he'd had time to speak to the bishop, which was what they called the padre, and his commanding officer about marrying Ellie at the earliest possible opportunity. He didn't want to footle about in a tent – he wanted to be back at base and talk to his darling girl.

He flew one sortie after another. When someone went into the drink or hit the deck it barely caused a ripple. They were too knackered to do anything more than fly, fight, eat and sleep. He returned to Hornchurch many times to refuel and rearm but was never there long enough to visit his quarters or make a phone call.

After a week his squadron returned to base. They were to have twelve hours respite and then they were on call again. He dumped his kit in the dispersal hut, for once found his own bicycle (the one Ellie had given him last Christmas that was painted red, white and blue) and wobbled his way around the apron to his quarters.

He wasn't sharing with someone in his squadron so didn't really know the chap as their paths rarely crossed. There were three letters on his bureau but he was too tired to read them now. He would have a shower, get into some clean clothes and sleep – but he didn't intend to do more than catch a couple of hours. He wanted desperately to speak to Ellie. He wondered if she'd been passed fit to fly – she might even be on her way to Scotland at this very moment.

His batman promised to wake him and so Greg was able to fling himself onto his bed and snatch the first decent kip he'd had in a week. The sound of aircraft landing and taking off was loud even in his quarters, but living in a tent the noise had been deafening.

When he was woken he slurped down his tea and felt ready to face the world. If things fell into place he could be married today – this would only work if Ellie managed to get a flip from Hatfield to here in one of the ATA Moths.

He picked up his mail and looked at the top envelope. He didn't recognise the handwriting. He looked at the other two; one was from Ellie, the other from his sister. He decided to open the first letter. A feeling of dread washed over him when he saw the signature – it was from Elizabeth.

Gregory,

I can't tell you how sorry I am to be writing this letter. You will be as appalled as I am to hear that I am carrying your child. If I hadn't been so incredibly sick I think I might have been able to deal with this before it became a problem. However, my mother guessed and you can imagine what happens next.

The announcement of our impending marriage will be in the paper tomorrow. We are good chums, from the same background, our parents are delighted, so we will just have to get on with it and make the best we can of the situation. Pa is getting a special licence so we can be married in our own church but if you can't get a pass I can come to your base and we can do it there.

    Elizabeth

He stared at the date. The letter had been written four days ago. The announcement would have been in *The Times*. There was nothing he could do about it. His darling Ellie was lost to him forever and in the most horrible circumstances. He hadn't even been able to tell her in person.

He collapsed on the bed and buried his head in his hands. His tears dripped through his fingers onto the discarded letter. He had no choice – a gentleman didn't leave a lady in the lurch. With any luck he'd go for a Burton himself because life wasn't worth living any more.

Ellie had had to travel all the way from Scotland in her flying gear and she was not only exhausted but felt like a boiled lobster. She made her way to the offices and was aware of several strange looks but thought it was because she was an unbecoming shade of beetroot.

Amanda saw her coming and grabbed her elbow and bustled her back outside. 'Don't go in for a minute, there's something you've got to see.' She rammed the front page of *The Times* under her nose.

There in black and white was the announcement of the forthcoming nuptials of the honourable Elizabeth Victoria Hamilton to Flight Lieutenant Gregory Arthur Dunlop.

For a moment, her world remained intact. 'What a coincidence, someone else in the RAF with his name.'

'No, it's your fiancé – or should I say ex-fiancé – he got Elizabeth pregnant and hasn't got any choice in the matter.'

'I don't understand. He loves me – we're getting married...'

Amanda put her arm around her shoulders. 'No, Ellie, you're not. I know Elizabeth Hamilton – she's had her eye on Greg since they had a fling a couple of years ago. She will have done this deliberately. She could have got rid of it – she's done that before – but she's made it impossible for him to back out.' Her friend paused as if hesitant to say anything else. 'I'm going to tell you something, a family secret, but you mustn't mention it to anyone else.'

'I don't need to hear any secrets. I've got to see him. I don't care if he cheated on me – what matters is that if he marries her it will ruin three lives. He will never love this Elizabeth, if he ever finds out she trapped him on purpose he'll not forgive her. He'll just do his duty to the child.' She couldn't accept that the man she loved was lost to her. If she saw him he would cancel his shotgun wedding and marry her. Amanda was still speaking but she'd not heard half of what had been said.

'Two years ago my brother got entangled with her and she tried the same trick on him. It cost the family thousands of pounds to get rid of her. They are all corrupt, the entire family will be involved in this.'

A flicker of hope stirred inside. 'If I can tell Greg he can pay her to go away like your brother did.'

'Wait there. I've got an idea. We might be able to stop that bitch if they're not already married.'

Half an hour later Ellie was sitting in the front seat of a Tiger Moth and her new friend was flying them to Hornchurch. As they had no RT they couldn't get permission to land so they circled the runway until a green light flashed and they came in.

Ellie was out of the aircraft before it had quite rolled to a stop. She jumped from the wing and looked towards the main building. She needed a lift – at the very least a bicycle.

A motorbike roared up beside her. 'Hop on, miss, I'll give you a lift.'

'Can you take me to Flight Lieutenant Dunlop's quarters, please?'

She charged in ignoring the shocked expressions of the two officers she passed who were half naked and on their way to the bathroom. She wasn't sure which room was Greg's. She could hardly barge into each one in turn.

Then an orderly pointed to a closed door. 'He's in there. He's getting married in half an hour – I reckon you've cut it a bit fine, Miss Simpson.'

Later she was to wonder how he knew her name, but now she just burst in to see the man she loved horribly changed. He was in his best uniform. His face was ravaged by grief and what little colour was left fled when he saw her standing there.

'You shouldn't be in here, Miss Simpson.' He remained parade ground stiff, no smile of welcome, his face shuttered.

'Greg, darling, it doesn't matter that you slept with her. I love you and you love me. We're meant to be together. This woman set out to catch you – don't let her ruin our lives like this. This isn't the first time she's done it.'

'I wish it could be different, but it can't. I cannot apologise enough for doing this to you. Your forgiveness is undeserved.' There were unshed tears in his eyes and she flung herself forward expecting him to take her in his arms as he always did.

Instead he held her away from him. 'Please leave. We both know you would never have been accepted by my family, would have hated being part of it. Look what happened between your parents. Better to have a clean break now. Marry someone from your own class. You will be happier that way. I know that I certainly shall.'

His brutal words shattered what remaining hope she had. He was a stranger to her now, someone she didn't recognise, he'd reverted to type. He was right. They wouldn't have suited – he was better off with someone like Elizabeth.

She scarcely remembered the journey back to Hatfield or being driven to her lodgings where she retreated to her bedroom and sobbed herself to sleep.

★

Greg held himself together until Ellie had gone. Then he smashed his fist into the mirror, the physical pain a welcome relief from the agony of losing her. The orderly rushed in and pushed him onto the bed.

'You sit here, sir, I'll see to your hand.'

By the time the pieces of glass had been removed from his knuckles, and his hand was bandaged, he had recovered sufficiently to leave the sanctuary of his bedroom and head for the small chapel where the ceremony was going to take place.

Several of his chums patted him on the back but no one congratulated him. Everybody knew that he was marrying a woman he didn't love because he had to.

Elizabeth was waiting for him. Thank God she'd had the decency not to parade in a white dress – that would have been too much. Whatever she had on, he knew it was haute couture and cost more than he earned in a year as an RAF officer.

She had brought her parents as witnesses to the ceremony. He repeated his vows like an automaton. He hadn't bought a ring but there was one for him to push over her knuckle. He scarcely looked at her but now she was his wife he supposed he had to say something.

He glanced sideways and her expression brought bile to his throat. Until that moment he'd not considered the possibility she was lying – that she wasn't in fact pregnant at all. Hadn't Ellie said something about Elizabeth deliberately setting out to trap him?

Her expression was triumphant. She had achieved what she'd always wanted. Her family were wealthy, but not in the same league as him.

He nodded to her, did the same to her parents. Then he turned and marched away leaving them stranded. He didn't give a damn what anyone thought – he'd done what he had to. But he had no intention of living with her, of having sex with her, of being anything more than a titular husband.

His dress uniform was tossed aside and as soon as he was correctly attired he headed for the sickbay. He wanted the doc to check his hand before he returned to duty.

'A couple of deep cuts, young man, they'll need stitching.'

'Right. I'm fit to fly.' This wasn't a question he was posing but a statement of intent. The doctor nodded.

'Absolutely. Pity it's your right hand, it's going to be a bit sore for a day or two. Would have been better to have used your left to punch the mirror.'

There was no answer to that. Amazing how quickly word had spread around the base – but then he'd done nothing but talk about Ellie, about his forthcoming marriage to her. They would all understand that he'd had no option. He done what any gentleman would do in the circumstances.

As far as he was concerned his marriage was meaningless, a bit of legal nonsense to legitimise the baby – if there was one. A faint glimmer of hope flickered through him. If it turned out she'd been lying and there was no child then it might be possible to annul the marriage if it hadn't been consummated.

He would cling on to this remote likelihood until the pregnancy, or lack of one, was obvious. He wasn't given to praying but he sent up a fervent message to the Almighty that Elizabeth had been lying and there was no baby. Because, if there was, the marriage must stand. He wouldn't abandon his child – he would be the best father he could be in the circumstances.

With his hand neatly bandaged he headed for the mess determined to get drunk. Win Co collared him.

'There's a kite arrived for you, Flight Lieutenant Dunlop. Get yourself to dispersal. You're needed.'

He wasn't asked if he was fit for duty despite the pristine bandage on his hand. He saluted smartly – it was that sort of moment. 'Yes, sir, I'm on my way.'

There was no respite for days and he flew sortie after sortie. Eventually there was a lull in proceedings and his squadron was relieved by one flown up from the West Country. Reports said the RAF were winning the battle of the air and the Hurricane squadrons had more kills than they did.

After sleeping for hours, he staggered out of bed and made his way to the bathroom. There he bumped into another chap from his squadron.

'We're being sent to someplace in Dorset for a week or two. Will be patrols, not much fighting.'

'Good show. We all need some R&R and this will be the nearest we get to any leave.'

'Did you know today is the bank holiday? Wish the bloody Huns had got the message and took the day off too.'

'That must mean it's a Monday, no bloody idea what the date is.'

'Fifth of August, old son.' The man's expression changed to sombre. 'Billy went for a Burton – did you know?'

Greg swallowed a lump in his throat. He'd taken crazy risks, done his best to get shot down but instead their squadron leader had been the one to die.

'I didn't know, he's got a wife and family, hasn't he? I don't envy Win Co having to write so many letters of condolence.'

He was unsurprised to be called to the commander's office. 'Dunlop, you've been promoted to squadron leader, effective immediately. I wasn't sure you were the right man for the job, but after consideration I decided to rubber stamp it. I want your word that you will put the safety of your men first in future.'

Greg's cheeks flushed. There was no need for anything more to be said. From now on he would shove his own misery to one side and concentrate on doing his duty – King and Country must come first.

He returned to his room where his batman had already sewn the new stripes on to his second uniform. He removed his jacket and handed it over so they could be added to this one as well.

'I suppose you know we're moving to Dorset for a week or two?'

'I do, sir. A nice bit of country air and a bit of peace and quiet will do you all good. Congratulations on your promotion, well deserved.' He nodded towards the neatly piled clothes waiting to be put into the kitbag. 'I'll have your packing done in a jiffy. I expect you'll want to get off ASAP.'

Greg shrugged into his other jacket before replying. 'I need to find out where we're going first. Wouldn't do to be rambling about Dorset looking for the new airfield.'

He ignored the small stack of letters on his bureau. Whoever they were from, he didn't want to know – they would only contain bad news of some sort.

Fourteen

Jack received a phone call from Fred which knocked him sideways. 'I can't believe it. That bastard dumped her and married some posh tart instead?'

'He did. I can't get hold of my Ellie, we're that worried about her. Someone in the village pointed out the announcement in the paper. Is there any chance you could go and see her?'

'As it happens, I'm out of action again – bloody shoulder sprung a leak and the medic has forbidden me to fly until it's properly healed. Don't worry, I'll go and see her today. I'll let you know how she is when I get back.'

It could take hours to get to Hatfield on public transport so he was going to see if he could borrow a vehicle of some sort. There were none available and he was resigned to hitching a lift to the station when someone yelled his name.

'Jack, you're in luck, mate. There's an ATA kite just arrived and you could probably cadge a lift to Hatfield with him.'

He pedalled furiously to the far side of the airfield and skidded to a halt beside the Tiger Moth. The pilot, a guy with grey hair and spectacles, was delighted to take him.

'You'll need something warmer on, it's damned cold in an open cockpit even flying as low as we have to.'

'I'll get my gear.'

The short flip to Hatfield reminded him of better times when he and Ellie had been running Glebe Farm Aero Club. He was still reeling from the news that Dunlop had dumped Ellie and done it so publicly. There was more behind this than he knew and he was determined to find out before he went after Dunlop and beat the shit out of him.

No one treated the woman he loved like this and got away with it.

On enquiry, he was told that Ellie was on sick leave but he was given her address. He snagged a lift into the village and found the house he wanted easily enough. He knocked on the door and it was opened by a woman in a wrap-around apron, her faded blonde hair under a scarf.

'Hi there, I'm a friend of Ellie's, Jack Reynolds. Her dad asked me to come and see her.'

'I'm so glad you're here. She's not come out of the room since she got back the day before yesterday. She's not eaten anything neither.' The woman dabbed her eyes with the corner of her apron. 'I thought her young man loved her. How could he be so cruel?'

'I don't know, ma'am, but I'm here to find out. Would you mind if I went up to her bedroom? I'll leave the door open.'

'You go ahead. I'll bring up a tray and leave it outside. Perhaps you can persuade her to eat a little something – or at least drink a cup of tea.'

He didn't bother to knock but pushed the door open quietly. The room was eerily silent, the curtains drawn, the huddled shape on the bed silent.

'Ellie, it's Jack.'

She didn't move, didn't react in any way. His stomach clenched and for a horrible moment he thought she'd taken her own life. In two strides, he was by the bed.

'Ellie, you need to speak to me. You can't hide away up here.'

The hump under the blanket stirred a little but made no response.

Then his instincts took over. He bent down and scooped her up in his arms and sat on the bed cradling her in his lap. He stroked her back, murmured loving encouragement until she relaxed. He'd expected her to start crying again but instead she put her arms around his waist and sighed. Moments later she was breathing evenly. She'd fallen asleep – perhaps this was the first time since she'd had the dreadful news.

Her arms felt right where they were. She was broken by this betrayal and he wasn't such a bastard that he'd take advantage of the situation. The fact that he was in love with her was irrelevant at the moment – she needed his support, not to be bounced into a rebound relationship just because he was there.

The door was wide open, as promised, and the landlady nodded and smiled. 'That's it, love, you give her a cuddle. It's what she needs, poor little lamb. I'll put the tray on the dressing table. Don't wake her up, let her get some rest, she's had precious little these last two days.'

After an hour his injured shoulder was protesting and he had no choice but to try and put her down on the bed without waking her up. As he started this painful manoeuvre she stirred.

'Jack, what are you doing here? I thought I'd been dreaming.'

He lifted her gently onto the bed. Her beautiful face was distorted by grief and a murderous fury filled him. Dunlop would pay for what he'd done. No one deserved to be treated the way Ellie had been.

'Fred called me and asked me to come. I'm back on sick leave, shoulder's still a bit ropey. I'm so sorry, Ellie, I know how much you love Dunlop. I thought he loved you, too.'

She sniffed and looked at the tray. 'I'm starving. Is that for me or you?'

'There's more than enough for both of us. Here, drink your tea first and then I'll hand you some sandwiches and cake.' God knows how there was cake – with rationing, such a thing was a rarity.

She started slowly but was soon wolfing it down and he let her eat her fill and then finished off what was left. Her colour was a little better, but there were black circles under her eyes, her hair was limp and she was still wearing her ATA uniform.

'Why don't you have a bath and get into something fresh? I'll take the tray downstairs whilst you do so. Come down when you're ready and we can sit in the garden – I'm sure your landlady will make us another cuppa if we ask nicely.'

'I'll be down soon as I can. It's time I got a grip. There's a war on. Nobody's died. We'll both get over it – I don't think it's possible to die from a broken heart.' She summoned a weak smile. 'Mrs Cooper must think she's got a lunatic for a lodger.'

In a remarkably short time Ellie joined him in the overgrown back garden. He'd found a couple of deckchairs in the shed and got them set up.

'You look a lot better. Come and sit down, we need to talk.'

She explained what had happened. 'I don't hate him. How could I? If you'd seen him you would understand that he was as devastated as I am. I don't suppose he's the only officer to do something like that. He was just unlucky that Elizabeth got pregnant.'

He took several swallows of tea to give him time to think of a response that wouldn't make things worse. 'He did something stupid but why the hell did he think he had to marry the girl? He could have…'

'No, he couldn't. A gentleman doesn't leave a young lady to become an unmarried mother. The taint would stick to the child. Being illegitimate would ruin his or her life.'

'Well, I'm bloody glad I'm not a toff then. The silly sod has ruined three lives by marrying someone he doesn't love. There'll be hundreds of little bastards running about after this lot's over. His child will have every opportunity in life – there's nothing having money can't smooth over.'

'You might be right, but it's too late now. He said we were from different backgrounds and that I wouldn't have been happy in his circle. There's truth in that statement. Imagine how much worse it would have been if we'd got married, had children, and then decided I didn't fit in?'

He wasn't going to argue although he disagreed completely with her theory. He wasn't a romantic by any means, but he was sure that if a guy and his girl loved each other enough they could overcome just about everything.

'I was going to knock his head off, but after what you've told me I think he's probably suffering enough already.' He reached across and squeezed her hand. 'In a few months you'll have got over this, be able to move on with your life – that poor sod has to live with a woman he doesn't love for the foreseeable future.'

She didn't want to talk about it any more. The thought of her beloved Greg being trapped in a loveless marriage was almost too much to bear. Far better to concentrate on her own life and try and forget about him.

'I can't tell you how pleased I am that you made the effort to come here. I haven't had the courage to ring Dad and hear him say he told me so. I've only been in the ATA a little over a week and already I'm on sick leave because my fiancé married someone else. They must wish they'd never taken me on. As long as no one mentions what happened I'll be fine.' She drained her mug and stood up. 'I didn't ask, but how did you get here?'

'I caught a lift with one of your lot. I'm hoping to get one back.'

'In which case, I'm coming with you. I need to demonstrate I'm not a silly girl but a professional member of their team. I'm ashamed that I gave in to my misery. If you hadn't come and sorted me out I might have been here for days like an abandoned heroine in a Victorian novel.'

Mrs Cooper tutted and fussed. 'I don't think you should be going back so soon, Miss Simpson. You've had a terrible shock.'

'I have, but I'm over it now. Thank you for your help and for the delicious lunch.' She looked around for her gas mask and haversack. 'Good grief! I came home without my essentials – I just hope I don't get spotted by a vigilant ARP warden.'

As always, they got a lift almost immediately. There was a constant stream of traffic back and forth from the airfield and anyone in uniform was bound to get picked up.

'Promise me, Jack, that you won't do anything silly where Greg's concerned.'

'I give you my word. I'm not a gentleman, don't want to be, but I keep my promises.'

She blinked back unwanted tears. Greg had made her a promise and he had broken it. It didn't matter why he'd done so, she could never forgive him for that. Strangely, his infidelity was easier to accept. She would always love him, doubted she would ever feel the same way about anyone again, but he was no longer a part of her life. From now on she would concentrate on being the best ATA girl she could be.

When she reported for duty Miss Pauline Gower, the woman who had persuaded the RAF and government to take on women pilots in the ATA, invited her into the office.

'My dear girl, what a dreadful thing to happen and so publicly, too.'

'Thank you for your concern, Miss Gower. I must apologise for being so feeble about it all. Engagements are broken all the time and I'm sure that other girls don't fall apart like I did. I give you my word it will not affect my work.'

'Good. There will be gossip in the pool, unfortunately both Elizabeth Hamilton and Flight Lieutenant Dunlop are well known to most of us as we move in the same circle. You must ignore it, Simpson, concentrate on what you're here for.'

'I will. Thank you for your concern.'

She was about to salute and quick march from the room when she remembered she wasn't in the WAAF any longer. Fortunately, she was the only one in the building as every other pilot was out on some delivery or other.

As she wasn't wanted for any administrative tasks she acquired some writing paper and wrote to her father reassuring him that she was fine. That it was all for the best. Next, she wrote a few words to Greg and enclosed the engagement ring in the envelope. It was quite possible this valuable item might not reach its destination, but she just wanted to be rid of it.

She refused any offers of a lift on her return to her digs as she wanted the exercise to clear her head. She joined Mrs Cooper and her three children for tea and then played French cricket in the garden until it got dark.

The next morning the crew room was full and she received several sympathetic glances but nobody said anything. Amanda came across with a chit. 'We're flying together today, Ellie, there are two Moths to bring back.'

'Good, much better to fly back than catch the train.'

She wasn't sure if being given the role of passenger on the way up was deliberate or coincidental. Whatever the reason, she was happy to be busy and not have time to think about Greg. The flight both ways was uneventful and she'd enjoyed the time she'd spent with Amanda.

The nine o'clock news spoke of victories in the air. She flinched when she heard the catalogue of losses and feared that either Greg or Jack might be on the dreaded list. Two days after her return she picked up a chit that appeared to send her to collect something from Southampton where the Spitfire was manufactured, and deliver it to Biggin Hill.

Overjoyed she showed this to Amanda. 'No, that's not for you, Ellie. We don't get to do more than deliver Moths. Look, that's not your name on it.'

Sadly, Ellie handed it back and got the usual long haul up north. 'I don't see why we can't do these other flights – we're just as competent as any male pilot.'

'Pauline is working on it. I'm sure that soon we'll be allowed to do more. By the way, did you know that Dunlop's squadron is somewhere in Dorset?'

'Why should I? He's none of my business now.' She turned away to hide the tears. Greg was married to someone else but that didn't prevent her feeling relieved he wasn't in the thick of the air battle at the moment.

Fifteen

Greg eventually got around to opening the letters that had been stacking up in his new quarters. As squadron leader he had a room to himself and he relished the privacy it gave him. He was able to behave normally with his men but needed time to let his guard down and try and come to terms with the ruin of his life.

There was a brief letter from his father congratulating him on his marriage, similar ones from his two sisters and mother. There were three from Elizabeth. He was tempted to tear these up and toss them into the waste bin. He opened Ellie's letter and her engagement ring dropped into his palm. Seeing it was agony. And not for the first time he wished he was dead. There was one with a handwriting he didn't recognise. This was the most interesting of them all.

He was now eager to open the first of the letters from the woman he had to call his wife. She demanded to know where he was, wanted access to the family home, thought she was entitled to a share of his wealth. The other two were in a similar vein – no mention of the pregnancy – no sign of regret or even the faintest flicker of affection.

This had been a calculated business deal to her. A marriage of convenience, if you like, but her convenience, not his.

He would ask the adjutant for personal leave – there was nothing much going on down here. They did regular patrols over the sea but most of the action was still over the capital. They were here to get some much needed rest and he'd already allowed those that had asked to have a twenty-four-hour pass.

There were things he needed to say to Elizabeth and something urgent he had to do. A letter wasn't adequate for what he had in mind. He sent her a curt note demanding that she meet him. He took his own kite, didn't bother to ask for permission, and landed on the immaculate lawn of his family's country estate.

As long as it didn't rain he should be able to get off again okay. The lawn was going to be dug up and planted with potatoes so it made no difference how much damage his Spitfire did. The shutters were closed, the place had been unoccupied since his parents had separated. His mother was now living in America and his father with his mistress somewhere.

The din he'd made when he landed would have alerted the only remaining staff of his arrival. A house of this size needed regular attention if it wasn't to decay, the grounds needing to be maintained as well.

His intention had been to arrive before Elizabeth but when he walked around to the front he saw there was already a Bentley, the chauffeur still inside, parked in the turning circle.

His jaw tightened. Whatever she might think, she wasn't going to get a toehold in his life and arriving early would make no difference to his plans.

The elderly butler had the door open. 'Mrs Dunlop arrived an hour ago, sir, I put her in the green room.'

'Thank you, Bridges. We won't require any refreshments. Mrs Dunlop won't be remaining here and neither will I.'

The old man nodded but made no comment.

Elizabeth was, as always, elegantly turned out. Their sordid encounter had taken place on the eighth of June, it was now the middle of August, which meant she would be around two and a half months and the baby would be due sometime next February if his calculations were correct.

'How are you, Elizabeth? Please sit down.'

Her eyes narrowed at his tone but she did as he suggested.

'Right. I take it you've had the pregnancy confirmed?'

'Of course. Our baby will be born in the middle of February.' She opened her mouth to continue but he cut her short.

'As I thought. There are things we need to get straight between us. I shall never live with you as your husband. There will not be a second child. You will not reside here, you can live at Siddons Hall in Surrey. I will pay all the bills, will make you an allowance and will pay any expenses for the child.'

She stared at him in incomprehension. 'I don't understand. We were always good chums, why are you being so unpleasant now?'

'I had an interesting letter from a friend of yours. Amanda Hoskins-Abraham.' He watched her colour fade but felt no remorse or sympathy. 'I should have known it wasn't a coincidence you were at that party waiting to pounce on me when I was at my lowest. It also appears that this isn't the first time you have been pregnant and that a friendly family doctor takes care of matters for you when necessary.'

She sagged, no glimmer of the defiance he had seen at the beginning of the conversation.

'I will not abandon my child. You will have the baby with you until the end of the war. Then he or she will live with me, but you will not. I think I make myself quite clear.'

'I never knew you could be so cruel. I am the perfect wife for you, could run this wonderful house and entertain your guests. Miss Simpson would never have done that successfully. She is the daughter of a farmer and the granddaughter of a fascist.'

This remark gave him pause. How the hell did she know this? Ellie's family had been assured the matter would be dealt with discreetly and Sir Reginald and his cronies, who had been on the list they had discovered, would be no threat to the country's security.

He hadn't sat down. Being on his feet made him even more formidable. He glared at her. 'I love her, I will always love her and I will always hold you in contempt. I intend to make very sure you regret what you did to us.'

Now she was on her feet staring at him with loathing. 'I'm glad I ruined your lives. I might be kept from my rightful place, but I can assure you I don't intend to be miserable or remain alone.'

He closed the gap between them. His fury made her take an involuntary step back. 'I intend to have you watched every moment of your life. If you are unfaithful to me I will divorce you instantly. I have nothing more to say to you. My butler will escort you from the premises.'

On cue Bridges appeared at the door. She stalked past them both and he heard the front door slam loudly behind her. He hoped he would never have to see her again but thought that having a child together might make that impossible.

'I'm handing the house and estate over to the government for the duration. It's going to be used as a convalescent home for servicemen and the grounds will be put into arable production. You and Mrs Bridges will be given an excellent pension and can retire to one of the cottages on the estate.'

He shook his butler's hand, much to his surprise, and then strode out. He hated this mausoleum of a place, had been miserable every moment he'd lived in it as a boy, and had no intention of ever residing there himself. Far better it was put to good use and not remain empty. Also, if it was occupied there was no opportunity for Elizabeth to attempt to move in herself.

Jack was on duty on 18th August and was discussing the progress of the air battle with a mate. 'So far I reckon we've got the best of it – one of ours but two of theirs each time.'

'We can't carry on like this, we're replacing the kites but can't produce new pilots quick enough. The poor sods that do come are so green they often get shot down on their first sortie.'

'Overcast today, maybe they won't come. Fancy a brew? The NAAFI truck has just arrived.'

The morning remained unblemished by any aerial activity and Jack was thinking he might be lucky enough to eat lunch before they were scrambled. Then the telephone rang and the orderly yelled through the window.

He ran for his Hurry and they were screaming down the runway and airborne in less than two minutes from the first shout. The RT crackled into life. A large enemy force had been seen approaching the coast. They were to join other squadrons and intercept. Then instructions changed and they were told to patrol at one hundred feet. There were thirty plus low level bandits approaching.

Jack saw nine Dorniers screaming towards Kenley, the Huns spread out their formation in preparation of attacking. The radio instructed him to attack from the rear.

The soldiers manning the anti-aircraft gun began firing. It was going to be bloody difficult flying at this height to avoid being shot down by friendly fire.

Despite his squadron doing their best to put them off the bastards dropped their deadly load. Having succeeded in their mission to cause maximum destruction to Kenley, the six Huns still airborne turned tail, hotly pursued by himself and the other Hurricanes.

He followed them up to 20,000 feet. They had practised head-on attacks and were now going to do one for real for a second wave of bombers was approaching Kenley. Flying directly at the Huns was working, as one by one they banked and left formation leaving them vulnerable to the fighters flying directly beneath. The bombs were falling in the surrounding area so no more damage was being done to the airfield.

He was out of fuel and ammunition and left the other fighters who had joined in the party to continue the good work and headed for base. The ops room must have taken a hit as all radio contact had vanished. He had to circle several times before he could find a bit of runway without craters to land on.

The air was full of smoke, the Hurricanes that hadn't managed to take off were destroyed and two hangars were on fire. He jumped from his kite, dumped his parachute and looked around in shock. There were unexploded bombs lying everywhere but the biggest danger was the fire. Buildings had been hit as well and it looked as if both the Officers' and Sergeants' Messes had been flattened. Far worse was the fact that the hospital and sickbays had been demolished. Fire engines were tearing across the damaged tarmac in the vain hope of saving the hangars and aircraft that were inside.

He ran towards the hospital. 'What you want me to do?'

'The doc's bought it, one of the sickbay attendants is badly hurt, but there was no one else in there today, thank God,' the fireman replied. 'I should see if you can move any aircraft out of reach of the fire, sir. We've got it covered here.'

Jack headed towards the inferno. The jets of water hitting the hangar were doing nothing to quell the flames.

There was nothing useful he could do here either. He might as well try and get his kite rearmed and refuelled and get back up there and leave the ground staff to deal with the devastation.

His Hurry now had another beside it and the flyer was standing beside his aircraft smoking a pipe. 'Jack, old fellow, we're not supposed to be here. Any suggestions as to how we're going to get any fuel?'

'Are we the only two to land? Where have they sent the others?'

'The Spits have gone to Nutfield, we were supposed to go to Croydon. I followed you in and got the message too late. Buggered if I know what we're supposed to do now. What a bloody shambles – can't believe those bastards did so much damage in just a few minutes.'

'I suppose we'd better make our way to Croydon. Not much good being here.'

'Righto! It looks like transport was hit as well so no chance of getting a vehicle.'

'The ops room might still be functioning, it looks as if it isn't too badly damaged. A bloody miracle considering everything else around it was hit.'

This was the sector headquarters and controlled operations not only for Kenley but all the other fighter stations in the neighbourhood. The telephone lines were down, unsurprisingly, but they were told to make themselves scarce and come back when things had been sorted out.

Jack turned to Stan Miller. 'I think we've been given permission to take a few days leave. I'm heading for Romford, got family there. What about you?'

'I'll go and see the little woman, she's billeted in Chelmsford. Means we both have to go to Liverpool Street.'

They avoided discussing how many of their squadron had been shot down – he'd seen one crash and there were probably more.

There was an hour's wait for the next train and he found a telephone box and called Fred. Mabel answered and was delighted to have him visit.

'I think Ellie might be coming, she said something in her last letter about having two days off.'

He hadn't seen her since visiting her at Hatfield. Her short letter had been cheerful enough. It would be good to see her, whatever the circumstances. In the end, she failed to come. He was disappointed but enjoyed his unexpected break.

When he rang Croydon he was told to collect a new Hurry from a depot in Kent and report with it ASAP. Kenley was out of action, but would be operational again by the end of the week. It seemed the Huns had also tried to attack Biggin Hill the same day but failed.

Sixteen

August drifted by and Ellie continued to ferry training aircraft to the north of England, flying them back occasionally. The Battle of Britain, which was what the Prime Minister had labelled it, continued in the air. The one phone call from Jack and his letter had been enough to keep her going. He thought he would probably get promoted again fairly rapidly because so many good men were being shot down.

News of a devastating attack on Kenley airfield was rapidly followed by a telephone call from Jack saying he was fine and spending a couple of days with her dad and Mabel.

Amanda had become a good friend and she spent her free time with her – not that she got a lot of that. She could go home when she had her days off but still couldn't face it. Romford was so close to Hornchurch that there had already been considerable bomb damage and civilian casualties. Knowing her father and Mabel were now in danger only added to her constant worry.

Ellie had learned that Greg had been promoted to squadron leader and that he'd given his estate over to the government to be used as a convalescent home.

She was sitting outside drinking tea, having just returned from yet another tedious train journey from Scotland, when Prunella joined her.

'There's been another raid on Hornchurch, a few injuries and some aircraft damaged but not too bad.'

Before Ellie could answer the siren wailed. The two of them, still carrying their tea, raced for the underground shelter. This was large enough to take all the personnel who worked at this end of the airfield – there was another one on the other side.

Carefully nursing her tea, she edged her way to one of the long benches that ran down either side of the shelter. The lights flickered, there was an ominous crump-crump as the anti-aircraft guns surged into life. The shelter was full, uncomfortably so, especially with the doors shut.

She didn't mind being confined, her one dread was that she would have to force her way to the curtained end of the shelter to use the primitive WC behind it. So far, she'd been spared that embarrassment.

'A friend of mine saw Elizabeth Hamilton, well Dunlop now, the other day. Your ex-fiancé has refused to live with her, has banished her to a small estate in Surrey and is going to take the baby away from her when she has it. I can't believe anyone could be so unkind.'

Ellie's initial reaction was shock that someone as considerate as Greg could behave in this way – then she wondered why Prunella had told her.

'It's none of my business, and I can't see why it is any of yours. Good, the all-clear's going.' She was on her feet and weaving her way through the crowd before her erstwhile friend could react. Amanda was due back in the next hour or two and she would ask her what she knew about the situation. The only possible explanation was that Prunella had been asked to pass the information on by Elizabeth but she couldn't see what Greg's wife hoped to gain by this.

Those that had emerged before her were milling about, pointing and exclaiming. There was a large crater in one of the runways and three new Mosquito bombers had been destroyed. As far as she could see there was no other damage, but losing aircraft was a disaster for the war effort.

The Junkers dive bomber that had inflicted the damage was no doubt being hotly pursued by a horde of Hurricanes or Spitfires. She hoped the Germans would be shot down.

As she was making her way back to the offices the familiar sound of a Tiger Moth approaching made her look up. It circled until given the green light and then came in to land smoothly. There were two occupants, the pilot had a passenger.

When he jumped down and removed his helmet she recognised him immediately. Jack had hitched a ride and come to see her. She shoved her empty mug into the nearest hand and tore across the apron to meet him. This was the first time she'd seen him since he'd come to comfort her.

He saw her approaching and was ready with open arms when she arrived. He picked her up and swung her around as if she was a child, laughing down into her face.

'I didn't know if you'd be here but my kite's in for repair and getting a flip across to Hatfield was too good an opportunity to ignore.'

'I'm so glad to see you, your letters cheer me up. How long have you got?'

'A couple of hours, no more, I need to be back at Kenley before dark. It's going to take me a bloody sight longer to return than it did to come.'

He kept his arm resting lightly on her shoulders as they headed for the offices. 'We had to take evasive action to avoid being caught up in all this.' He gestured towards the bomb damage. 'Don't worry, our boys will get him before he reaches safety.'

'Sit here, I'll get us some tea and biscuits and then we can talk. There's something I need to ask you to do for me.'

He was dozing when she returned but quickly sat up and took his mug and a handful of biscuits.

She told him what she'd just heard. 'I know I shouldn't be interested in anything Greg does now, but I'm curious as to why Prunella thought I should know.'

'I don't mix in the same rarefied circle as she does, but I expect there's a couple of guys who will know the gen. I'll ring you when I hear anything worth passing on. Now, tell me what you have been doing these past weeks? You certainly look a lot better than you did last time I was here, but you're too thin. You need to eat more.'

'That's not very polite – you should say how well I look, not that I'm skinny.'

'You're like a little sister to me and I can say what I want. Have you been to see Fred and Mabel?'

'No, but I have my two days off next week and I'm going to spend it at Glebe Farm. I wanted to give them time to get used to being married. I do hope Mabel isn't still living downstairs as she was when you were there.'

'I think of them as my parents now, I hope you don't mind that I went to see them without you?'

'Of course I don't. Surely your squadron will be given a rotation somewhere quiet soon? You can't go on sortie after sortie indefinitely. I know Kenley is back in action, and that you had two days' respite, but you deserve a proper break.'

'That's what I was talking about. The Win Co said we're just waiting for a replacement lot and then we're going to Exeter. Not sure how long we'll be there and it won't be easy getting from there to Romford, but I'll do it if I can.'

'I don't hear anything from George, I must assume he's still alive and flying. You appear to be the only brother I've got left, in fact the only real friend.'

'I'll never let you down, honey, you can rely on that.'

Something flashed across his eyes and for a moment she thought he might mean something more than just being like a brother to her. Then he laughed and he was the old Jack again.

'It's about time you girls were allowed to do a bit more than fly Tiger Moths. They can't get the new aircraft to us quick enough or get the spare parts to repair the damaged ones. Any sign that the powers that be intend to use you girls in the same way as they do the chaps?'

'Pauline's working on it. Two more girls joined us last week. There's a ground training school at Whitchurch, outside Bristol, where we've been told new male pilots are being trained so the service is obviously expanding rapidly.'

'How many ATA pools are there now?'

'Eight, I think. This is now an all female pool. The men have transferred.'

'I don't see that it would take much instruction for someone with your experience to fly a fighter.'

'That would be wonderful. Don't get me wrong, I'm very happy doing what I'm doing, but there are a lot of things that could be improved to make our life easier. Pauline said she's trying to arrange for one of us to fly a taxi service to take the flyers where they need to go so they don't have to catch public transport. Also, it would be so much easier flying back from Scotland than travelling on that wretched night train.'

His visit flew past and she walked with him to the gate. Without hesitation, she hugged him and he responded. He scrambled into a lorry and waved before vanishing behind the canvas curtain at the back.

The guard grinned. 'He's a lucky bloke, miss. Hope he appreciates you.'

Jack overheard the remark and was tempted to peer between the canvas and the edge of the lorry to see Ellie's reaction, but thought better of it. He wasn't comfortable about making enquiries into Dunlop's private life, but as she'd asked him to do it, he had no choice.

They weren't leaving for Exeter until the following morning at the earliest, and he might not be able to go with them if his kite wasn't fixed in time. It all depended if the reserve squadron turned up. The life expectancy for a new fighter pilot could be as little as a few hours. It was usually the first time the poor buggers were involved in a party that they went for a Burton. If they survived that encounter with the Huns then they were halfway there. They soon learned how to spiral away from the fighters, keep an eye out for anything on their tail, and hide in the clouds when necessary. Practising attacking bore no comparison to the real thing.

He got back just before dark and immediately checked in with his ground crew. 'How's it going? Will it be done tonight?'

'Not a chance in hell, sir, you'll have to join the rest of your mates later. They're leaving at dawn as the other squadron arrived this afternoon.'

'Fair enough. Thanks, guys. I'll check in first thing for an update.'

The mess was heaving and a lot of the blokes were strangers – they must be the new bods. He sunk a couple of pints, played a few games of darts and then left them to it. It didn't matter how knackered they were, how many sorties they'd flown, the Brylcreem boys, as they were affectionately known, always found time to get drunk.

He was there the next morning to see them take off and fly in formation across the airfield. He'd been told to report ASAP but no direct order had been given. This gave him an idea. He wandered into the admin offices and casually enquired if Greg's squadron had returned to Hornchurch. It had.

His batman had packed his kitbag so all he had to do was sling it over his shoulder and head for his Hurry. He left Kenley at midday and headed west, but instead of continuing towards Exeter he landed at Hornchurch.

He taxied to the far side of the apron. He didn't want to get in the way of any fighters taking off or landing. The weather was overcast, the clouds were low, hopefully that would put the Huns off. He hitched a ride in a passing service vehicle and announced himself to the adjutant.

He saluted smartly. 'I'm looking for Squadron Leader Dunlop, sir. Any chance that he's available?'

'He's here somewhere. Try the mess, if he's not there he'll be in his quarters.'

Jack wasn't asked who he was, or why he was there; he guessed just being an RAF officer gave him reason enough to be here. The bloke probably thought he was based here and he wasn't going to disabuse him.

Despite the fact it was early afternoon the bar was busy, the air heavy with blue smoke and raucous laughter. If he didn't know better he would have thought the young men in here hadn't a care in the world.

Dunlop was sitting on his own at a table nursing an empty glass. He approached him and tapped him on the shoulder. Jack had thought his instinct would be to punch the guy in the nose but the man who looked up at him was a stranger. The poor guy had aged ten years, lost even more weight than Ellie, and had flecks of grey in his blond hair.

'Greg, I need to talk to you. Is there anywhere quieter we could go?'

'My room – nobody comes in there.' He didn't ask why Jack had come and just stood up like an old man and headed for the exit.

They didn't exchange a word and Dunlop gestured towards a battered armchair and slumped on the bed himself. 'Have you come to punch me? Go ahead – I'll not stop you.'

'I thought about it, but seeing you I've changed my mind. There's nothing I could do to you that's as bad as what you're doing to yourself.'

'In which case, what do you want if it isn't to break my jaw?'

Jack repeated what Ellie had told him and explained that she wanted to know why Elizabeth's friend had told her.

'I expect she's trying to cause trouble. She deliberately trapped me into marrying her but I rather think she's regretting it now.'

'Do you actually intend to take away her baby?'

'When the war's over, yes. I can't take responsibility for a child at the moment, but as soon as I'm free he or she will live wherever I am.'

'That's a bit harsh, not like you. Don't let what happened change you into a hard bastard. You aren't the first guy to be trapped into a shotgun marriage and won't be the last. If you don't want to be married to the woman then get a divorce.' Why the hell was he suggesting this? If that happened then the slim chance he had of being able to marry Ellie himself would be gone.

'I have every intention of doing so. I'm having the woman watched night and day and as soon as she invites a lover into the house I'll know and get things in motion.' His shoulders straightened and for the first time he looked directly at him.

'How's Ellie? I'll never marry again unless I can persuade her to forgive me.' He shrugged hopelessly. 'No woman in her right mind would take on someone like me with a child in tow, would they?'

'Don't know, but Ellie's a great girl. If you survive the war and are free, then who knows?'

'One can but hope. Anyway, how are you here? Shouldn't you be at Kenley shooting down the bloody bombers?'

'My squadron left for two weeks in Exeter, my kite wasn't ready so I couldn't go with them. I'm on my way there now.'

'Piece of cake down there, that's where we went. You will get scrambled, but not every day. We came back fighting fit.'

Jack felt sorry for the bloke. He shook his hand. 'Good luck, Greg, keep safe. Don't worry about Ellie, she'll get over it and you've got to do the same.'

'Thank you, keep an eye on her for me. I know I can count on you.'

They parted not exactly friends but certainly not enemies. Out of the three of them involved in this disaster the one he really felt sorry for was Elizabeth. Dunlop was not a man he'd want to cross himself – he hadn't realised what a hard bastard he was until now.

Seventeen

When Ellie reported at nine o'clock Amanda greeted her with excitement. 'Pauline's done it again. From today we can fly any non-operational aircraft and she thinks when things calm down a bit they might let us fly the fighters, too.'

'That's good news!'

'We've got to do a short test flight before we start. I'm doing mine tomorrow and three are doing it now. I wonder if that means we'll get promoted and get another stripe?'

'I like being an officer of any sort, but it's not the same in a civilian organisation as it is in the services.'

'Another thing, in future we have to clock in at eight o'clock, everything else is pretty much the same.'

'Where do I find out when I'm doing my test?' asked Ellie.

'Sorry, I should have looked for you. It's on the noticeboard in the operations room.'

Ellie dashed inside and saw she was down to do it that afternoon.

Her instructor, a RAF chap who obviously didn't approve of female ferry pilots, was waiting for her beside the plane. He didn't smile so neither did she.

'Ellen Simpson,' she said and stood military straight in front of him. He pursed his lips and then jerked his head in the direction of the aircraft. She had already spoken to the girls who'd successfully completed their test and believed she knew enough to be able to fly it successfully.

This was the first closed cockpit aircraft she'd flown, but the instrument panel and everything else was pretty much the same. There was a checklist they had all memorised by its initials and she quickly ran through it making sure the disapproving officer behind her was aware she was doing it. Once completed she called the all clear and said contact.

Fortunately, the engine fired and the prop began to turn. She taxied from the apron onto the runway and waited for the green light. She also did a visual check to ensure there were no random aircraft waiting to land. Hatfield wasn't an operational RAF base so at least there was no danger of being in the way of a dozen fighters screaming down the runway to take off in pursuit of a German.

Once airborne she forgot about the man sitting behind her and just enjoyed flying something different. She did, as instructed, three circuits and bumps and each one was immaculate. She taxied the Lysander back to where it had been when she got in, switched everything off and scrambled out.

If memory served her right she was the last to go up today. The RAF chap jumped down behind her. 'Excellent, Miss Simpson, the best so far.' He smiled and offered his hand. 'I don't think ATA, in your case, stands for "Always Terrified Airwoman".' He handed her a signed form and, ignoring his comment, she all but skipped back to the office to hand it in.

From that moment on things changed. She might be the youngest in the pool, but she was one of the most experienced, and until her performance in the Lysander she hadn't really been accepted into the group.

She was kept busy delivering Lysanders to various parts of the country. When she was flying she couldn't think about anything else so the busier she was the better she liked it. The air battles continued and one morning when she checked in the girls were discussing a lightning attack that had taken place at Kenley.

'The Huns hoped to surprise them but radar picked up the bombers and the Hurricanes were already in the air and waiting for them,' someone said. Ellie's first thought was relief that Jack was still in Devon.

'Was there much damage?'

'Not on the aerodrome, Ellie, but a lot of bombs fell on houses nearby and there were dozens of civilians killed as well as half a dozen airmen. The armoury blew up and the control tower has been hit as well. Let's hope we don't have to deliver anything there for a day or two.'

'How dreadful. I suppose it's only a matter of time before civilians are bombed deliberately and not just military targets.'

'My chap works at the Air Ministry and told me on the QT that if the Germans continue to attack our airfields we won't have enough air power to protect us.'

Ellie thought whoever Daphne's boyfriend was he shouldn't have been so indiscreet. This wasn't the sort of news that should be bandied about. Knowing they could be on the brink of defeat was demoralising and not at all helpful – especially to the men fighting to protect the country.

Amanda obviously agreed with her. 'That's quite enough of that, not the sort of thing you should be talking about. The chits are ready so shall we get on with what we're supposed to be doing and stop gossiping?'

There was a murmur of approval and Daphne muttered an apology and hurried away. The weather was warm and dry – ideal for delivering aircraft when you couldn't fly above 2000 feet – but this also meant the attacks from the Luftwaffe continued to be ferocious. Not only were they raiding several times in the day but had also started coming at night. Even though their targets appeared to be the RAF there was a horrific amount of collateral damage as bombs were dropped indiscriminately on civilians and their houses.

At the end of the month she had her two days' leave and snagged a lift into London. This was the first opportunity she'd had to visit Glebe Farm and she was looking forward to seeing her father and Mabel. It would have been better to be away from the constant noise, wail of sirens, sound of ack-ack and the worry that someone she knew could be killed at any moment; she was well aware that Romford was in the firing line.

Travelling around the country carting a parachute was annoying but at least it gave you something solid to sit on. She hadn't told her dad she was coming just in case something cropped up, so was quite prepared to walk home. All she had was her haversack and overnight bag and the exercise and fresh air would do her good.

She'd given her ration book to Mrs Cooper, her landlady, but hadn't asked for it back. There was always plenty to eat on a farm, especially one like hers that had poultry, dairy and pigs.

The dogs sensed she was approaching down the drive and raced towards her barking in excitement. She knelt down to greet them and then, with them dancing around her ankles, she arrived at the farmhouse.

Dad was on his way to greet her. 'Ellie love, you should have told us you were coming tonight. Mabel's not here, she's visiting a sick relative in Chelmsford.'

She embraced him. 'Then who's looking after you?'

'Vera, one of her friends in the village, is staying until she gets back. She's sleeping in my Mabel's old rooms.'

She slipped her arm through his and they walked to the house. There was no sign of the temporary housekeeper, but then it was almost nine o'clock. 'I've not eaten since lunchtime, Dad, will it be all right to get myself a sandwich?'

'You don't have to ask, love, you have what you want. This will always be your home and don't you forget it.'

With a mug of tea and a ham sandwich she went to join Dad in the garden. He wasn't given to idle chatter, liked to sit quietly until he had something pertinent to say.

'I can't tell you how sorry we are about what happened with Greg, Ellie love.'

She'd been dreading this conversation but strangely, found she could answer without tears welling up. 'I'm fine now, thanks. It was a dreadful shock, but in a way far worse for him than it is for me. I suppose you know why he had to marry that woman?'

'In the family way, is she?'

'She always wanted to marry him. She got pregnant deliberately – it happened the night of Neil's funeral.'

'He was engaged to you, Ellie, no excuse for what he did. Whatever you might think now, you're better off without a man who does that sort of thing. I'll say no more about it. You won't believe it, but I heard from your brother the other day.'

'How is he? Is he still cosying up to our fascist relatives?'

'Whatever you think, love, they're your family too. He's left the RAF, some sort of ear problem which means he can't fly, he's working at the Air Ministry. There's a wedding invitation too, I don't know the date but it's in a week or two.'

'Are you going?'

'Not likely. I'm glad he's safe and happy, but he's made his choice and I doubt I'll see him again.'

'I agree. I don't want to speak to Mum, George or Sir Reginald again, but I'm glad she's still got her favourite son in her life. Does she know you and Mabel married?'

He chuckled. 'I doubt it. I've never been happier, but I don't regret having married your mother. If I hadn't, you and Neil wouldn't have been born.'

He puffed on his pipe, leaving her to her thoughts. The blackbirds were singing their final songs, the chickens were back in the barn, it would be dark soon. She inhaled the sweet, clean country air and was just enjoying a moment of peace when the sky was rent by the wail of an air raid siren. It was coming from Romford – but it probably didn't mean they had to scuttle into the shelter.

The familiar roar of two squadrons of Spitfires tearing into the sky made it impossible to talk. Greg would be leading his men into battle and she sent her love and good wishes his way. This time her eyes brimmed and she was glad her dad couldn't see her crying.

Eighteen

Hornchurch was being attacked so often that Greg, when he was not on duty, never bothered to get undressed. Fleeing to the shelters in his pyjamas wasn't something he intended to do. The people he had watching Elizabeth reported nothing untoward. She was not noticeably pregnant, and if reports were true was well liked in the area. The staff he'd employed to run the house were loyal to him – God, they'd better be as he was paying them enough – and the only people she'd invited to stay with her were relatives and female friends.

The sorties were unrelenting and if they continued at this rate the RAF would have no aircraft or functioning pilots. The outlook was grim. He'd written condolence letters to six families so far and the bods who had replaced his men were little more than boys and had not nearly enough flying experience to keep them safe.

He threw away any letters from his wife and family unread. He saw an announcement in *The Times* that Ellie's estranged brother, George, had married his fiancée and this just rubbed salt in his festering wound.

Getting drunk wasn't an option, not when they were scrambled several times a day. When would this bloody attrition be over? It could only be a matter of time before Britain was defeated and the jackbooted bastards were marching up the streets of London. The Germans were concentrating their attacks on RAF airfields and the loss of life and aircraft was horrific.

Then, at the end of August, for some inexplicable reason the Luftwaffe stopped coming. After one day without action even he was smiling occasionally. The pause in hostilities didn't last and the raids increased in severity. London was heavily bombed. Hitler obviously thought it would destroy the morale of the British people, as he hadn't managed to destroy the air defence to obtain a victory.

The short respite was over and once more he and his comrades were fighting desperately to shoot down the invading bombers. Sometimes he was leading his squadron into battle four times a day. On one of the rare occasions when they'd been scrambled but seen nothing, he was ambling along enjoying the Kent countryside, thinking about the breakfast he'd left uneaten hours ago.

The golden rule for fighter pilots was to always watch your tail. However empty you might think the skies, they were full of snappers. He was jerked from his complacency by a searing pain in his leg. Then to his horror there was the sound of someone shaking pebbles in a metal bucket right outside the cockpit. He was under attack. Not stones but bullets.

His leg didn't hurt, but when he glanced down he saw blood oozing over the top of his flying boot. Two

Hurricanes drew alongside and glanced in at him. He managed a thumbs up and they peeled away, off to find another target to destroy. He assumed they had shot down whoever had attacked him. He bloody well hoped so, because his head was beginning to spin and he didn't think he'd survive a second skirmish.

His kite was no longer responding. He was flying at 20,000 feet in an aircraft that was going to crash. He was about to lose consciousness and inevitably death would follow. For a second he closed his eyes thinking this was what he wanted – an end to his impossible situation.

But then he realised he didn't want to die. Life, any sort of life, even one without his beloved Ellie, was better than the alternative. He made a split second decision to bail out. He thought he would probably be unconscious before he was low enough to land. The Spitfire could probably be landed safely despite the damage, but not by him.

They didn't receive any training about the use of parachutes for jumping out at such a height. There were various techniques talked about, but his mind was becoming woozy. He would get rid of the canopy, undo the straps and then pull the stick as hard as he could. Hopefully this would catapult him out.

He didn't have time to test the theory as he was lifted out of the cockpit and thrown into the wind. He was tossed like a rag doll, head over heels, his limbs out of control, unable to think straight. The air had hit him like a sledgehammer but it was short lived. He had left the aircraft when it was travelling at almost 400 mph. No wonder it felt as if he'd walked into a brick wall.

Then natural air resistance kicked in and he slowed to a sensible speed. Nothing was real. He was in a silent world, in no pain, and no longer worried about dying. He was to learn later that the loss of blood and lack of oxygen had caused this strange, dreamy state.

When he left the thin air and fell into the denser atmosphere his brain started to work again. He realised he needed to get down fast if he was to survive. He recalled being told not to pull the ripcord until you could actually see the ground. He emerged from the cloud into sunlight and saw the Kent countryside spread out below him; the parachute opened with a crack and he was jerked upwards.

The noise in the cockpit, plus the earphones and the RT, meant you never heard anything else. Now, as he floated down he could hear car horns, cattle and even the occasional human voice.

The ground hurtled towards him. Because of his damaged leg he landed heavily and tumbled over and over, to sprawl face down, the breath knocked out of his lungs.

He was only alone for a few moments when two land girls arrived at his side. 'Jolly good, you're still alive. Betty's gone to call for help. You're losing a lot of blood and the sooner you get to hospital the better.'

He didn't have the energy to reply but managed a weak smile. The girl was busy tying a makeshift tourniquet above his knee. 'Your Spitfire crashed in the next field. I don't suppose the cows will give any milk for weeks.'

That was the last thing he remembered until he opened his eyes in Orpington Hospital three days later.

'Welcome back, Squadron Leader Dunlop, we didn't think we would see you again.'

Ellie enjoyed her short break at Glebe Farm, though she missed Mabel, who she thought of as her mum now. But she was glad to get back. Although the sirens had gone off several times a night they didn't go into the Anderson shelter. Bombs dropped on Romford but so far nothing had fallen on the farm.

There was now serious talk of setting up a taxi service for the ATA pilots so they didn't have to waste so much time on public transport. The idea behind this was that they were taxied to where they were collecting whatever aircraft they were ferrying, and then the same thing in reverse.

'That's all very well, Amanda, but the aircraft we fly at the moment only take one passenger so I can't see it working,' Ellie said as she waited for her morning chit.

'They're going to use Puss Moths and Stinsons initially, they can take three passengers. I expect they'll have to think of something else, but this is a start. Also, in future, instead of us taking a kite all the way to Scotland we take it to the next ferry pool and then someone from there does the next leg.'

'Makes excellent sense to me. I don't know how you did it during the winter months, it's been bad enough doing it in the summer.'

'It's a pity we can't coordinate our time off so we could go to London, dress up and have a good night out.'

'I'm not one for posh frocks, but it would be great to go to a show, concert or the pictures. You're off next week, aren't you?'

'I am, and three of us are going to book into a hotel and have dinner somewhere splendid.'

'I'm sure you'll have a good time.' She flinched as a swarm of fighters screamed overhead. She'd never get used to it, knowing that it was highly likely one of the planes wouldn't come back.

The next week she ferried two Lysanders, one to Cornwall where she managed to hitch a ride back, and the other to a deserted airfield in the middle of Kent. She handed over the paperwork to an anonymous man who was taciturn to the point of rudeness.

There was little chance of getting a lift back from there and she was resigned to lumping her parachute and overnight bag for miles to the nearest bus stop or station. She didn't get back until the small hours and decided there was no point in returning to her digs so she would get a couple of hours' sleep in the common room.

The building was eerily quiet, no one around apart from the guards patrolling the perimeter and the soldiers manning the guns. As it was a warm night she decided to take a chair outside rather than remain in the stuffy room. The night was noisy, the factory next door never slept.

The hair on the back of her neck stood up as she heard the ominous drone in the distance of heavy bombers. She scrambled to her feet and stared towards London. The city was surrounded by barrage balloons suspended at just the right height to prevent low flying fighters and bombers from getting in.

The sky above the city was suddenly lit up by searchlights, even from this distance she could hear the air raid sirens wailing. Then squadron after squadron tore into the night sky to try and intercept the Germans before they dropped their bombs. These brave boys could fly in the dark, but she couldn't see how they would find any targets until it was too late. The inside of a fighter cockpit was too noisy for them to be able to hear anything outside – maybe they would be able to see the flicker of exhaust fumes or something like that. She would ask Jack next time she saw him.

She watched as the capital was bombed. The horizon turned orange, the smell of smoke drifted over Hatfield. Amanda was there. She prayed her friends would turn up the day after tomorrow and laugh about their experience in a communal air raid shelter. The underground stations were also being used to protect people from harm. The Germans would be bombing the docks, not the West End, so she was pretty sure they would be safe.

The raid was over in half an hour but the flames continued to light up the sky. She couldn't sleep now, just had to hope she would be able to remain alert until she got to her bed tomorrow. The admin members of the

ATA usually arrived early so they could sort out who was doing what.

Just before six o'clock the telephone rang and she dashed into the office to pick it up.

'ATA, Hatfield.'

'To whom am I speaking?' a plummy voice demanded.

'Ellen Simpson speaking, sir.'

'Good God! Just the gal I wanted. Your young man has been shot down and is fighting for his life at Orpington Hospital. Get here as soon as you can if you want to say your farewells.' The line went dead.

The speaker hadn't identified himself but she assumed he must be a doctor. She was listed as Jack's next of kin, which must've been why they had called. Hastily she scribbled a note to Pauline, the CO, explaining she'd been called away on a family emergency. Orpington wasn't far from Hatfield so if she was lucky and managed to get a lift she should be there in an hour. She refused to consider the possibility that she was going to lose Jack as well as Neil. In the weeks since Greg's betrayal they'd become closer, had managed to speak on the telephone occasionally and shared weekly letters.

Despite the hour she got a lift quickly in a vehicle delivering parts to the de Havilland factory.

'Don't often see you girls around so early, miss. Where do you want to be dropped off?'

She explained and his expression changed to one of sympathy. 'It ain't that far, I'll take you all the way. Don't fret, miss, you'll be there in time.'

She arrived at the hospital only to find the reception area deserted. The place was vast, she'd never find Jack without assistance. She ran along the corridor until she saw a nurse sitting at a desk in a small office.

'Excuse me, sister, I got a telephone call saying Flight Lieutenant Reynolds has been shot down and is critically ill. The doctor told me to come at once.'

'Just a moment, I'll make a phone call and see if I can locate him for you.'

Ellie listened to the one sided conversation but couldn't work out what was going on. The nurse replaced the receiver with a puzzled frown. 'There is no one of that name been admitted here. Are you sure you've got the right hospital?'

'Definitely. Now I come to think of it, the doctor didn't say his name. Could you check if a fighter pilot was admitted recently?'

The nurse nodded and rang a different number. This time when she replaced the receiver she smiled. 'Do you by any chance have any connection with Squadron Leader Dunlop? I think he's the young man the consultant was referring to.'

Ellie gripped the edge of the table to hold herself upright. How could this have happened? Somehow, she managed to nod. 'Yes, it must be him. Can you tell me where he is?'

The young woman in crisp blue cotton gave her the directions. What she must have thought about her being involved with two young men Ellie could only imagine. Greg had a wife, however much he disliked her, and she should be the one who had been called to his bedside.

Nineteen

The hospital smelt of disinfectant, which was good, and boiled cabbage, which was less appealing. Greg was in a side ward. Ellie didn't think this was a good sign as only the most dangerously ill were kept separate.

The door to his room was open. When she took another step she would be visible to anyone in there. She wasn't sure she was ready to see him – wasn't sure if she was still in love with him. One thing she did know was that she didn't want him to die.

This thought galvanised her into action. She couldn't stand dithering outside when her presence might save his life. She took the all important step and froze in the doorway.

The man in the bed, a frame over his legs, was a stranger to her. The Greg she remembered had been young, handsome, had golden hair and smiling blue eyes. This person was haggard, his hair dull and flecked with grey. There was a blood transfusion dripping into his arm. His complexion matched the sheets.

Then he turned his head. His eyes widened and he was her Greg again. She forgot everything, that he had married somebody else, that they were no longer together, and flew across the room.

'I asked for you but I didn't think you'd come. There's something you need to know in case I don't make it.'

Her eyes filled and her throat constricted. She couldn't speak so just took his hand in hers. He didn't need sympathy, he needed to fight.

'Don't be ridiculous, Squadron Leader Dunlop. You're not going to die. Your country needs you – your unborn child needs you.' His eyes had closed and she wasn't sure he'd heard her. 'Greg, I have forgiven you. Don't be so feeble. We can't be together which is sad, but not the end of the world.'

His eyes flickered open and he almost smiled. 'That's what I wanted to tell you. We can be together if you can forgive me. I've applied to have the marriage dissolved.'

'What do you mean? How can you do that? Of course I forgive you, I love you.'

He spoke again and this time his voice was firmer. 'The baby isn't mine. I've discovered she was already pregnant when we slept together. I wrote another will making sure she gets nothing and you get it all.'

'I can't believe it. How could she do such a wicked thing? And don't talk about wills, let's talk about how soon we can get married.' She smiled down at him. 'In fact, I don't care if we don't get married. I'm quite prepared to live in sin with you, as long as we're together.'

'That's all I needed to hear, darling girl. If you've been as wretched as I have these past few weeks I can only apologise again.' His colour was improving and his grip on her hands was firm. 'I must say you look quite lovely in that uniform. A lot better than I do, I dare say.'

'I should certainly hope so.' She stretched out beside him resting her head on his shoulder. Then she told him how she'd asked for Jack as she had thought it was him who was critically injured and they laughed together.

He drifted off to sleep for a few minutes and she propped herself on one elbow so she could look at his face. He was far too thin, there was oil ingrained in his cheeks, there was grey in his hair – but now he would start to get better.

'Greg darling, as soon as you are well enough to come out of hospital you must convalesce at Glebe Farm. I'll leave the ATA if they won't give me compassionate leave and look after you.'

'Are you sure that Fred and Mabel would want me there after what I did?'

'Once I've explained what happened, and they see how happy I am, they will be delighted to have you.'

There was a slight sound at the door and she looked over to see the nurse smiling in at them. Ellie had expected to be told to get off the bed but this didn't happen. It must be because her visit had obviously made Greg so much better.

'I love you, sweetheart, I don't deserve a second chance but I'm going to take it.' He drifted off to sleep. She was desperate for the loo and a cup of tea. A piece of toast would go down well, too.

She waited for a few minutes but he didn't stir. His breathing was shallow but regular. Slowly she edged her way forward. 'I love you, I'm just going to get a drink. I'll be back soon.' He didn't respond. He wouldn't even know she had gone as she didn't intend to be more than a few minutes.

She stopped at the nurses' station. 'He's asleep. Can you tell me where the lavatory is, please? Also, is there anywhere I could get something to eat and drink at this time of the morning?'

'The WC for visitors is in the foyer. I'm afraid there's nowhere open so early, but I'll make you a cup of tea at the nurses' station and have it ready for when you come back.'

'That would be so kind. I won't be long.'

The nurse was already on her feet and walking briskly towards Greg's room. Ellie could go in search of what she wanted knowing Greg was in the best possible hands.

The hospital was now busy, the night shift had been exchanged for the day. The corridors were full of bustling nurses, orderlies and nursing assistants. She was on her way back and was surprised to find the pleasant nursing sister not sitting at her station.

The door to Greg's room was closed. She could hear the murmur of voices inside. The doctors were with him so she might as well go and find that cup of tea and come back later. It was very early for them to visit. A prickle of unease ran through her. She'd only been gone a quarter of an hour, surely he couldn't have deteriorated in so short a time?

As she turned to go the door opened and two grave faced men in white coats emerged and strode off down the corridor. She looked across at the bed just as the sister was pulling the sheet over Greg's face.

'No, he can't be dead. He was just talking to me...' She couldn't continue. The nurse carefully folded the sheet back again. Ellie wasn't aware that she'd moved but found herself by his side. She stretched out a tentative hand and touched his cheek, already it felt different, not quite cold but different.

She stared at the man she loved, the man she was going to spend the rest of her life with, and something inside her died as well. A world without him in it was too awful to contemplate. She understood now that she'd been able to recover so quickly because in a small corner of her heart she'd always believed that one day they would be together again. How could life be so cruel as to snatch him away when they were finally going to be together as they should be?

When she kissed him for the last time his lips were cold. This wasn't Greg. It was a shell, he had gone forever. She prayed it was to a better place, that there really was another life for those that died. If she'd known she would have stayed at his side and he wouldn't have had to die alone.

'Miss Simpson, come with me. You've had a dreadful shock. Thank God you got here in time to say your farewells. I believe Squadron Leader Dunlop was just holding on until you arrived.'

Ellie turned away from the shrouded shape on the bed. She was about to explain that she wasn't the person who should have been here but realised that was incorrect.

Elizabeth might be his legal wife, but she was the woman he loved and the right person to be at his bedside. She couldn't think about the legal ramifications of what he told her – not now – but it was some small comfort to know that wicked woman would get nothing.

'If I'd known what was going to happen I wouldn't have left him.'

'He didn't regain consciousness after you left, Miss Simpson. I was with him when he died but he wouldn't have been aware of his surroundings at that point. I'm so sorry for your loss.'

She was numb. There were things she should do but her brain refused to function. She swallowed a few mouthfuls of oversweet tea and then put it aside. 'May I use your telephone? There are things I need to arrange.'

Once she was alone she rang Kenley. Jack would know what to do.

The telephone rang and Jack, like the other guys, was already on his feet waiting for the order to scramble.

'Hey, Flight Lieutenant Reynolds, urgent phone call for you, sir,' the orderly yelled through the window.

Everyone resumed what they were doing and he ran for the office. 'Reynolds here.'

'Jack, Greg's dead. I'm at Orpington Hospital and I'm not sure who to contact.'

He didn't ask what she was doing there, that could come later. 'I'm on duty, Ellie, there's nothing I can do at the moment. I can't stay on the line. Ring Hornchurch and speak to his CO. I've got to go. I'll come and see you as soon as I can.'

The receiver had only been replaced a second when it rang again. This time it was for them. He pushed all thoughts of Ellie and Greg to one side and concentrated on staying alive and stopping the bastards from getting any more bases.

This time they all returned safely from the sortie and he went straight to the adjutant to ask for compassionate leave at the end of his shift. 'I've been on duty every day for the past two weeks, God knows how many sorties I've flown. The squadron can manage without me for twenty-four hours. Death in the family.'

'Right, sorry for your loss. Make sure you're back this time tomorrow.'

He wasn't asked who had died and Jack didn't volunteer the information. He threw a few things into an overnight bag and then rang Hatfield. He was told that Ellie was delivering a Lysander but was expected back at any moment.

Getting to Hatfield from Kenley was a bugger if you didn't have your own transport. He had the best available – his Hurry. There were no bods to use his kite so he was going to go AWOL with it. He would face the music when he got back.

His ground crew asked no questions and he supplied no answers. 'I'll be back tomorrow. Not going far.'

He taxied across the apron and waited for his turn on the runway. No doubt someone in the control tower would report that he'd flown off without permission. Too bad. Ellie needed him and being put on a charge was fine by him.

He landed at Hatfield and parked the kite out of the way. He nabbed a bicycle from outside a hangar and cycled across to the offices. Someone must have seen him coming – one of the benefits of having such distinctive hair – and Ellie came out to meet him.

She fell into his arms and he hugged her. 'Right, let's find somewhere quiet where we can talk. Tell me what happened.'

When she had finished his eyes were moist. 'What did his CO say when you rang?'

'He had already been informed of Greg's death and that someone would be contacting Elizabeth. He said he was glad I got there in time to say goodbye.' She was too choked to continue and he handed her his handkerchief. When she recovered she continued. 'He's going to tell me when the funeral is and I'm going to go – I hope you'll come with me.'

'I will if I can get the time off, which is highly unlikely. Why don't you get Fred and Mabel to come? After all they knew him as well as I did.'

She sniffed and nodded. 'I'll do that. But I'm afraid that's not all.' She told him about the will and that Greg had been seeking to get the marriage put aside.

'Sod me! That's not good. What are you going to do?'

'I'm just ignoring it. I don't think the will is read until after the funeral. Time enough to worry when someone contacts me. I expect that woman will try and overturn it – but Greg wanted me to have his estate and I'm going to fight for it.'

'I can't tell you how sorry I am that just as things were sorting themselves out he died. Anything I can do to help, you only have to ask.'

'I suppose I should be grateful he died knowing we could be together after all. But it's no comfort to me – it just makes it so much worse. If that woman hadn't interfered we would have been married and maybe I would be having his child.' She turned away, not wanting to show him her tears.

'I made him a promise, honey, that I would look out for you if anything happened to him. He wrote to me the other week, he didn't tell me all this, but wanted to be sure you wouldn't be on your own if he bought it.'

'I only want a good friend, Jack, nothing else. I don't think I'll ever want anything else from you or any other man.'

'I didn't mean anything else. I know how you felt about Greg and I don't expect to replace him. You're a girl who can look after herself and I can't see that changing.' He squeezed her shoulder affectionately. 'I just want you to know I'm here if you need me.'

She managed a watery smile. 'That's if you're not fighting to keep Britain safe. That must always come first. And don't die as well.'

'I'll do my best to stay alive, honey, and you do the same. Let me know the time of the funeral and I'll come if I can. Also, if you have any trouble from his wife don't try and handle it yourself. Make her speak to your solicitor.'

'In which case, I'd better get on and find myself one. I didn't tell you, did I, that three of the girls from here were caught in the air raid in London the other night? Luckily, they weren't hurt, but lots of people were. Sometimes I wish I had become a doctor – being a ferry pilot isn't nearly as useful.'

'It damn well is. Without the ATA the RAF wouldn't be able to function so well. Our new crates wouldn't get to us on time.'

'True, but at the moment only the men can fly operational aircraft. Pauline, that's Pauline Gower our CO, is hopeful we'll be able to at least fly single engine fighters sometime soon.'

He hugged her again and then pedalled back to his Hurry. Although he'd been given a twenty-four hour leave of absence, he hoped that by returning in a fraction of that time he might be forgiven for taking his kite with him.

Greg had been shot in the leg – he shouldn't have died from that. He thought the poor sod had given up the will to live. No – the man had everything to live for, he would have wanted to stay alive so he could be with the woman he loved.

Jack loved Ellie, was prepared to remain celibate for the foreseeable future on her behalf, but if she died he wouldn't want to top himself. You only got one go on this earth and, as far as he was concerned, you owed it to yourself to experience as much as possible and stay alive however bloody awful things might seem.

Twenty

No one at the ferry pool knew that Ellie had visited Greg just before he died. When his name appeared on the list of deaths there were several speculative looks, especially from Prunella. Throughout the interim between her visit to Orpington Hospital and the announcement of the funeral she'd kept working as if nothing catastrophic had happened, as if she wasn't in real physical pain.

The way she felt when Greg had been forced to marry Elizabeth had been unpleasant but now it was as if there was a splinter of wood lodged somewhere inside her where her heart used to be. Every breath was painful, sheer willpower carried her from day to day. The only respite from this unrelenting agony was when she was flying. Up there she had to concentrate on what she was doing, put everything aside, there was no room for her grief in the cockpit of an aircraft.

The Prime Minister's radio broadcast three days later did nothing to reassure her, or anyone who was also listening, that the worst was over. Ellie was sitting in the operations room with her friend – she only returned to her digs to sleep so she didn't have to interact with the family. Being sociable was too difficult at the moment. Ellie hadn't even told Amanda about her visit and what she'd learned, but she was aware that Greg had died.

The effort of the Germans to secure daylight mastery of the air over England is, of course, the crux of the whole war. So far, it has failed conspicuously. For Hitler to try to invade this country without having secured mastery in the air would be a very hazardous undertaking.

Nevertheless, all his preparations for invasion on a great scale are steadily going forward. Several hundreds of self-propelled barges are moving down the coasts of Europe, from the German and Dutch harbours to the ports of northern France, from Dunkirk to Brest, and beyond Brest to the French harbours in the Bay of Biscay.

'The RAF are fighting to save the country, but at such a dreadful cost.'

'I heard on the grapevine that we are losing more pilots and aircraft than are being replaced,' Amanda said gloomily.

'They will have to recruit more women to help collect operational aircraft. There must be a hundred or more female civilian pilots eager to do their bit.'

'I know Pauline's working hard behind the scenes. You look exhausted, Ellie, you should take your days off as planned.'

'I would if I wasn't needed. If I was in the services I wouldn't get leave, so it's only fair I do as much as they are for the war effort.'

She'd made the decision almost immediately not to attend the funeral. She'd said her goodbye to Greg. The ceremony was for his family and she wasn't part of that circle. It was hard to comprehend that the grief she was feeling was being experienced by hundreds of other family members. Not only were servicemen and women being killed, but civilians were losing their lives and homes in the daily raids, too.

Landing and taking off at any airfield in the vicinity had become hazardous. Because of the frequent raids it was often difficult to get a clear run and not get in the way of fighter aircraft roaring in and out.

The day of the funeral was 15th September – it seemed strange to hold a funeral on a Sunday but it was no concern of hers. She arrived early, as always, and joined the others waiting to discover what they would be doing that day.

Her chit stated she was to taxi an Air Ministry chap from Biggin Hill to the Spitfire factory in Southampton. This was the first time she'd been given a duty that involved doing more than delivering an aircraft. The fact that she had to fly in and out of a busy fighter base would be a challenge. Exactly what she needed today.

One of the more experienced flyers took her to one side. 'It's going to be tricky landing there, they were badly damaged at the end of last month and are not fully operational yet. Be very careful coming in, won't you?'

'I would have checked for myself, but thank you. I suppose the man is going there to see how close they are to being 100 per cent.'

'Very likely. It's all Hurricanes there, you know.'

'That I did know. I'd better get off, I don't want to keep the bigwig waiting.'

The sympathetic glances she received indicated most were aware of the significance of the date. In the space of a few weeks she had lost the man she loved twice over. She wished with all her heart that she had slept with him that day.

She went through her preflight checks, the ground crew pulled the chocks away and she taxied to the end of the runway to wait her turn to take off. The weather was fine but the Meteorological Office had forecast rain and cloud by lunchtime. Hopefully, she would be on her way home by then and wouldn't have to hang about waiting for the weather to clear. The haversack with her overnight things always travelled with her, as did her parachute.

Biggin Hill was the other side of London and she had a choice of flying around the perimeter of the city or taking the shortest route. As the man she was collecting was important she decided not to risk being late by taking the more circuitous journey. She had plotted her trajectory carefully on her map but thought she could rely on visual clues and shouldn't need to use her compass.

By following either the railway or the main road, and making sure she crossed the Thames at Richmond, she shouldn't have any difficulty finding the airfield she wanted. She closed her mind to the thought that she would be flying over the hospital where Greg had died – she didn't want to think about him today.

She took off neatly and climbed to the regulation 2000 feet. They had no RT, had to rely entirely on observation. She was no more than halfway when from the open cockpit she heard the distinctive wail of air raid sirens. Her hands clenched on the stick. There was nothing she could do about it. She had no idea how close the bombers were. If she stayed where she was the fighters who would be screaming into the air at any moment should be able to see her. They flew at 20,000 feet so if she continued where she was everything ought to be fine.

Her heart was thudding uncomfortably. Her pulse raced. Should she land or continue? The ack-ack began from below her – she hoped they didn't think she was an enemy aircraft. Was she likely to be shot down or shot at? What should she do?

To her horror she saw half a dozen Junkers dive bombers approaching. She was directly in their path. Should she climb or dive? Were the guns more dangerous than the Germans? She decided to go up.

She pulled back the stick and pointed the nose towards the high cloud. They were forbidden to fly above the cloud but she ignored this rule. Better to risk clouds than being shot down by enemy or friendly fire.

The Tiger Moth responded gallantly. Her breath hissed through her teeth as she emerged above the cloud bank into bright sunlight. It took a moment for her heart to stop thudding. She scanned the horizon and saw nothing untoward. All she had to do was maintain her direction and pray she didn't get in the way of any bombers or fighters from either side.

She checked the compass. Okay so far. If she continued on this line she should be above Biggin Hill in ten minutes. It was strangely quiet up here; the cloud must be muffling the sound of the battle below her.

Time to descend. Flying through cloud was a strange experience, like going through fog but fresher smelling. The damp was seeping through her Sidcot suit and flying jacket by the time she exited. Her calculations had been perfect. Then she stiffened in horror. Two squadrons of Hurricanes flying at maximum speed in search of Luftwaffe intruders were heading straight for her.

Instinctively she closed her eyes. Stupid. Taking evasive action would be even more stupid. Better to continue and let them avoid her – they were faster and more manoeuvrable.

Two fighters passed so close she could see the pilots in their cockpits. Her aircraft was tossed about by the fighters' slipstream. One of them laughed and the other had time to wave. Nothing fazed the brave men of the RAF. Her brush with death, if that's what it was, made her smile.

The one working runway was now clear and she did the required circuit and made a perfect landing. There was no need for her to go in search of her passenger as he was waiting in a service vehicle for her arrival.

He shouted up to her as she taxied to a stop. 'Stay where you are, I'm in a frightful rush. Well done for getting here in one piece. Bit of a flap on, don't you know.'

Minutes later she was airborne again and heading for Southampton. The Spitfire factory, indeed any factory, was a target so she hoped the Huns were concentrating on London today and she'd have no more excitement.

After delivering her passenger she left her aircraft to be refuelled and went in search of some lunch. A little after two o'clock she was ready to depart but one of the ground crew stopped her.

'I shouldn't go yet, miss, all hell's broken loose over London. Far too dangerous to be scudding about up there at the moment.'

'Oh dear! I want to get back before the weather worsens but it looks as though I'll have to find somewhere to sleep tonight.'

'You can bunk in with me, love, if you like?'

She took his comment in good part and laughed. 'Thank you, but I'll find a B&B somewhere.'

As it turned out there was a bed going spare in the WAAF accommodation block and she accepted the offer gratefully. She listened to the nine o'clock news in the crew room and was relieved that both raids had been thwarted.

The next morning she was able to take off at dawn – the sky was usually free of enemy and friendly aircraft then – and landed safely at Hatfield just as the girls were arriving for their shift.

After filing her flight report and filling in her logbook she headed for the office to see what they had planned for her today. Her passage was blocked by Prunella.

'You bitch. Don't think you can get away with it.' This snarled comment was accompanied by a hard shove that sent Ellie flying backwards. Her feet became tangled in her parachute straps and she fell painfully to the floor.

'What in God's name is going on here? Prunella, have you lost your senses?'

Ellie was helped to her feet and her attacker was bundled away. Amanda collected the discarded chute and handed it to her. 'Are you okay? I'd better take you to sickbay so you can be checked out.'

'I'm absolutely fine.'

'Have you any idea why she pushed you over?'

'I'm afraid I do. I'll explain it to you when we've got more time. I had a really scary trip yesterday – what about you?'

Over a much needed mug of tea she regaled the room with her near misses. Amanda brought over the chits. 'Nothing so exciting today for any of us. We're taking a couple of Lysanders up north. Should be well away from the action.'

One of the secretarial staff poked her head through the door. 'Ellie, Pauline wants to speak to you.'

'Right, I'm on my way. Don't wait for me, Amanda, no doubt we'll catch up tonight.'

This interview was inevitable and she was dreading having to explain to her CO why she'd been attacked.

When she'd finished Pauline shook her head. 'Good God, what a mess. Not your fault at all, Ellie, I can see how it happened. No excuse for Prunella's behaviour. I've dismissed her immediately from the service. You can't just ignore this – have you got yourself a decent lawyer?'

'I haven't, but I know I should have. I find that if I don't think about it at all I can cope.'

'A tragic story, but there you are, there's a war on. You won't be the only girl in the same situation.'

'Having a fortune left to them when those that don't know the truth will think it should have been left to the wife?'

Pauline smiled. 'Of course not, I imagine your position is unique.' She scribbled on a piece of paper and pushed it across the desk. 'Contact this firm. Excellent chaps. Give them my name and they'll look after you.'

'Thank you, I'll do it when I get back. I can't see that another day or two will make any difference.'

The flight was as expected and she landed just before lunch. Amanda was waiting for her, obviously eager to hear the full story. They got a lift to the nearest station and went in search of a café.

'Now, Ellie Simpson, tell me all.' When she'd finished her friend was staggered. 'Have you any idea what you've been left? Surely Greg didn't own the family estates as his father is still alive?'

'I've no idea – but I'm pretty sure it's a lot of money and most people would think it wouldn't be right for me to have it.'

'After what you've told me I don't think Elizabeth has a case. Let's hope the legal people agree with us.'

'But she's his wife, his widow now, and I'm nothing at all in the eyes of the law.'

'Stuff and nonsense. You're the woman he loved, the woman he would have married, intended to marry once he'd had this thing with Elizabeth dissolved. If anyone is entitled to inherit from him it's you and not the person who tricked him and ruined your lives.'

'I suppose this conversation is academic. I'm certain his family and Elizabeth will fight the will – they'll take it to court if necessary.'

'Let them. Remember, he sent for you, not her. He knew that his will would be null and void after he married and deliberately wrote another one, again leaving everything to you. He must have had some evidence that the baby wasn't his – hopefully whatever solicitors you use will be able to find this out. If you don't want the money yourself then you could set up a charity of some sort in his name.'

Twenty-One

Birkett & Ellisons had their main office in St Martin's Lane, not far from the National Gallery, and Ellie made an appointment to see them the following morning.

'Why don't you come with me, Amanda? We could go to the Empire, or one of the other cinemas nearby, and see a film afterwards and then have tea somewhere.'

'I'd love to. It's amazing that everyone goes about their daily business as usual even though there's a good chance there will be an air raid at some point during the day.'

'Hitler isn't going to break our spirit. British people are resilient and stick together when things get tough.'

'Absolutely. I must say I'm surprised you've not heard from the Dunlop solicitors. Surely they must know where to find you?'

'It's only been a week since the funeral. I expect the letter's in the post. I was thinking, why don't you come back to Glebe Farm instead of going out for a meal? I'd love to introduce you to my dad and stepmother.'

'That would be splendid. We don't want to travel in the rush hour so we must make sure we go to an early showing.'

'I'll leave you to check what's on, shall I? I'm sure there's a list in the newspaper somewhere.'

That night Ellie returned to her digs immediately after her shift. Mrs Cooper greeted her as if she'd been missing the evening meal for weeks, not days.

'There you are, Miss Simpson, the children and I were beginning to worry because you haven't been getting your rations.'

'Sorry, I've been so busy and getting back really late. This is the first time I've finished early. I'm away for two nights, I'm going home to see my parents.'

'Then you'll want your ration book...'

'No, you can use whatever you want. Don't forget my dad's a farmer, there's always plenty to eat there. I'll try and bring you back some eggs – they'll be cracked ones, but perfect for scrambled or an omelette.'

'Ta ever so much, that would be smashing.'

Ellie was meeting Amanda at the station to catch the nine o'clock train. Her appointment was at ten thirty so she should have ample time to get there. The constant daylight raids had stopped and now the Germans were coming at night. She'd heard them flying overhead last night and dreaded what might have happened, what she might see.

The train was packed, mostly with people in uniforms, but a fair number of pinstriped businessmen in bowler hats as well. Apart from the lack of seats, the absence of station names and all the gas masks hanging around people's necks, it could have been a normal day in normal times.

'You never said much about what happened when you were up here last, Amanda.'

'Not a lot to say. We spent most of the day underground and then came home. Most of the bombs fell on the docks so apart from a lot of smoke in the East End of London there wasn't much to see.'

Ellie stepped out of the train and almost choked. The air was thick with dust. She looked around but nobody else was bothered, they all strode off to do what they'd come for so she supposed she must do the same.

Amanda sensed her dismay and slipped her arm through hers. 'Chin up, old thing, pretend everything is fine. It's the only way to get through this.'

There was no actual bomb damage on this side of London but for there to be so much smoke in the air must mean there had been a devastating attack last night. How many civilians had been killed? How many homes and businesses destroyed? She didn't want to know – she had to push such thoughts aside and concentrate on her own contribution.

There were no buses to be seen but the underground was functioning. They were waved through the barrier. There was barely room to stand because of the piles of rubbish, blankets, buckets and so on that had been left behind by those that had sheltered there during the raids. The smell was appalling.

With some relief she jumped on the train. She was jammed into a corner, separated from Amanda, but being in uniform meant she was treated with respect. There was no point in worrying about her friend, she would get off at Charing Cross as planned and wait on the pavement.

Amanda joined her. 'It doesn't look as if any bombs dropped here. It's the East End that's getting hammered every night.'

'I don't want to talk about it. One thing at a time. I've lost the two people I loved most in the world in the last few months. I know it sounds callous, but I can't deal with anyone else's grief. I'm barely coping with my own.'

She walked briskly in what she hoped was the right direction and no more was said on the subject of the blitz. When they arrived at the smart offices of Birkett & Ellisons they were immediately ushered into a waiting room and plied with not tea, but excellent coffee.

'It was worth the journey just to drink this,' Amanda whispered.

'I can't remember the last time I had any. I wonder where they get it?'

'I wonder if there's going to be a second cup.'

An elderly clerk escorted Ellie up to a large, well appointed office on the first floor. A surprisingly young man limped across the expensive rug to shake her hand.

'Good morning, Miss Simpson, I am David Humphrey, the junior partner here. Please take a seat.'

'Thank you for seeing me so promptly. As you can imagine this matter has been preying on my mind and I need to get it settled.'

'I have obtained a copy of Squadron Leader Dunlop's will. Do you wish to read it or shall I summarise?'

'I should like a copy, obviously, but for the moment please just give me the gist.'

Her hands were clenched in her lap and she was having difficulty swallowing. This meeting made it all far too real. She bit her lip in the hope she could keep the tears from dripping down her cheeks and embarrassing both of them.

'The will is quite explicit, Miss Simpson. You have been left everything he owned to do as you like with. There are no provisos, no other beneficiaries.'

'I see. Exactly what have I inherited?'

He reeled off a list of funds, stocks and shares, houses, farms and foreign interests. Her head was spinning by the time he finished.

'I'd no idea he was so wealthy in his own right. I knew his family were rich, but I assumed he only had a moderate income until his father died and left him the rest.'

'His wealth was inherited directly from his maternal grandfather and his paternal great-uncle. None of these items come from his father.' Mr Humphrey tapped the papers in front of him. 'It is my opinion, and I can assure you I have taken advice on this matter, that the terms of the will are inviolate. This is a will written after he was married. Squadron Leader Dunlop married Elizabeth Hamilton because she told him she was expecting his child.'

'He told me just before he died that he had evidence to the contrary.'

'That is correct, Miss Simpson. His solicitors have forwarded three affidavits, signed and witnessed, that categorically state she is expecting the baby at the beginning of January and not the end of February. He was also attempting to have the marriage dissolved.

'Therefore, it is our opinion that you are under no legal or moral obligation whatsoever to relinquish any of your inheritance. I understand that you and Squadron Leader Dunlop would have been married yourselves before he died if Miss Hamilton had not intervened.'

She sniffed and wiped her eyes. 'We would, in fact if he had…' She dug her nails into her palms in an effort to prevent herself from completely breaking down.

He was looking at her as if expecting an answer but she couldn't remember the question.

'I beg your pardon, what did you ask me?'

He repeated it and this time she was able to respond.

'Yes, we were to be married. I tried to persuade him not to marry that woman but he was too much of a gentleman to allow her to become a social pariah.'

He cleared his throat. 'We are of the opinion that the marriage would eventually have been set aside. That you would in fact have been Mrs Dunlop.'

'I would.' She couldn't continue. Grief at what might have been if only her darling Greg had survived overwhelmed her.

The solicitor waited for her to recover before continuing. 'Do you wish us to handle probate for you, Miss Simpson?'

She wasn't exactly sure what this entailed but she knew she didn't want anything to do with it. 'Yes, please do so.' She stumbled to her feet then managed to pull herself together. 'I don't want any of the money – I want to set up a charity for injured RAF men. Can you arrange that as well?'

'I shall give it some thought, Miss Simpson, and we can discuss it when you come back when probate has been settled.'

Amanda was waiting for her at the bottom of the stairs. She took one look at Ellie's face and bustled her back into the waiting room.

'Sit down, Ellie, I'll ask for some more coffee. Take your time, it's all been a terrible shock.'

After another drink she was beginning to feel more in control. Her tears dried and she was able to explain what had been said.

The elderly clerk came in with a tray holding a plate of pastries and sandwiches plus another silver jug of coffee. 'Good, I asked them to send out for something to eat. You stay here. I'm going to ask your solicitor some questions.' The clerk was hovering at the door. Amanda beckoned him in. 'Right, I want you to witness this. Ellie, do I have your permission to act on your behalf in this matter?'

Ellie had no idea what she meant but nodded anyway. 'Yes, you do.'

Her friend vanished and she poured another cup. She hadn't been hungry until she saw the dainty, crustless sandwiches and assortment of pastries that had been placed on the central table. Why had Amanda rushed off to speak to Mr Humphrey? She couldn't think of anything else they could possibly wish to know.

She took a bite of a sandwich but couldn't swallow it and had to spit it into her handkerchief. She was awash with coffee and didn't want any more – in fact she didn't want to stay here a moment longer than was necessary. Neither did she want to go to the cinema. What she wanted was to go to Glebe Farm and pretend that neither her brother Neil nor Greg were dead.

As she waited she began to think about what she'd learned. Even though she had no wish to be a beneficiary, she was determined that the Hamilton woman wouldn't get her greedy hands on it.

The door flew open and Amanda appeared. 'We can go now. These chaps seem to know what they're doing and won't let you down.'

She didn't want to talk about it any more – Greg was dead. That was all that mattered. No amount of discussion and debate was going to change that.

Once they were in the street she turned to her friend. 'I'm really sorry, but I don't want to go the cinema. Would you mind very much if we went straight to Romford?'

'Actually, I'd prefer it. I know it won't be exactly quiet being so near Hornchurch, but at least we can pretend.'

Being in uniform meant they didn't need tickets when they travelled. She supposed that an ATA uniform shouldn't qualify as this rule only applied to service people – but the guard didn't query their lack of tickets.

She was shocked to see the bomb damage in Romford as they walked through. 'The fact that all this was caused by collateral damage, bombs meant for Hornchurch, doesn't make it any better. In fact, I think it's worse.'

'You're right, Ellie. Civilian losses are mounting up. Thank God for the civil defence and so on. What do the people who've been bombed out do? The East End has been raided day and night for weeks – it must be horrendous there.'

'Not just the East End, Oxford Street was hit last week, wasn't it? D H Evans and Bourne & Hollingsworth were badly damaged and John Lewis was completely burned out. I read in the paper that it looks like a charred skeleton with its blackened walls and gaping windows.'

'Hang on, I think that car is going to offer us a lift.'

It was a camouflaged RAF car driven by a smiling WAAF. 'Want a ride? I'm going to Brentwood to collect some bigwig who has been visiting his son at the posh school.'

'Thanks, if you could drop us off at the end of the lane that leads down to our farm that would be helpful.'

'ATA girls, aren't you? Ever so smart those uniforms are. Not like this one which fits where it touches.'

'We are. I was a WAAF until a few weeks ago. I know exactly what you mean – the passion killers were the worst. We can wear our own undergarments.'

They were dropped off and she and Amanda strolled down the drive enjoying the fresh air. The cows were grazing contentedly in the adjacent field and the sound of female voices carried from where the gang were working.

'The only help my dad's got here now are the land army girls. He's delighted with them, especially as Mabel doesn't have to cook for more than the two of them now.'

Where were the dogs? Usually they were racing towards her by this time. Then she heard them barking in the distance and stopped to peer through the hedge. Sure enough, they had either seen or smelt her and were tearing across the stubble.

'Hang on, we're about to get company.' The two animals wriggled through a gap at the bottom of the hedge and were soon squirming in ecstasy as she and Amanda patted them.

The two days passed quickly and this time she was sorry to leave. On the train back to London her friend asked her why she hadn't told her parents about the will.

'There's no point in worrying them unnecessarily. Nothing's going to happen for months so I'm going to forget about it and try and get on with my life.'

Twenty-Two

Jack, like the rest of his squadron, was permanently knackered. He had no time to think about anything but attacking the Huns and trying to stay alive himself. Personnel changed, too many of his friends vanished, some to hospital but many to a wooden box like Greg.

The CO had a stroke and was carted off a gibbering wreck to be replaced by a Canadian guy. They were discussing this new arrival in the mess one night.

'I heard that he got his AFC for testing the strength of the balloon cables,' one of the blokes said.

'How the hell did he do that?' Jack asked as he swallowed a third of his warm beer.

'He had an old Fairey Battle which had been fitted with armour plated wings.'

Jack choked on his drink. 'Sod me! They're bloody horrible aircraft at the best of times – something like a cross between a Hurricane and a cucumber.'

Another guy joined in. 'I'd rather fly the latter than a bloody Battle, let alone one with modified wings. Flying deliberately into balloon cables must mean our new CO has balls of steel.' The bloke raised his glass and they drank a toast.

Jack finished his drink and refused a refill. They were on duty at five and he wanted to read the letter that had arrived from Ellie and then get some kip. In fact, he should tell his men to do the same, this was the first shift they'd had off for weeks and sleep was more important than getting smashed.

His promotion to flight lieutenant had made him second in command in his squadron, but they were all adults and must make that sort of decision for themselves.

There was a small kitchen that the batmen used to make tea but obviously any officer was free to use the facilities if they wanted to. He made himself a brew and took it into his room. He was no longer sharing, one good thing about being promoted he supposed. Another was the slight increase in pay – he thought most of the men spent the bulk of their wages in the mess, but he was more cautious.

He too, had written his will leaving everything to Ellie, he had a tidy sum invested in war bonds from the proceeds of selling his two aircraft. She didn't need his money, especially now Greg had made her his beneficiary. However, he liked the thought she would have something from him if he went for a Burton.

The information in Ellie's letter didn't surprise him. He would never have married a girl he didn't love even if she was having his child – certainly not until he was certain she wasn't lying. If Greg had listened to Ellie he might still be alive today. Being so cut up about what happened had probably made Greg more vulnerable to attack.

The Hamiltons and Dunlops would appeal against the will, but he doubted they would succeed. He was pretty sure there was some legal thing that said a widow and her children must be provided for – he wasn't sure where this left things for Ellie. She might have to settle something on the Hamilton woman, but hopefully not have to provide support for the little bastard.

The raids on London intensified and the Huns were also bombing cities throughout the country. Word in the mess was that the attacks on the airfields had moved to raids on cities because of the British attack on Dresden. It was bloody bad luck for those who lived in London et cetera, but if the raids on the air bases had continued the RAF wouldn't have been able to continue to protect the skies above Britain.

There was scarcely a moment to think about anything but stopping the bombers every night. Then at the start of October the weather changed and there was thick fog over London. They remained on call but no one was scrambled. Even Hitler had more sense than to send his bombers out in such conditions.

Ellie wouldn't be flying either – the ATA weren't allowed to fly unless the weather conditions were optimal. He joined the queue at the telephone and rang Hatfield. Sure enough she came to the telephone.

'Jack, I was just thinking about you. I hope you're all grounded too.'

'We are, thank God. The Met Office says this is set in for a few days. I can't leave the base, could you possibly come here?'

'I could if I can hitch a lift. Hang on a minute, I'll go and check if I'm allowed off base. My official days off start tomorrow but it doesn't look like I'll be going anywhere today.'

He heard a clatter as she dropped the receiver. A few moments later she was back. 'I can come. Can I bring a friend?'

'Bring whoever you like, there's a distinct lack of female company at Kenley.'

She laughed. 'In which case, Flight Lieutenant, I'll invite anyone who has a day off. We'll need somewhere to sleep tonight, we won't want to be hitching back in the fog and the dark.'

'Don't worry about that, something will be arranged. I'll send word to the gate to expect you.'

'If you wait a minute I'll go and find out exactly how many of us there'll be.'

Again the clatter, but this time he had to wait longer. The guy behind him in the queue wasn't impressed. 'Get a move on, there's a queue waiting to use the phone.'

'I can see that, not blind you know. I'm in the process of arranging for a group of ATA female pilots to come and visit. My friend has gone to find out how many can come.'

This news changed the atmosphere. 'Jolly good, that's news worth waiting for.'

Ellie picked up the receiver. 'There will be seven of us – is that too many?'

'No, you can't have too much of a good thing.'

'We are setting off now, don't know how long it will take, depends on transport. We should be there around lunchtime.'

He hung up and grinned at the expectant queue behind him. 'There will be seven girls coming – I think that calls for a bit of a party.'

Word soon spread through the Officers' Mess and even Win Co was on board with it. There were a dozen or so WAAF working on the base as well as civilians in various domestic roles. Everyone was invited and within a couple of hours he was certain there would be plenty of females to go around.

He spoke to the catering staff and they were happy to provide some sort of running buffet. There was already a piano in the mess, but someone brought in a record player and a pile of records as well.

'We can make this a dance rather than a party, there's plenty of room now we've pushed the tables and chairs against the wall,' an Australian guy said.

'Great, nothing like a jitterbug to make an evening go with a swing,' Jack said.

'Jitterbug? Don't know that one, mate. Is it a Yank dance?'

'It is. I'll show you. It's popular in the nightclubs here, too.' He checked the titles on the discs and was delighted to find a selection of Glenn Miller and Benny Goodman. These would make the evening a success.

The fog got thicker and the mess got gloomier. When midday came and went and there was still no sign of the girls he began to think they wouldn't get there.

'Cheer up, Jack, we've still got our own popsies even if your ATA girls don't make it.'

The fog wasn't too bad when Ellie and the girls set off and they managed to catch a lift in an army lorry much to the delight of the soldiers sitting in the back.

'Hop in, ladies, plenty of room inside,' one of them said as he leaned out and offered a hand.

She, like the others, was quite capable of climbing into a lorry without any assistance and they all ignored the waving hands. Once settled, sitting close together, in the space between the two rows of soldiers, the ribald remarks began.

It was hard not to laugh as the comments were harmless enough, if a bit near the knuckle. Although she didn't join in the banter, hearing the light hearted talk and jollity raised her spirits a little. The last two weeks had been the longest in her life. Knowing she wasn't the only person suffering unbearable grief didn't help at all. One consolation was that she could fly every day. When she was up there she felt closer to Greg somehow. Nonsense, of course, if there was an afterlife – which she doubted – you certainly wouldn't find it in the sky whatever people might think to the contrary.

The seven of them scrambled out at the station and caught the next train into London. 'A lot of the roads will be closed, blocked by rubble or unexploded bombs,' Amanda said. 'It's going to be easier to catch the tube. The Northern line would take us as far as Morden and hopefully we can get a lift from there to Kenley.'

The fog, raids and bomb damage didn't seem to have depressed the Londoners' spirit. People chatted, shoved and moaned as always but she didn't hear anyone complaining. As she clung onto the pole by the door in the tube it gave her pause for thought. She scanned the faces, apart from looking tired, and a bit grubby in some cases, nobody looked miserable. She couldn't tell which ones of them had suffered a loss in the family and by the law of averages there must be several passengers who were grieving.

Greg wouldn't want her to be sad, he'd want her to get on with her life. She remembered someone telling her that the first few weeks after the death of someone you loved were the worst, once you'd endured those, things started to improve. That's what she would hang onto – that by Christmas the loss would be bearable. Although whatever anyone said she doubted she would ever truly get over it.

Amanda was rocking beside her and nudged her in the ribs. 'I know it's hard, Ellie, but try and put it aside just for today and enjoy yourself.'

'I think it would have been so much easier to lose him if we'd been married as we should have been. I feel cheated, robbed of what was rightfully mine. I'll never forgive that woman for what she did to us, she'll get a penny over my dead body.'

Until she'd spoken she hadn't realised she felt so strongly about it. This hate, this anger, would get her through the bad weeks. Far easier to hate than to grieve.

'That's the ticket, fighting talk. Everyone's behind you and will give you whatever help you need.'

Good grief! Ellie looked at the others – some of them she didn't even call close friends. She wasn't sure she was comfortable with them knowing her personal business like this. Fond as she was of Amanda she wished her friend was less indiscreet. In future she might be a bit less forthcoming about her personal life.

By the time they reached Morden the train was almost empty and they had all got seats. When they emerged, the fog had worsened. 'I can hardly see my hand in front of my face,' one of the girls said.

'How far is it to Kenley from here?' Amanda asked her.

'Too far to walk. If we can find a telephone box I'll ring and see if they can organise a lift for us otherwise I don't think we're going to make it.'

'I'm not spending the night anywhere but in a bed,' a determined voice said. Her shape was so indistinct Ellie had no idea who was speaking.

'If we don't stay together we're going to get lost. I suggest we hang onto each other's jackets. Who is volunteering to lead the crocodile?'

'Just a minute, I think there's a ticket chappie, or maybe a guard, over there.'

The man was only too happy to help. 'You girls are a wonder, flying them aircraft like what you do. I'll give Kenley a call and see what I can organise. Stay in the station, you'll get blooming lost if you go out there in that.'

Despite the fact that it was only the beginning of October it was decidedly chilly. By the time the promised transport arrived Ellie was regretting her impulsive decision. The last thing she wanted to do was be jolly, dance and drink cocktails.

Then suddenly things were better. 'Hi, ladies, your chariot awaits.'

Without hesitation Ellie rushed forward and threw herself into Jack's arms. He held her close and she breathed in his familiar aroma of engine oil and soap. When he gently released her she smiled at him. 'I'm so glad to see you. I won't introduce you now, we'll wait until we're somewhere more convivial.'

He had managed to borrow an ancient truck, hardly comfortable, but in the circumstances anything was better than hanging about outside in the fog. The journey to the base was slow, the driver crawling along by the curb in the hope that he wouldn't get lost.

She was jammed in between him and Jack on the front seat, the other girls were travelling in the back. The engine of this old vehicle wheezed and groaned but eventually it got them to their destination, much to her relief.

The security check at the gate was non-existent – the barrier was raised and they were waved through uninspected.

Jack jumped out first and then swung her out. From nowhere a dozen boys in blue appeared and surrounded the truck. The girls were assisted to the ground and escorted inside. It was hard to be sad in the face of such an enthusiastic welcome.

'Come along, honey, and meet the guys in my squadron. Unlike some of the old farts they surely appreciate the work you girls are doing.'

Her hand was still in his as he led her forward and she didn't have the heart to pull it free. The sound of *Five O'Clock Whistle* from the Glenn Miller orchestra belted down the corridor. Half a dozen giggling girls in pretty floral frocks dashed past.

'Good, I'm glad you found some other female guests. I really don't want to dance with anyone apart from you and I would have had to if we'd been the only ones here.'

He pulled her to one side, allowing the others to surge past. When they were alone he looked closely at her. 'I shouldn't have done this. It's too soon, isn't it?'

'No, it's exactly what I need. Maybe for a few hours I can forget what happened and just enjoy the moment.'

He nodded and pulled her a little closer. 'If it gets too much, just tell me and I'll take you to my quarters. Against all the regulations, but sod it, there's a war on and your needs come first today.'

There was food, coffee, tea and drinks from the bar – everything had been thought of. Despite the fact it was early afternoon everyone was behaving as if it was a normal night-time party. Seeing the dozens of young men in RAF blue was too much for her. Some of them even sounded just like Greg.

She pulled her hand from Jack's. 'I'm sorry, I can't do this, it's too soon. I should never have come.'

He was about to answer when a pretty girl in a WAAF uniform grabbed his hand and dragged him onto the makeshift dance floor. Ellie retreated hastily. She asked for some paper from the adjutant's office and wrote a quick note telling Jack she had gone home.

Twenty-Three

Ellie marched off into the fog determined to return to Romford whatever the weather conditions. It wasn't dark yet, and a small amount of light filtered through, so she could see just enough to find her way back to the underground station.

Luck was with her and the train arrived a few minutes after she did. Once she was safely inside she stopped worrying that Jack might appear to drag her back. Three nights at the farm would be better for her than trying to forget at a party.

By the time she arrived at Liverpool Street station it was heaving with businessmen determined to get home before it got dark and the trains ground to a halt. There was no point in finding a seat as Romford wasn't many stops.

Being sure you were at the right station was difficult when you could see, but with the thickening fog and falling darkness she just had to pray she'd counted correctly. She'd only taken a few steps along the platform when she realised she'd missed her stop and got out at Shenfield.

She had two choices – cross to the other side and wait for a train going back to London or see if she could get a lift to Romford. The chances of this happening were becoming more remote by the minute as the weather worsened. She went to speak to the stationmaster.

'I don't rightly know when the next train will be here, miss, there's not been nothing getting through this past hour. Last I heard the fog's too thick to move around Chelmsford and everything's backed up waiting for it to lift.'

'Would you mind very much if I waited in the ladies' room anyway? I don't have anywhere else to go.'

'You help yourself, miss, but I reckon you're in for a long wait. Do you need to make a telephone call to let someone know you're safe?'

'Thank you, that's very kind of you. However, I'm not expected anywhere so nobody will be worried.'

She groped her way over the bridge and down the other side and located the waiting room. As expected it was unoccupied. There wouldn't be many people wanting to go to London tonight, or any other night. If it wasn't for the fog there would be bombs dropping indiscriminately and she certainly wouldn't want to risk her life just go to the cinema or theatre.

It got darker and darker and no trains arrived at the station on either side. On balance, she thought it was better being stranded here than at Liverpool Street station or, even worse, trapped on one of the trains that was stuck on the line.

When it had snowed so badly over the winter the soldiers had cleared the roads and the railway track, but there was nothing they could do about fog. She didn't regret abandoning her friends, they deserved to have a good time, and she hoped Jack wasn't too upset about her sudden departure.

She loved him, of course she did, but not the same way she'd loved Neil. She was pretty certain his feelings were not at all fraternal. He'd kissed her more than once and she'd seen that tell-tale flash of darkness in his eyes afterwards.

Better to stop seeing him before she had to hurt his feelings. From now on there should be no phone calls, and certainly no meetings, perhaps just the occasional exchanged letter. She hoped he found himself a young lady he could love and who would be able to love him in return. He was an attractive man, and wouldn't remain single for long once he knew she was off limits.

There were no blackout blinds on the waiting room windows therefore there were no lights allowed when it got dark. Fortunately, she had her torch and was able to make her way to the WC when she needed it.

She wished now she'd eaten something before she dashed off as her stomach was rumbling. At three o'clock she heard the unmistakable sound of a train approaching the platform. She rushed out and saw the faint flicker of a lantern. There must be a guard on the platform too.

'Will this train stop at Romford?' Her voice echoed down the platform but received an immediate response from the ghostly figure at the far end.

'Yes, miss, you hop on when it arrives.'

She did exactly that and was unsurprised to find it full of disgruntled passengers who'd been delayed for hours, but unlike her they hadn't had access to a functioning WC.

As far as she could see the fog wasn't any better than it had been when everything had ground to a halt, but as long as it got her back to Romford she didn't care how slowly it went.

Her parents were delighted to see her and she decided to tell them about her deathbed visit to Greg and the legal ramifications of his new will.

'Well I never did!' Mabel said as she dabbed her eyes with the edge of her pinny. 'What a dreadful thing to do. I'm so sorry, lovey, that you didn't get to marry your young man.'

'You stick to your guns, Ellie love, don't give that woman a penny. Greg wanted you to have it and you'll be honouring his memory by keeping it.'

'There's another thing, Dad, I've a dreadful suspicion that Jack doesn't think of me as a sister. Next time he comes down could you please make it clear that as far as I'm concerned he's a brother – nothing else.'

'I'm not surprised. You're a lovely girl – why shouldn't he fall in love with you?'

'I'm sorry he has, but there's nothing I can do about it. I'm going to write him a letter explaining how things are, which should be enough. If you and Mabel confirm this next time you see him so much the better.'

Writing the letter was harder than she thought it would be, but it had to be done. She blotted the paper, folded it and put it in the envelope ready to be posted when she left.

Jack might be upset but he was a pragmatist, he wouldn't sit around moping, but get on with his life and hopefully find himself a new love interest.

Having got this out of the way she was able to spend her time walking with the dogs and thinking about what might have been. The more she did this, the harder her resolve. She decided that just keeping the money wasn't punishment enough for the woman who had ruined her life and possibly caused Greg's untimely death.

What she was going to do about it she wasn't quite sure, but there was no rush to get her revenge. The longer she had to plan, the more effective it would be.

Jack enjoyed the party but he would have enjoyed it more if Ellie had stayed. He hadn't been worried about her safety, he trusted her, she was a resourceful girl and would find her way home without his interference.

The fog lingered for another day, giving them all time to catch up on their sleep and be ready to scramble when the order came. Ellie's letter was no surprise to him. He wasn't going to give up on her, whatever she said. She had loved Greg and the poor sod had only been dead a couple of weeks. She wouldn't be ready to think about another relationship for months, if not years.

Her suggestion that he find himself a girlfriend might be sensible, but until he was certain Ellie was out of his reach he had no intention of tangling himself up with anyone else.

*

The mayhem over London continued and he and his men fought tirelessly to protect the city. He had no time to think about anything but his job. Liverpool and other cities were bombed repeatedly – God knows how the civilians were coping.

There were no further letters from Ellie and he missed them. She'd made her position clear and he wasn't going to intrude where he wasn't wanted. The news said the Battle of Britain had been won by the RAF, that Hitler had indefinitely postponed his intention to invade. That much was true, but God knows how they were going to win the war.

Then Hitler turned his attention to Russia at the end of October and the nightly raids on London began to tail off, which meant a welcome lull in their sorties. The following week his squadron was told they were being posted to North Africa to join the Western Desert Air Force which already had Wellington bombers, Blenheims and Gladiators.

He had kept his distance as Ellie had asked but wanted to speak to her before he left. They were all given a forty-eight hour pass before they departed and he was determined to see her face to face one last time.

This time he got permission to use his kite to fly to Hatfield. He didn't check if she was there, just took off in the hope she would turn up sometime in the next two days. As before, he landed and taxied to the far side of the apron.

An erk offered him a lift to the ATA building and he jumped in beside him. The time was mid afternoon, the weather was decent for a change, and the only people there were the girls in the office.

'I'm hoping to see Ellie Simpson. Is she likely to be back today?'

The girl smiled and checked her list. 'She should be arriving at any moment, Flight Lieutenant, she had to deliver a Lysander to Kent but has got a lift back.'

'Thank you. Any chance of a cuppa whilst I wait?'

She pointed towards the room next door. 'Help yourself, and there are biscuits in the tin and there might even be a bit of cake left.'

The smell in here was different, a feminine aroma. No residual cigarette smoke or stale beer fumes. There was a knitting bag on a side table, a chess board, a pile of books and magazines and a bridge set. No overflowing ashtrays in here.

He didn't have long to wait before he saw a Tiger Moth circle and land not far from his Hurricane. If this was Ellie then she would know he was here. He hoped it didn't mean she would vanish and not come to speak to him.

It might be better to wait outside. He took his mug with him and was standing by the door when she pedalled up on a battered bicycle. He'd expected her to be cool but instead she dropped the bike and ran towards him, her face radiant.

'Jack, I can't tell you how glad I am to see you after so long.' She smiled, looking like the old Ellie he used to know. 'It's my fault, but I was so miserable then I couldn't cope with anything else.'

This was going better than he dared hope. He explained the reason for his visit. 'I'm hoping you will write to me again whilst I'm away. It could be bloody years before I get back to Blighty. Knowing you're here, having your photograph in my pocket, will give me something to stay alive for.' This was a risky thing to say as it implied there might be something more between them than just friends. He braced himself for a brush-off.

'I'd love that. I've missed our exchange of letters.'

He knew he was grinning like an idiot but he couldn't help himself. 'I'll take that, honey, it's more than I expected. I've got two days before I leave, would you come with me to Glebe Farm so I can say goodbye to Fred and Mabel?'

'You've timed it perfectly, Flight Lieutenant, I'm just starting my two days free as well. Wait there, I'll speak to Pauline.'

She returned a few moments later looking pleased with herself. 'We can take the Tiger Moth, she said they could manage without it for a couple of days. I hope the grass isn't too long on our strip or it could be a bumpy landing.'

There was no question as to who would be flying, he was definitely the passenger. This didn't bother him as Ellie was as a good pilot as anyone he knew and that included the blokes he flew with.

On the short flip to Romford he relaxed and enjoyed the view. He was glad he'd put on his flight suit again as it was damn cold in an open cockpit at the beginning of November.

The airstrip they'd used when they were running the aero club together was usable, but only because the grass had stopped growing when the frost started. She taxied the kite up to the hangar and switched off the engine.

She was out before him and ran across to peer in through the window of the building. He joined her. 'Look, Jack, it's still there. I like to check every time I come home. I'm afraid we'll have to walk. Do you want to shove your flight suit with mine somewhere in the Moth where it won't be seen?'

He did as she suggested and just hoped nobody would come down here and steal it. He'd have to pay for another one if he lost it.

The little dogs raced, barking loudly, to greet them when they were still a quarter of a mile away from the farm. He had casually slung his arm around her shoulders and she hadn't shrugged it off. She smiled up at him.

'The good thing about all this noise is that Mabel will know someone's coming and it must be either me or you. They don't bark at strangers, only for family.'

Twenty-Four

Mabel already had the kettle on when they walked into the kitchen. 'You should have given us a ring, Ellie, and let us know Jack was coming with you. You'll have to make up his bed, but yours is always ready.'

Ellie hugged her. 'I'm sorry, we didn't know we were coming until an hour ago.' Mabel was suitably impressed when she heard how they'd travelled.

'Just like the old days. Your dad has gone into Romford to the bank – not sure what it's about. It's none of my business.'

'I'm sure he'll tell you when he gets back. After I have my tea I'll do the bed. As you weren't expecting us why don't we all go into Romford tonight and find something to eat there?'

Mabel looked relieved. 'If you wouldn't mind, lovey, that would be grand. Fred and I are going to a whist drive in the village hall and I don't want to miss it. We did ever so well last time.

'We've got a lovely group of land girls who have taken over the dairy and the pigs. I'll shut the chickens up when

I get back. We don't have any trouble with foxes now we've got the dogs.'

'We can drop you off, go into Romford, and then pick you up on the way back.'

She left Jack downstairs and quickly sorted out his room. The fact that Greg had once slept in the other bed was no longer as painful. She was concerned about her dad's visit to the bank, he never went anywhere that forced him to put on a collar and tie. In fact, as far as she knew, the last time he'd been into town was when he'd redrawn his will at his solicitors last year leaving the farm to Neil and her. She blinked back unwanted tears. The farm would be hers now.

The dogs started barking and a few minutes later Jack's Austin Seven drove into the yard. He'd left the car here when he'd joined up. They were together in the sitting room. He sensed her unease.

'Don't worry, honey, give the guy time to talk to his wife.'

She couldn't help laughing. 'Sometimes, Jack Reynolds, you sound more like a Yank than a Brit.'

He returned her smile. 'Spending four years out there with a flying circus rubbed off. It just slips in.'

There wasn't long to wait before her dad and Mabel came in. He looked pleased. Whatever he'd been doing had been successful. He didn't like being hugged, but she did it anyway and this time he responded.

'Good to see you both, couldn't have timed it better.' He and Mabel sat together on the sofa; she and Jack resumed their seats in the armchairs.

'My will was useless so I've been to rewrite it. I needed to take care of Mabel, Ellie love, I'm sure you understand.' He smiled lovingly at his wife before continuing. 'If I die then the farm comes to you and Jack, but Mabel will stay here until she goes too. I've set up an annuity for her, so you two will be able to run the farm without interference.'

She exchanged a glance with Jack. He was looking equally shocked. 'If that's what you want, Dad, then I'll go along with it. But it's not something any of us have to worry about at the moment. Jack and I are more likely to...' She stopped, horrified at what she'd been about to say.

Jack smoothly covered up her gaffe. 'We're more likely to be living the other side of the country by the time this happens. It's not going to be for years. Mabel's quite capable of running the farm for us, aren't you?'

'I don't know about that, Jack, and I don't want to think about it. My Fred's just going to change into something more comfortable and then we'll be ready to go.'

Ellie hadn't forgotten that everything took place in the afternoon because of the blackout and the raids. 'What time does it finish? I take it you get something to eat whilst you're there?'

'We all take a contribution and have ever such a nice tea. It finishes just after seven – it's dark then but them blooming Germans don't come until later so we can get home safely.'

Her parents hurried out chatting – not something her dad usually did. Mabel was making him happier than he'd ever been in his life and she was glad for him.

'I don't want to run the farm, not with you or anyone else. I thought I did, but...' She stopped as something occurred to her. 'I don't think George will be pleased if he discovers he's cut out of the will.'

'How will he know?'

'He won't, of course. Dad's fighting fit now and will be around for years. Why didn't you tell them you're going to North Africa – isn't that why you came with me?'

'Plenty of time, we've got another two days here. I'm more concerned about being in Romford so early. Will the movies be open?'

'I should think so. Nobody wants to be caught in an air raid in a cinema so I expect everything closes down early nowadays.'

'As long as we can get something to eat. I seem to remember there's a good fish and chip shop next to the pub by the station.'

'That suits me. I'll check the paper and see what's showing.'

'Don't bother, we'll go in, whatever it is. Bound to be something worth watching even if it's only the cartoon and the newsreel.'

Jack drove, after all it was his car, and she sat in the back with Mabel who was clutching a tin filled with sausage rolls.

'We'll be outside at seven. Good luck with the cards,' Ellie called after them as they vanished into the village hall followed by other couples with similar tins.

'Do you mind if we eat before we go to the movies? Seeing all that food has reminded me I've not eaten since breakfast and that was hours ago.'

'Then you've done better than me, Jack, as I haven't eaten since last night. I had such an early start I missed breakfast at my digs and didn't have time to grab anything in Kent as my lift was waiting.'

'Let's hope the fish and chip shop's frying.'

He didn't need directions, he was familiar with the neighbourhood having lived there for several months last year. Not only was the place open, there was a queue of like-minded customers waiting patiently outside. The smell of vinegar, hot fat and chips made her mouth water.

To her embarrassment the queue stepped aside and insisted they went first.

'Only right,' a woman in curlers said without moving the cigarette from between her lips. 'Anyone in uniform gets served first as far as I'm concerned.'

It would have been churlish to argue so they thanked the queue and stepped up to the counter. Ten minutes later they had the newspaper wrapped parcels and were heading to the pub. It was too cold to sit outside but the landlord didn't mind them taking the food in as long as they had a couple of drinks.

When the last greasy chip was eaten she licked her fingers, carefully folded up the paper and finished her lemonade. 'That was absolutely delicious, thank you, Jack. Exactly what I wanted.'

They found a litter bin outside and disposed of the rubbish and then headed for the Vogue Cinema. The other one had closed down at the beginning of the war, which was a shame. She was delighted to see *Rebecca* showing as well as the news and obligatory cartoon for the children. They bought their tickets at the kiosk and were shown to their seats by an usherette with her torch pointed to the ground. The girl had decided they were a courting couple and the seats they were offered were in the back row.

As the film had already begun she could hardly make a fuss and disturb everyone else. Those sitting on the end had to stand up to let them past and there were a lot of muttering complaints until they found the two empty places in the middle of the row.

Jack didn't take advantage of this, his hands remained firmly in his lap. She rather liked sitting close to him, she didn't feel so alone.

When they emerged two hours later it was dark and they needed their torches to make their way back to the car. This time she put her arm through his knowing that if she stumbled he was strong enough to keep her upright.

They were halfway there when the siren coughed into life. 'Bloody hell! Where's the nearest shelter?'

'I've no idea. There must be one somewhere. Should we go back to the cinema and go into theirs?'

As they dithered about the wailing increased and was then drowned out by Spitfires taking off from Hornchurch. Her heart was thudding so loudly she could hear it. Then the unmistakable drone of bombers approaching filled her with terror.

The searchlights slashed the sky, the anti-aircraft guns began their thumping accompaniment. Then fighters added their machine gun fire to the general cacophony as they dived to intercept. Too late to do anything but cower against the wall. He put his arms around her and stood in front as if he could protect her with his body.

The bombs started screaming down and she screamed with them. Jack rocked her in his arms and that helped a little. Suddenly the night was bright. He swore. This shocking language jerked her back to common sense as nothing else could.

'Incendiary, Ellie, stuck in the wall just above us. We can't stay here, it's far too dangerous.'

She didn't need to be told that this bomb was like a torch and would attract further bombing. He took her hand and they fled for their lives.

A bomb dropped on a row of houses on the other side of the road. The explosion threw them to the ground. She couldn't breathe. Her mouth was full of dust, her ears were ringing – but she was still alive.

'Come on, sweetheart, we've got to get out of here. There must be a bloody shelter somewhere.'

He dragged her to her feet. She couldn't move. Was frozen by what she saw. Two minutes ago there had been a row of houses and now there was a gaping hole. All that was left of the house was the back wall and part of the bedrooms. Curtains were blowing at the broken windows and a rag rug dangled from the edge of the remaining floor. There was no chance anyone who had been in that building could have survived.

'Ellie, come along, now.' He punctuated this sentence by shaking her shoulders. It did the trick and her mind focused again.

'We're not far from the station. There's bound to be a shelter there.'

Screaming bombs continued to fall. The devastation would be terrible. There was no need to use their torches, the many fires burning in the town made it easy to see. They ran through the deserted streets flinching at the explosions. The British fighters were flying just above the rooftops in pursuit of the bombers.

They met a dust covered ARP warden, his tin hat askew. 'Quickly, down there, into the shelter before you get blown to smithereens.' He grabbed her arm and shoved them both down a slippery flight of steps. The door clanged shut behind them.

The sound of children crying, people talking, their voices loud with fear, echoed up to her. Jack put his arm around her waist and guided her into the communal shelter. There were candles in jam jars and a couple of lanterns for illumination.

On either side were the benches, they were crammed full of women, children and old men. Jack was the only man in uniform and she the only woman.

'Budge up, Daffy, let the nice lady sit down, why don't you?' The woman who'd spoken had a smelly baby on her lap and two other children squashed in beside her. One of them, presumably, was called Daphne.

'Thank you, you stay where you are. We can stand up at the end.' Ellie smiled down at the children but they didn't respond.

She and Jack edged their way between the knees to a space at the far end where the curtain hung. The appalling smell made her gag.

Carefully the two of them sidled back until they were able to breathe again. The shelter shook a few times and they were liberally covered with plaster from the ceiling, but at least they were safe. After an interminable time, the ARP warden who had been standing with his ear pressed to the door at the top of the stairs, yelled down to them.

'All clear's going. That's it for tonight, thank the good Lord, off to your beds.'

As they were standing in the central passageway it made sense for them to leave first. They emerged into the cool night air thankful to be alive.

'What do the families do if they go back and find their house has been destroyed? If they have no beds to go to?'

'Someone will take care of them. I just hope my car hasn't been blown up. It will be a long walk back.'

There was still sufficient light for her to see her watch without shining her torch onto it. 'It's after eight, my parents will be beside themselves. They will have seen the raid over Hornchurch and Romford and know we've been caught up in it.'

'Then we'd better get a shifty on.'

The car was unscathed apart from a thick covering of dust. It started first time, much to her relief. Jack drove slowly and she held her breath every time they turned a corner, expecting the road to be blocked, but they escaped from Romford safely. Once they were away from the town driving was easier even with the tiny lights they were allowed on the car.

'Bomber's moon tonight, but at least we can see to get home.'

That was all he said on the remainder of the journey and she knew he was angry that he hadn't been at Kenley and able to join in the fracas. She didn't know much about the Western Desert where he was going to be deployed, but it had to be safer than here.

Twenty-Five

January 1941

Ellie had continued to work, ferrying whatever aircraft she was given since Jack had gone. As many of the women at Hatfield were married she had volunteered to work over Christmas – after all the war didn't stop because it was supposedly a festive season.

The lack of a Christmas dinner for those working was a necessity of war. The ferry pool had agreed not to exchange gifts but to put some money into a charity box to help those who'd been bombed out. She rang Glebe Farm and wished her parents a merry Christmas and wished she could do the same for Jack.

The last letter she'd had from him, heavily redacted, told her he was suffering from the heat and hated sand but was otherwise all right. On balance, she was happier with the cold than she would be in baking hot desert temperatures.

Probate was slow because, as expected, the Dunlop and Hamilton families were appealing against the will.

She had instructed her solicitor to delay things as she had a plan of her own to settle the matter.

That woman – she couldn't bring herself to call her either Elizabeth or Mrs Dunlop – had remained in the house Greg had assigned to her. What she didn't know was that the staff she was employing were still loyal to Greg. Now they were reporting to her.

The baby, supposedly due at the end of February, was born on 3rd January weighing a healthy eight and a half pounds. Definitely not almost two months premature. This letter from the housekeeper was accompanied by several snapshots of the baby, a boy, and the mother.

She showed this to Amanda. 'Leave this to me, Ellie, you don't have to be involved. I'll contact the news desk at the Daily Express and speak to William Hickey. You know, the chap who writes the gossip column.'

'You can't do that, it would be too unkind...'

'You couldn't do it, you're far too nice, but I could. My brother's never been the same and she deserves to suffer.'

Reluctantly she handed over the photos and agreed that her friend could give the story to the newspaper. She listened whilst Amanda spoke to someone and was immediately offered an appointment.

'There, piece of cake. I'm going to Fleet Street tomorrow. I promise you won't be mentioned – this will be about how that bitch tricked a good man into marriage and ruined his life.'

'What about the will? Won't you have to mention that?'

'No, they will just want the dirt on the Hamiltons. I'll make sure that what they did to my brother is in the piece too. I can bet the court case will be dropped when it's published.'

What Amanda was going to do was unpleasant, probably unkind, but that woman deserved everything she was going to get. She had ruined too many lives and shouldn't be allowed to play the victim. The baby that had just been born would otherwise grow up believing he was a Dunlop which was blatantly untrue and Greg wouldn't have wanted that.

She thought she could now move on and think about a future that didn't include Greg. Only the charity had to be set up and then she could put it all behind her. She would always love him, but he was gone and she was still here and must make the best of it.

Although the nightly bombing raids on the city had slowed over the past few months, there was always the risk that the Luftwaffe would appear. British bombers were now flying nightly to German cities and doing the same to the civilians there. She hated to think of anyone suffering in the same way that people were over here, even if they were the enemy.

Liverpool, Coventry, Portsmouth, Southampton, Birmingham – she could go on with the list of cities that had suffered catastrophic damage. There had even been a handful of ATA pilots who had lost their lives – these had not been due to enemy action but to pilot error or mechanical failure. The most recent and tragic of these losses had been Amy Johnson, her death still shrouded in mystery.

Reports said that the most famous of the ATA girls had flown above the cloud, something no one was supposed to do, and come down over the Thames estuary where she'd run out of fuel. A brave sailor had dived in, attempting to save her as she'd been seen alive, but he too had perished.

Her ex-husband was also a member of the ATA – it must have been very difficult for him to carry on as wherever he landed people knew who he was and commiserated with him. When Greg had died not many people knew of their connection. He, another name on the growing list of fatalities in the RAF and she, barely recognised as part of his life. This was why she was so enraged with the woman who had taken away her right to grieve publicly. The so-called widow was about to get her comeuppance.

Amanda left early for her appointment with a briefcase filled with the evidence needed to persuade them to run the story. 'I'll let you know how it goes when I get back.'

'No, thank you, I'd rather pretend it's nothing to do with me.'

The William Hickey column had used to be just society gossip, but since the war started the tone had changed and it was now more about social and other important issues.

Ellie was half hoping that he wouldn't want to run it or let it appear somewhere else in the paper. With any luck there would be too much war news to run a scandal story.

The man Amanda met wasn't called Hickey, he did identify himself but she promptly forgot his name. She explained why she'd come, gave him the whole story and presented him with the signed affidavit, the photographs and everything else pertaining to the matter. The fact that both the Dunlop and the Hamilton families had continued to maintain that the baby was Greg's, despite clear evidence to the contrary, showed them in a deceitful light.

With the papers about her brother's case to read as well, the reporter took his time scanning what she'd given him and looking at the photographs. 'This is indeed a remarkable story, Miss Bradshaw. We should certainly like to run with it – there's nothing our readership likes better than a good family scandal.' He paused and steepled his fingers. 'You do realise that your brother will not come out of this unscathed. There will be those that turn against you for making this public.'

'I'm no longer part of that set. The Hamiltons deserve everything that's coming to them and if I'm collateral damage, then so be it.'

'In which case I shall print this.' He nodded. 'Good for you. It is a constant source of amazement to me to what lengths some people will go to in order to get their hands on money. Both families merit what they get.' He flicked through the photographs and held up one of herself in her ATA uniform. 'I shall use this one. Are you sure you won't be dismissed when this comes out? From what I know of your unit a lot of the women and the men will be friends of these families and not take kindly to what you're doing.'

'I might be ostracised by some, but Miss Gower will ignore it. She's more interested in my flying abilities then my popularity.' She stood up. 'When will you run the story?'

'Sometime this week. With the death of Amy Johnson fresh in everyone's mind it's the ideal time to run something else about you brave ATA girls.'

This time Amanda felt obliged to speak. 'Do you know what the RAF call us?' He shook his head and half smiled. 'Always Terrified Airwomen.'

This was a good point to leave and she left him chuckling. Perhaps she had better speak to Pa and her brother and let them know what to expect. The whole story had focused on her family's involvement and Ellie hadn't been mentioned by name, neither had the will. Amanda prayed the reporter wouldn't bother to investigate as then Ellie would also become notorious.

She turned back and banged on the door. She opened it but she didn't go in. 'I'm sorry, there's something you should know, but I don't want this to be public.' She explained about the money and that it was all going into a charity.

'Excellent. I'll keep Miss Simpson's name out of this – she's suffered enough.'

'Thank you, much appreciated. Toodle pip.'

As soon as she returned to Hatfield, Amanda spoke to Pauline. 'I thought you ought to know what's coming.'

'Good for you, I admire your spirit. It won't go down well with some of the girls, but I'll make sure you're kept busy.'

Satisfied that finally her beloved sibling would have had his revenge she went in search of Ellie.

'I'm so glad they won't drag my name into it. Let's forget about it and talk about something else.' Ellie held up three letters. 'I had all these arrive from Jack last week. The censors cross out so much there's very little left to read. One thing I do know is that he'd rather be here in the cold than there in the baking heat.'

She rang and told Dad about Amanda's revenge and he was shocked but understood why her friend had done it. Later that night something that had been bothering her made her introduce the topic again.

'Your life will be untenable once the story's printed.'

'Pauline has promised me nothing will change as far as she's concerned. I don't care if I'm ignored, as long as it doesn't interfere with my work.'

'Whatever happens, I'll support you. The problem is that half the girls here are either good friends with one or other of the families or are related to them in some way. They'll close ranks and make your life absolute hell.'

'We're not at school now, Ellie, we're adults working in a man's world. I doubt there's anything they could do that will make the slightest difference to me. If you want to distance yourself from me, I'll understand. We don't both need to be sent to Coventry.'

'I don't think anyone wants to be sent there. The city was flattened the other night. Hundreds of civilians died.' Ellie didn't want to talk about this, she knew how bad things were in the cities but had an ostrich-like approach to each disaster. If she didn't talk about it, read about it, or hear it on the nine o'clock news, then she could ignore it.

'There's always a Daily Express in the crew room so we'll know immediately from the attitude of the other women when the story appears. It will be worth it,' Amanda said.

Three days after her visit to London she returned from a delivery to the same remote airfield she'd taken a Lysander to a few months ago and immediately detected a frigid atmosphere. If they were treating her like this what must it be like for Amanda?

The only thing they could do was ignore it. However, she wanted to see what had been written for herself. She wasn't so naïve as to think that newspapers printed the truth, they printed what would make a good story and get them more readers.

One of the women, a crony of Pauline's, all but threw a copy of the paper in her face. 'Well, Simpson, I expect you're pleased. Amanda Bradshaw has let the side down. Turned on her own. Disgusting behaviour, if you want my opinion...'

'Actually, Deborah, I don't. What was disgusting was the way Elizabeth Hamilton tricked my fiancé into marrying her and by so doing ruined both our lives and caused his death. This was the second time she'd done this to someone.'

One of the other girls looked less hostile. 'Hang on a minute, that can't be true.'

'Greg was so unhappy it affected his ability to fly. He would never have been caught by that Messerschmitt before he was manipulated into marrying that woman. He was a fantastic flyer, one of the best in his unit.'

Those who had been waiting to ambush her became less hostile, apart from Deborah who continued to mutter threats under her breath.

'I haven't seen the story myself, excuse me whilst I read it.' Ellie said.

William Hickey, or whoever the journalist had been, had printed the exact truth. No embellishments, no sensationalising, just the unvarnished truth. She tried to take it in as an impartial reader and was convinced that no one could fail to be horrified by what had happened and have every sympathy for Greg and for Amanda's brother.

The fact that Elizabeth Hamilton was now labelled as the mother of a bastard child bothered her not at all. Unfortunate for the infant, but by the time he was an adult his conception would be forgotten.

There were photographs of Elizabeth and her family and a comment that they had refused to answer any of the accusations.

The following day she received a letter from her solicitors saying the families had dropped their appeal against Greg's will. She wrote back with the instructions to invest the money in the war effort and then put the matter from her mind. The charity could be set up when the war was over.

Twenty-Six

June 1941, Western Desert

Jack, unlike a lot of the guys in the squadron, had adjusted well to the blistering heat, sand flies and mediocre accommodation. The food was monotonous, basically beef and hard biscuits, but perfectly edible. The only thing that really got him down were the constant sandstorms. He didn't enjoy flying into the unknown and for the first time had had the dreaded fear in the pit of his stomach before operations.

There was, of course, a desperate shortage of water and showers were a thing of the past. The bloody sand got into everything and most days he wished he was back at Kenley. The strips they had to use were hazardous but so far no one in his squadron had gone for a Burton although there had been losses elsewhere.

Getting to North Africa had been different. Their kites had been loaded onto ships and taken to Africa and then they'd had to fly in stages to where they were based now. The whole process had taken more than three months.

Only the bombers had the range to be able to fly directly. Even the uniform was different – blue serge would be too dammed hot in the desert. They were now in sand coloured gear with short sleeves and short pants – much better than boiling in winter weight stuff.

Initially the Hurricanes had been used to dodge about the place, landing on makeshift airfields to try and kid the Italian reconnaissance planes they actually had more aircraft in the area than they actually had.

The brown jobs were having a rough time. They'd been driven back and forth across the desert and hundreds had been captured. At least the boys in blue could make a run for it – aircraft moved faster than tanks. From what he'd heard the German pilots that strafed fleeing soldiers were good at their jobs. They aimed the Stuka at the target and let the bomb go at the last minute whilst machine gunning the soldiers as they dived for cover. They flew so low the poor buggers could have got flattened by the fixed undercarriage.

Tobruk had been abandoned in April but now the army were attempting to retake it – at least that's what he thought was going on. Lines of communication between the two arms of the services were not great and he just did as he was ordered like everybody else.

They were scrambled and, as always, he carried all his belongings in his Hurry. You never knew where you would be told to land on your return so better to keep things with you.

He was Yellow Leader today, but they were intercepted by 109s and all hell broke loose. He saw one of his mates go down, smoke pouring from the engine. He circled as Jimmy landed in the sand.

The 109s had been driven off and the other guys were long gone, chasing after them. He would go down and rescue Jimmy. The landing was successful. Jack opened the cockpit and stood up.

'Quick, hop in, and we'll get the hell out of here.'

The only way they could both fit in the cockpit was if they discarded their chutes.

'Thanks, mate, I thought I was a goner.' He scrambled in the cockpit and Jack sat on his lap.

'Anyone for the skylark?' He opened the throttle and the kite began to move. Then a tyre burst, the wheel dug in and the kite tipped onto its nose.

'Bloody hell, we'll have to walk back. There's a couple of trucks over there, maybe we can use one of those?' Jack said as he jumped onto the wing. Jimmy followed. 'Grab my kitbag, I don't want to leave it for the Huns to find.'

'My kite's about to go up in flames. We'd better be quick. They'll be all over us in a minute.'

They buried his belongings under some brushwood and then ran to a nearby wadi and threw themselves behind the rocks.

'I can hear trucks coming. Keep your head down.' Jack pressed himself into the sand and held his breath, expecting to be seen at any moment.

They were Italians and began to search the area. They found his possessions and it could only be a matter of time before they were captured. Two Italians were no more than a couple of yards away when darkness fell and they were called back to the trucks by their commanding officer.

He remained flat on the ground for another ten minutes before he thought it safe to move. 'We'd better go east rather than west. I know it's shorter in the other direction but far riskier.'

'Okay by me, you outrank me, I'll just follow your orders.' Jimmy was an excellent pilot but not too strong on initiative.

'We'll leave it a bit longer and then use the North Pole star to navigate.' It was bloody cold at night and for the first time he wished he was wearing his blue serge uniform. His flight suit had been abandoned and now belonged to the enemy.

The desert here wasn't like the Sahara but scrubland with plenty of rocks and brushwood to hide behind during the day. He rationed the small amount of water they had to a few sips every hour during the day and none at night.

Flying boots weren't meant for long hikes but at least they kept out the scorpions and the sand. After two days hiding, they were walking, more like staggering, as the lack of water and food was taking its toll. On the third night Jimmy poked him in the back.

Jack stopped. Somehow, they'd managed to wander into an enemy encampment. There were the shapes of tanks and trucks surrounding them. Cold sweat trickled down his back and his mouth was even drier – if that was possible.

There was nowhere to hide. All they could do was creep forward and pray they wouldn't be spotted by an alert sentry. Things were going well when suddenly the lights went on and there were shouts in German.

He dropped to his face in the sand, Jimmy landed beside him. He was motionless, kept his head down until the voices stopped and the lights went out. They were safe – for the moment. He gripped Jimmy's elbow and they began to inch forward on their hands and knees. Progress was too slow but he daren't suggest they stood up in case they were seen. The sentries would be more vigilant now.

Dawn would soon be here and he feared they would be captured. Then he saw a ring of brushwood just ahead and they crawled towards it. It was a dried up, abandoned well. Perfect to hide in.

Exhaustion made them both sleep soundly despite the danger they were in. Then he was jerked awake by the sound of gunfire and the whizz of shells flying overhead. They wouldn't be heard if they talked during the racket.

'I'm going to take a deco. With any luck it's our blokes firing at the Huns.'

He scrabbled upwards and slithered to the edge of the brushwood and carefully parted the branches. He could see guns firing and was certain he could hear English being shouted.

'What do you think, Jimmy? Shall we make a run for it?'

'My bloody feet are finished, I can't walk another night, don't think I can run. You go on.'

'Don't be so bloody stupid. One last push and we'll be safe.'

Jack heaved his companion to his feet, put his arm firmly around his waist and then put his head down and belted towards the gunfire. They ignored the commands to stop. If the gunners couldn't bloody well see they were friendly, then sod them.

The gunners were not exactly welcoming despite the fact he and Jimmy were speaking English and wearing RAF uniform. The water they were given was the best thing he'd ever drunk and he could forgive them their surliness just for this gift. The guards were sent for and they were suspicious, too.

Jimmy was done. He couldn't walk and when Jack had recovered sufficiently he stood up and took command. He was a bloody officer, they might be brown jobs, but he still outranked them.

'Get off your arse and fetch the medics with a stretcher. That's an order.'

This did the trick and Jimmy was carried away to be treated and he was escorted to Brigade HQ. He explained who they were and where they'd been for the past three days and the CO was suitably impressed.

'Good show, Flight Lieutenant. I'll have you transferred to your unit. No doubt they'll be delighted to see you as you chaps are in desperately short supply.'

On their return they were greeted with enthusiasm as they'd been given up for lost. Jimmy wouldn't be able to fly until his feet healed but he was cleared for duty and a spare kite provided.

He'd lost everything he possessed. He no longer had Ellie's letters, or any of his documents. He patted his top pocket. At least he still had one photograph to keep him safe. He thought if things continued to deteriorate he was going to need it.

July 1941, Hatfield

Ellie had now added Fairey Battles, and the noisy Harvards, to her repertoire of Lysanders, Proctors and Tiger Moths. Lt Col Moore-Brabazon had been in discussion with Pauline and they were all expecting to be given the go ahead to fly operational aircraft at any moment.

She arrived as usual and the day's assignments were chalked up on the blackboard outside the Hatfield operations room. As always, the pilot's name was on one column and the aircraft they were to fly was in the other.

Next to her name and the names of four others, was the word Spitfire.

Someone grabbed her elbow. 'Look at that – you lucky devil. I'd give my eye teeth to be flying a Spitfire.'

Amanda took her chit and left to deliver a Lysander somewhere. She felt sorry that her friend was the only one not getting this opportunity.

The four others were, unfortunately, from Elizabeth's set and so ignored her as they always did. She didn't mind, she was used to it now. There were more girls joining the ATA and these were mostly foreign pilots who had come to do their bit. In fact, there were now more pilots like her than the posh lot.

She sat in the corner and studied the information she had got on fighter planes. It all seemed pretty straightforward and she was sure she'd have no difficulty when it was her turn to do a couple of circuits and bumps.

A captain from the ATA's technical department at White Waltham arrived soon afterwards and to her delight she was called out first. This was an honour, but also added pressure. Pauline must have decided she was the most experienced flyer and therefore if she couldn't fly a fighter then nobody else would be able to.

Her heart was pounding whilst she was pulling on her flying suit – she'd never been so nervous. Two of the women appeared in the doorway. 'I say, Simpson, good luck. We're counting on you.'

'Thank you, I'll not let you down.'

She climbed in, buckled on her parachute harness and taxied away. Whilst she was waiting for the green light she took several steadying breaths. There wasn't much room in the cockpit for her, must be a very tight squeeze for a man.

The light flashed and she pushed open the throttle. She'd been told to do a couple of circuits and a three point landing. The Spitfire tended to pitch backwards and forwards but she pushed the throttle and pulled gently on the stick and all was well. She shifted her left hand to the stick and with her right pulled at the undercarriage lever. She climbed steadily, loving the power, the feeling that the kite was just waiting to tear across the sky. The controls were light, but it wasn't easy to fly because of the pitching instability.

Her short flight was over too soon. For the first time since Greg had died last September she was genuinely happy. She'd just successfully flown the same plane that he had flown every day. It made him seem closer somehow. Not only that, but she was the first woman to fly an operational aircraft.

She taxied back to the small group of anxious spectators. 'Piece of cake, girls, it's a joy to fly and you'll have no problems at all.' Many of the flyers couldn't really be classified as girls, they were married, had children even, but they were all in the same unit, so girls it was.

The captain nodded and gave her the thumbs up. Now she seemed to be included in the group and was happy she could answer their questions. Everyone completed their test with flying colours. When the last one landed they all cheered.

'Ellie, we thought we might pootle up to town and have dinner in St James's at the Ecu de France. If we pool our petrol coupons we can borrow a car. You will come with us, won't you?'

'Thank you, I should be delighted. We've done something amazing today and we deserve to celebrate. We've shown that women can fly operational aircraft and with any luck we'll all be flying Spitfires soon.'

The five of them piled into a battered vehicle belonging to the ATA. She didn't offer to drive, that would be pushing it, but wished she had as Joan was a shockingly bad driver and crashed the gears continuously.

After her second champagne cocktail she forgot her reservations about these women as they had now apparently forgiven her for her part in the exposé.

The nightly raids on the city had stopped in May but there was still the occasional attack. She was almost relieved when the siren went and they had to pile downstairs into the cellar and wait for the all clear.

At least down here Joan might have a chance to sober up. Ellie didn't fancy being driven back by someone who was drunk at the wheel, especially as there was no moon tonight.

'Here, why don't you have another drink, Ellie? See, they have a bar already set up for such an eventuality.'

'No, thanks, alcohol really doesn't agree with me. I wonder if I can get a coffee instead.'

'Jolly good,' Joan giggled. 'Would you mind awfully being the one to drive us home? Everybody else is going to be decidedly squiffy.'

'I should love to. Why don't you grab that table in the corner before it goes and I'll bring over the drinks?'

Coffee was available and she had the entire pot to herself. Her companions were now flirting with a group of army officers and she left them to it. Harmless fun, and today was a day that everything had changed for them.

She wished she could tell Jack her good news. She'd not had a letter from him for a couple of weeks and was getting a bit anxious. Although the news never gave the full story, she was getting good at reading between the lines and was fairly sure things were going really badly in the Western Desert. Reports had told of hundreds of soldiers being taken prisoner and being shipped to POW camps somewhere in Italy. This was marginally better than being in Germany, but either option was horrible.

Eventually the all clear sounded and she marshalled her group of inebriated ladies into some sort of order and chivvied them up the stairs and out into the fresh air. There was no need for torches, the sky was bright with orange flames. Somewhere in the city there would be devastation and death. She thanked her lucky stars that today they had been spared.

Twenty-Seven

Ellie was disappointed when she found she wasn't to fly a Spitfire the next day but start a Moth on its journey to Scotland. She was to collect it from a private airstrip where the owner had finally decided to donate it to the RAF for training.

This meant lugging her parachute onto the train and then catching a lift to her destination. The weather, which had started fine, began to close in and the clouds were low and the thunder rumbling in the distance by the time she arrived.

The owner, a rotund gentleman with a handlebar moustache, was somewhat shocked to see a female pilot and for a while she thought he wouldn't allow her to take it. Eventually he agreed.

'She has a full tank, young lady, and will take you wherever you want to go.' He turned and stomped off, leaving her to complete the preflight checks and spin the prop herself.

Taking off reminded her of her days as a flying instructor and as soon as she was airborne she checked her map and compass and headed for Hawarden pool near Chester.

She'd been flying for about half an hour when the weather closed in. She would have to land somewhere and wait it out. It was too dark and damp to see clearly on her map what was down below.

She circled a few times and then saw a grass patch – the runway – if that's what it was. It was going to be tight even for a Moth. She took the longest run she could, skimmed over some greenhouses, flew very low and slow with flaps down and more by luck than judgement touched down by a hedge. By applying a little judicious brake, she was able to slither to a halt without careering into the hedge at the other end.

As she taxied in she saw a group of people waiting to greet her. A man approached her in the gloom. 'What the bloody hell do you think you're doing? This ain't an airfield. You could have killed Billy on his tractor.'

Only then did she see a tractor cutting what she'd thought was an airstrip but was in fact a hayfield in the process of being harvested. Although why this was being done in the dark and damp she had no idea.

'I beg your pardon, but he was in no danger. Why do you think I circled a couple of times and had a second run at things.' She dropped down to the ground and the man's expression changed to incredulity.

'Blow me? A blooming woman. I didn't know the RAF had girls in their ranks.'

'I'm in the ATA, sir, I'm delivering this aircraft to Chester. It will then be taken to Scotland to be used to train new RAF pilots. I apologise for landing in your field, but I had no option as I'm not allowed to fly in bad weather.'

'I should think not, come along with me, miss, my Ada will make you a nice cuppa. Your plane can go in the barn so it don't get too wet.'

'Thank you, but it can stay where it is. A bit of rain won't hurt. I could really do with a hot drink, thank you very much for being so understanding. I don't suppose you have a telephone I could use?'

He chuckled. 'Don't hold with them newfangled things meself. I could get someone to cycle into the village and make the call for you if you like?'

'No, it's not urgent.'

After a delicious afternoon tea which reminded her of Glebe Farm, the storm passed and it was safe to leave. She thanked the farmer and his wife again, scrambled into her flight suit and climbed into the aircraft. She buckled in, one of his labourers kindly spun the prop for her, and she taxied to the far end of the field. The tractor driver had wisely removed himself and his vehicle to safety in the barn.

Her heart was in her mouth for a few seconds and she thought she was going to snag the undercarriage on the hedge, but all was well and she soared into the air. When she landed at Hawarden nobody had been unduly bothered by her absence, everyone knew an ATA pilot had to land when the weather was bad.

She handed over the paperwork and signed the necessary forms. 'If you hurry there's an Anson leaving and it can take you halfway to Hatfield,' she was told by someone in the office.

There were three other ATA members clambering in when she arrived – none of them were female. The racket inside the aircraft made conversation impossible and she was content to snooze until they landed.

She was offered overnight accommodation, as often happened, in a spare bed in the WAAF block and was able to report for eight o'clock the following morning at Hatfield.

Her smile was wide when she spotted her name next to a Hurricane. She and the other qualified women were to go to Southampton and then deliver new aircraft to Kenley. The Anson that had just returned her was to be their taxi.

When they arrived at the factory the five of them marched proudly to the office and handed in their chits. Joan was their spokesperson. 'We have come to collect five Hurricanes for delivery to Kenley.'

Ellie had expected there to be some reaction to the fact that they were female but the man just nodded, pushed over the usual pile of paper and they signed the necessary forms.

'I think we should fly together, ladies, and arrive at the same time. Let's make a real impression. Show the bigwigs that we can do the job as well as any man.'

The Met report was excellent, they should have an easy flight as long as no one tangled with barrage balloons or fighter squadrons taking off. Although they had only half an hour's flying experience in a fighter, Ellie was confident none of them would have any difficulty.

They took off one after the other and flew in perfect formation. She was, she decided, born to fly a fighter. She was in the position Jack flew, directly behind Joan on the left. There were low clouds but they flew beneath them. Then driving rain made things difficult and as the visibility decreased she thought it safer to drop out of formation just in case she collided with one of the other Hurricanes.

The rule was to land as soon as possible in these circumstances. To her relief an aerodrome appeared beneath her and she circled and prepared to land. Then to her astonishment the four she was following shot past her. What the hell was happening?

Ellie swung round and roared after them, this time at the rear of the group. After they had flown for a while she noticed the petrol gauge on the upper wing showing it was dangerously empty. She opened the throttle and flew level with Joan and tried to indicate the problem. Surely the rest of them would be as low on fuel as she was?

For some inexplicable reason Joan veered away violently. She twisted and turned as if trying to get rid of her. After an extraordinary few minutes Joan dropped the nose of her kite and pointed to an airfield which had appeared through the rain. This must be Kenley.

Ellie had so little fuel she was forced to land without the usual circuit or waiting for the leader, Joan, to land first. She taxied to the edge of the apron, switched off and walked across to speak to Joan.

'I was out of petrol…'

'And who the bloody hell are you?' A furious man with a giant moustache faced her from his cockpit.

She pulled off her helmet.

'Good God! It's a woman!'

He jumped out and landed beside her looking less angry. She looked around and finally understood she hadn't landed at Kenley at all, she had no idea where she was.

Quickly she explained and he laughed. They were joined by the other three RAF chaps and she was escorted with due ceremony to the Officers' Mess where she was treated like royalty. She had followed an RAF formation instead of Joan and the other girls. Heaven knows where they were.

'This is Biggin Hill, my dear, and we could do with another Hurricane. I'm commandeering yours, those blighters at Kenley have got more than enough.'

'I'm not sure I can do that without getting arrested. Might I use your telephone?'

When she explained to Pauline her predicament her CO laughed. 'He's right, Kenley have got four new aircraft – leave yours with him. I'll send a taxi for you first thing. Hang on a minute, I'll check where you're going tomorrow.'

Ellie could hear rustling of papers and then Pauline returned. 'Back to Southampton, this time to take Spitfires to the docks at Liverpool.'

August 1941, Western Desert

Jack was promoted again, and was now a squadron leader leading a new batch of guys who'd just arrived across country. Most of the men were reasonably experienced which would hopefully keep them alive longer than if they were raw recruits.

He desperately wanted to return to Britain, hated being ordered to machine gun the poor sods on the ground. Somehow it had seemed fairer attacking the bombers in the air or fighting a Messerschmitt. What he was doing now felt like murder. It was what was happening to their guys, but it didn't make it any easier.

He'd just received a letter from Ellie and had shared the news around the mess. His mates had raised a glass to her and her fellow ATA girls. It was quite possible she had actually flown one of these newly arrived kites to Liverpool herself.

He was due for home leave as he'd flown double the number of sorties most of the guys had. The only way he was going to get this was if he got shot down and that just wasn't an option. He was determined to stay alive so he could get back to Ellie. The letters had become his lifeline and he was pretty sure her tone had changed over the months and she might now have feelings for him too. Nothing had been said, of course, this must wait until they met again.

The tannoy blared and he and his men bolted for their Hurrys. A tank regiment was being strafed and needed their urgent assistance. This was a sortie he didn't mind.

The RT crackled. He was given the coordinates and gave his squadron their orders. Basically, they were to follow him and shoot the hell out of the Huns.

The mission was successful, they drove off the Germans and none of his guys were shot down. He continued to scan the sky for lone fighters but it was clear. He was approaching home base when the RT burst into life again.

'Sandstorm here, Yellow Leader, don't attempt to land.' The operator gave him fresh coordinates and he checked that everyone knew they weren't going home.

This wasn't an unusual occurrence; the bloody sandstorms were a permanent menace to this posting. However, this was the first time it had happened when he'd been airborne. They were flying at altitude, no sand up here, but they could no longer see the ground.

The new destination appeared to be as dangerous as their own airstrip. None of them had sufficient fuel to continue flying. They would have to risk landing or crash somewhere in the desert.

He sent his men down one by one; they all landed safely. He was now flying on fumes. The engine coughed and the prop stopped spinning. He was going to have to glide down – not ideal – but he'd done it several times before.

The silence was unnerving. Only when the engine failed did you realise just how noisy it was in the cockpit. He radioed in this predicament and they were waiting for him. As he neared the ground he was surrounded by sand, so thick he couldn't see a yard ahead. Not only without power, now he was without vision.

The undercarriage was down. The RT said radar indicated he was on the right trajectory, the airstrip was clear, he had to trust his judgement. Suddenly the wheels hit the deck. The nose bounced up, he'd misjudged his angle, had been travelling too fast. The kite slewed sideways and tipped onto one wing. There was a searing pain in his left arm and then nothing.

★

He came round in a field hospital. A smiling nurse held the cup to his lips and he swallowed gratefully. He was about to ask how badly damaged his arm was then his stomach clenched. He no longer had a left hand – his arm had been amputated from just below the elbow.

He turned his head away, couldn't speak, needed time to adjust to this horrific information. One armed man? What use was he to anyone? His dreams of marrying Ellie evaporated.

He wasn't allowed to wallow in self-pity for long. A medic gripped his good shoulder and shook him awake.

'Good morning, Squadron Leader, you'll be glad to know you're being shipped home as soon as you're fit enough to travel. You won't be able to fly, but chaps like you are needed behind a desk, too.'

Jack didn't answer. The doctor nodded and left him to contemplate his future. He didn't want to remain in the RAF if he couldn't fly. He wasn't the sort of bloke who'd settle into office work.

When his CO came into visit later that day he asked about being discharged as unfit for duty.

'If that's what you want, Jack, then consider it done. Shocking bad luck, could have happened to anyone.'

Over the next week whilst he recovered he had ample time to think. He had written a brief letter to Ellie telling her of his accident but not of the decision he'd made. That was something he wanted to tell her in person. He would remain a member of the RAF until he returned to

Britain. Then he would be demobbed. His back pay was going to be impressive but he was too depressed to even consider going on a spree. He didn't intend to spend it, he had had other things on his mind and none of them were positive.

Twenty-Eight

Mrs Cooper handed Ellie a letter when she returned to her digs. 'This came today, it's from your friend in the desert.'

'Good, I was becoming a bit worried as I haven't heard from him for a while.' She slipped the envelope into her pocket to read later. She always spent time with the children of the house if she got back before they were in bed. As it was only six o'clock and they were still up; she played a noisy game of Ludo and another of Snakes and Ladders before they retired.

Her job kept her so busy nowadays that she was rarely back in time for tea but her landlady always made her something tasty and a mug of cocoa before bedtime. She had some bad news for Mrs Cooper and hadn't wanted to tell her whilst the children were up.

'I'm very sorry, but I'll be leaving here at the weekend. I'm going to see my family for a couple of days and then I'm being sent to a different ferry pool. I won't be living in this area any more.'

'Oh, I'm so sorry, we've loved having you with us these past few months. Do you think another girl might come to me instead?'

'I'm certain of it. One of the reasons five of us are being moved is because lots of new pilots are joining from abroad. You wouldn't believe how cosmopolitan we are. We've got Americans, Polish, Irish, South African and Australian girls with us now.'

'Fancy that! If you'd be kind enough to put my details on the noticeboard, hopefully I'll have someone straightaway. I couldn't manage without the money now, what with everything being so expensive.'

'I'll put the notice up first thing so you can expect to get a flood of eager applicants tomorrow. I've really enjoyed staying here, I doubt I'll find anywhere so pleasant where I'm going.'

They said goodnight and she left Mrs Cooper washing up the supper things. With the blackout closed she was able to put on the bedside light and read her letter.

Ellie,

I'm writing this from hospital. I'm being discharged from the RAF as I'm no longer fit for service. I should be back in Britain in a few weeks and will come and speak to you in person.

Best wishes
Jack

She read the letter again. Something catastrophic must have happened to Jack or he wouldn't be leaving the RAF. Some small comfort was that he obviously wasn't critically injured. Her imagination ran wild at the possibilities – had he been burnt? This was a common injury for pilots but he probably wouldn't be discharged so soon if that was the case. Her conclusion was that he'd been maimed in such a way he couldn't remain in the RAF. Then even that possibility seemed unlikely as he could hardly come and visit her in person in a wheelchair because he'd lost his legs or something equally horrible. Then she recalled that her brother George had been forced to leave the RAF because of a perforated eardrum – it could be something like that and she was worrying unnecessarily.

There was nothing she could do until he contacted her. She checked the date on the letter, surprisingly it had only taken a week to reach her so she would be at the Hamble base before he got back. If she wrote her reply immediately and posted it first thing he should get it before he left and know not to come to Hatfield in search of her.

She and the other four women who had pioneered the flying of operational aircraft were going to be based with men and their duties were to deliver Spitfires. Then, as more women were trained, the men would transfer and the pool would be all female.

The following morning she pinned up the postcard for Mrs Cooper and it was immediately pounced on by one of the new pilots. 'Is this where you've been staying, Ellie?'

'Yes, I can highly recommend it. Excellent food, comfortable room and delightful family. It's a bit of a trek if you have to walk but I've managed to get a lift every morning without fail.'

The girl, and she wasn't much older than Ellie, removed the card and put it in her pocket. 'I've got to do a test run this afternoon, circuits and bumps to prove I'm qualified to be here. So I'll go now and bag this for myself. The B&B I stayed in last night was grim.'

The crew room was busy as always at this time of the morning. Amanda greeted her with a hug. 'I've just been told I'm coming with you – I can't believe my luck. It wouldn't have been the same without you here.'

'That's good news. Are you going home tomorrow or would you like to come with me again?'

Amanda blushed. 'Actually, old thing, I'm going to meet Rodney's parents.'

Rodney was one of the men in the ATA, the only reason he wasn't operational was his age. At forty he was considered too old. In her opinion he was too old for her friend, a fifteen year age gap wasn't ideal.

'I didn't realise you were so serious or that he still had parents alive for you to meet.' Her friend looked hurt and Ellie regretted her snide remark. 'Sorry, that was unkind. I really like him. Have you asked him why he never got married?'

'Of course I have. He was engaged but was jilted at the altar and this rather put him off the whole business. I know you think he's a bit long in the tooth for me, but I love him and that's all that matters, isn't it?' Amanda was called to the operations room giving Ellie time to think.

In her opinion love was overrated. All it had brought her was pain and heartache. If she ever did get married, and she supposed one day she would want a family of her own, it would be for practical reasons, not romantic ones.

Over the past few months she had begun to believe that maybe Jack would make her an ideal partner. If she wasn't going to marry for love then she wanted her future husband to be someone she liked and respected, someone who would be a good father and companion to her. He didn't have to be wealthy, she had more than enough money of her own.

Losing Greg, allowing Amanda to ruin the lives of his unwanted wife and child, had changed her, made her harder and she really didn't like the person she'd become. How could she be contemplating marrying a man she didn't love? It would be so unfair to Jack.

The war must also take some of the blame. It was unrelenting. However much the newspapers and newsreaders tried to disguise it, things were not going well for Britain. They might have prevented Hitler from invading but she could see no way they could win; eventually his superior forces would wear them down.

Pushing aside such morbid thoughts she smiled at Amanda when she returned. 'I really like him, he shares your love of flying and will make you an ideal husband.'

Amanda's shout of laughter turned several heads in the direction. 'Good God! I'm not going to marry him. I said I love him, marriage is not on the cards.'

Ellie was confused. 'Then why are you meeting his parents?'

'His family breed steeplechasers. It's been ages since I had a good gallop, that's why I'm going down to his family home.'

'Then why didn't you say so?'

'I'm sorry, I couldn't resist it. There's a war on, in case you haven't noticed, we've been given licence to behave how we like and by God I'm going to take every advantage of it.'

Ellie didn't smile. 'Just make sure you don't get pregnant like Elizabeth did – otherwise you'll have to marry him whether you want to or not.'

'That too will be taken care of. I suggest you find yourself a lover, let your hair down a little, you're becoming old before your time. There must be dozens of unattached Brylcreem boys who would be only too happy to show you the ropes.'

This suggestion was so outrageous Ellie had to laugh. 'I can't think of anything I'd rather do less. I would have slept with Greg but he was too much of a gentleman. I don't have any religious or moral principles on the subject, it's just that sex with a stranger doesn't appeal to me.'

'I'm not suggesting you hop into bed with the first attractive man you meet. I'm just saying it's time you began to live again, it's been nine months since Greg died. He wouldn't want you to mope about any longer.'

Now was the time to tell Amanda about Jack's letter but for some reason she refrained. She didn't want anyone to pity him. He was a proud man, he deserved to keep his dignity intact.

September 1941, London

Jack was sick of the sympathetic glances he got because of his empty sleeve. If they only knew about the excruciating pain he had where his arm used to be. His first task must be to use his accumulated coupons to buy himself some clothes.

Being out of uniform wasn't right, but he'd had no choice. He was going to fly or leave. He wasn't going to see Ellie, that would be too painful, so he would write to her again, make up some nonsense about relocating to America as he had no ties in the UK.

In fact, maybe that would be a good move. He had friends out there, maybe it would do him good to get away from here where he was constantly reminded he could no longer do his bit for the war effort.

Despite having sufficient coupons there was nothing for him to buy. He must remain in his ill-fitting demob suit unless he was prepared to go down to Glebe Farm and collect the clothes he'd left there when he joined up.

She was already at Hamble, in Hampshire, so she could deliver Spitfires all over the country. She could hardly get back to Essex on her two free days so it would be fairly risk-free to nip down there and collect his things.

The more he thought about this the better he liked the idea. Fred and Mabel could tell Ellie how things were and he didn't have to see her or write to her himself. She didn't deserve to be tied to a cripple, a one armed man was no use to anyone and certainly not someone as lovely and perfect as she was.

Decision made he headed across London to Liverpool Street and caught the train. He had to buy his ticket – another thing about being a civilian he didn't like. Strangely, they hadn't asked for his uniform back – he still had it in his kitbag. He'd leave it at the farm if Fred didn't mind.

He wasn't sure if he was imagining it, but people didn't seem to want to meet his eye, even those he knew quite well from his time living at the farm and running the aero club. Nobody offered him a lift, probably because he was out of uniform and they thought he was a draft dodger. With his kitbag over his left shoulder they wouldn't be able to see the empty sleeve.

Night was falling by the time he trudged down the lane that led to the farm, but the dogs were there to greet him. He was some distance from the house when Fred appeared in the gloom.

'Is that you, Jack? You should have rung, I'd have come and got you.'

There was no comment made about his arm and for that Jack was grateful. Time enough to explain everything when he'd had a stiff drink. He hoped Fred had alcohol in the house as he could do with something stronger than tea.

They walked around to the back and slipped in behind the blackout curtain that hung a foot behind the door. Fred reached over and removed the kitbag from his shoulder. 'Go in the sitting room, lad, I'll bring you a whiskey.'

There was no sign of Mabel who would normally come out and greet him. Jack could hear the sound of crockery rattling in the kitchen. He had missed supper but his appetite had deserted him since his accident and he wasn't hungry. He must have lost a stone at least in the past month and he'd already lost weight whilst living in the desert.

He slumped onto the sofa, closed his eyes and let his thoughts drift. He didn't know what he was going to do with the rest of his life, he thought he had it planned, but now he was at a loss.

'Here you are, Jack lad, get this down you.'

A glass was put in his remaining hand and he opened his eyes sufficiently to guide it to his mouth.

'Good thing it wasn't your right one, son, it would be a right bugger to learn everything again.'

The whiskey slopped onto his chest as he sat up abruptly. 'Bloody hell! You're right. I should be thanking my lucky stars that I'm not dead and that it was my left hand that bought it.' For the first time since his accident he smiled.

'Mabel's making you a bite to eat. Seems to me you need a bit of feeding up before you do anything else. Have you spoken to Ellie?'

Jack drained the glass and Fred filled it to the brim again. 'I wrote to tell her that I was out of the RAF but didn't tell her why. I don't want to speak to her or see her at the moment.'

'She's bound to ring once she's found new digs and I'll tell her you're here recuperating. She'll be imagining the worst, lad, so I'll tell her it's just your left hand, nothing too bad.'

'I'd be grateful if you don't mention I'm here. I'll go and see her once, well, when I know what I'm going to do next.' He put the full glass down, he'd not eaten since yesterday morning and didn't want to get drunk. 'I was hoping that Ellie and I might make a match of it one day, but that's out of the question now.'

He waited for Fred to contradict him, to tell him he had his blessing to ask his daughter to marry him, but an uncomfortable silence remained.

'Thank Mabel, but I'm going to turn in.'

It was strangely difficult to stand up with only one arm, he'd no idea why this was as he'd never used his left hand to push himself to his feet. Perhaps it was a balance thing or maybe all in his mind. The pain he felt where his arm used to be was certainly imagined. The doc told him this could last a few weeks or years – he hoped it was the former.

Fred didn't call him back. Jack was on the bottom step when he reconsidered. Food was rationed, not only would it be wasteful to refuse what had been prepared for him but also impolite. Being an officer and mixing with the toffs must have rubbed off on him.

He returned to the sitting room. 'Sorry, I'm not myself at the moment. I do need to eat if I'm going to get fit again.'

'Good lad, I can hear the tray coming. Set yourself down again. I expect you'd prefer coffee, but you can't get it for love or money nowadays.'

'Anything is fine.'

He hadn't sat down as he would only have had to get up again when Mabel came in.

'Here you are, I wasn't sure what you wanted so I've brought along a bit of everything. There's cheese on toast, scones, a bit of cold beef from yesterday's roast and bubble and squeak.' Mabel beamed at him and put the tray down on the central coffee table.

'It smells delicious, you shouldn't have gone to all this trouble. I'd have been satisfied with a sandwich.'

After a few mouthfuls, he realised he was ravenous and ate more than he had in months. He'd been so busy eating he'd not paused between bites to speak. Definitely not the behaviour of an officer.

He wiped his mouth on the napkin and sat back. 'Thank you. That was excellent.'

'You're half starved, Jack love, I can't tell you how glad we are to have you back. Now you're safe we don't have to worry too much about this wretched war.' Mabel took his empty plate and handed him a second mug of tea.

'Romford has been bombed several times, people have died. We've even been down the shelter ourselves a couple of times but don't bother any more.' Her happy smile faded. 'Oh… I'd forgotten… You and Ellie were caught in a raid last time you were here. I'm so sorry…'

'It was a long time ago. Thank you so much for the food, I haven't enjoyed anything so much since I was here last. I'm hoping you'll let me stay until I've sorted out what I'm going to do next. I'll pay for my keep…'

'You'll do no such thing, lad, you're a son to us, you're family. It doesn't matter how long you stay – this is your home.'

Jack had got the hang of undressing one handed and it didn't take that much longer than it had done when he'd been able bodied. He didn't bother with pyjamas. Just being able to sleep in clean sheets knowing he wouldn't be tumbling out of bed and racing for his aircraft at any moment was great.

He half smiled in the darkness. Jimmy had said not long before the crash that he'd give his right arm to be back in Blighty. Jack had given his left arm and he still wasn't convinced the sacrifice had been worth it. A lot of the guys he'd flown with wouldn't survive until the end of the war. The mortality rate in the RAF was horrific. He must try and be glad he wasn't going to be a name on the list of fatalities.

Twenty-Nine

October 1941, Hamble

Ellie's delivery chit this morning was to take a Spit to Ternhill. She scrambled into the cockpit, buckled up and did her preflight check. The Merlin engine thrummed powerfully. She signalled she was ready to go and the chocks were pulled away. The Spitfire was nose heavy on the ground and it didn't do to overuse the brakes.

She soared into the air. Every time she flew one of these aircraft she thanked the powers that be she'd been given leave to do so. It was a joy to fly, responsive, fast and exhilarating. The first time she'd gone up she'd indulged in a little acrobatic flying but had now got over the initial excitement.

After an uneventful flight she landed perfectly at the fighter squadron base and climbed out. There was a row of pilots lounging on the grass waiting to be scrambled and they greeted her with wolf whistles and exuberant waves. She was used to this response and returned the gesture with nonchalance.

The Hamble all female ferry pool had been formed from the nucleus of experienced pilots. Veterans one might say. Every week women were added to this group having just completed the comprehensive courses at the ATA training school.

An Anson taxi dropped in to pick her up and return her to base. Amanda was waiting for her as they shared digs a mile away. They both had dilapidated bicycles as the cottage was so remote they would never have got a lift from there.

'Have you heard anything else from Jack?'

'No, he must be back but obviously doesn't want to see me. I'm going to take your advice and start going out. There's a party tomorrow night at that huge house we cycle past every day. Everyone at Hamble has been invited.' She wobbled dangerously as her wheel dropped into a rut and almost somersaulted over the handlebars. Once she was stable again she continued. 'If you're not seeing Rodney, will you come with me?'

'I was going to ask you the same thing. I wish we could put on an evening gown. It's hard to feel glamorous, even in this uniform, especially when other women will be looking so elegant.'

'I shall wear a skirt and silk stockings, that's quite elaborate enough for me.'

'Let's hope we don't have an overnight stop and miss it.'

'We both have our days off starting tomorrow evening and ops always try to get us back for that.'

Amanda hopped off her bike and leaned it drunkenly against the fence. 'We've both been stranded by bad weather, but the Met reports for the next few days are good.'

They had been fortunate to get this cottage to themselves. The owner had moved to Canada for the duration and was renting it out to ATA girls. The only drawback to this was that they had to find time to shop, do their own laundry, and prepare their meals. Someone came in once a week to clean so that was one job they didn't have to do.

As they were civilians they were as restricted by the rationing as everyone else. There was a farm at the end of the lane where they could get milk, eggs and butter, but for everything else they had to rely on the mobile shop that came to the end of the lane three times a week.

'Omelettes again tonight, Amanda, but we can have stewed apples and cream for pudding.'

It was Ellie's turn to cook this week and her friend had to do the laundry and ironing. Rotating the jobs was working well so far. She was rather enjoying the independence as it was the first time she'd had to look after herself.

Her twenty-first birthday last week had been spent delivering a Spitfire to Norfolk. There had been nothing from her estranged mother and brother George to mark the occasion. Dad and Mabel had sent her a card but no gift. Jack had forgotten but he had the excuse of having been seriously injured in the line of duty.

As none of her ATA friends even knew the date of her birthday the day had passed unnoticed so she would consider attending the party as a belated celebration. She hadn't put the card on display as she hadn't wanted to draw attention to the occasion.

Whilst washing up she changed her mind. 'Amanda, I forgot to tell you but I was twenty-one on Tuesday. I...'

'Good grief! The most important birthday in your life and you neglected to tell any of us? No wonder you want to go out tomorrow. Did your family forget?'

'No, I just didn't put the card up.'

'No present? How rotten is that?'

'I'll get it when I go home next, so the card said. I don't want a fuss made. Lots of people must have had significant birthdays but no one remarked on it, did they?'

'Well, you're probably right. Anyway, we can have a jolly good time tomorrow.'

As expected they were home in good time to get ready for the party, which in her case meant clean underwear and silk stockings.

'Ellie, you can't possibly go like that. I've decided that as we're civilians we don't have to wear our uniform when we're out if we don't want to.' Amanda held up two glamorous evening gowns. 'We're about the same size so either of these would fit you. Which one do you want to borrow?'

'The blue is beautiful, it's cut on the bias and not too low. I've got shoes that will go with it. Are you sure? What if I get wine on it?'

'Then we can get it cleaned or you can buy me a new one. Don't forget, you're a very wealthy woman now.'

She didn't want to be reminded about Greg's money. 'The money's not mine, and anyway it's tied up in investments. However, I do have quite a lot in a Post Office account if I can ever find the book.'

'I was joking. I don't give a fig if the dress is ruined as long as we both have a good time. Rodney's going to collect us. I hope you don't mind if he stays the night.'

'As your bedroom is the other side of the cottage I won't even know he's there. Just remind him there's no lock on the bathroom door.'

Her hair was long enough to put up and she'd got adept at putting in kirby grips and pins to hold it in place. She stepped into the beautiful silk gown, loving the soft slither against her bare skin. All she had in her room was a small dressing mirror so she couldn't see the full effect.

Amanda tapped on the door and came in holding a darker blue Kashmiri wrap. 'You're going to need this… Wow! You look absolutely splendid.'

'Thank you, and you look amazing too. This is the first time we've seen each other in mufti and I must say we both scrub up rather well. Burgundy is perfect with your fair colouring but I shouldn't do too much jitterbugging if you don't want an embarrassing incident.'

'It is a bit revealing, but it's my favourite evening gown. Come on, Rodders is waiting outside.'

They didn't bother to lock the cottage, the likelihood of there being any intruders was remote, and anyway they had nothing much worth stealing.

'Good evening, ladies, forgive me for not coming in to escort you but if I let this damn car stall I'll never get it started again,' a cheerful voice called from the darkness. Ellie wondered where he got petrol for his car as civilians had so few petrol rations.

The moon was no more than a silver sliver, not bright enough to see by. They found their way to the car using their torches. Once they were settled Rodney revved the engine and the car bucketed down the lane.

Ellie was thrown against the side of the car when a wheel dropped into a pothole. He drove the way he flew, fast and furious with total disregard for the circumstances. Thank God the distance was short; she was going to find herself another lift as she had no intention of travelling with him ever again. If he was dangerous now he would be lethal when he'd had a few drinks.

The sound of the revellers already at the party could be heard when they pulled up alongside a dozen or so other vehicles. They all looked black in the gloom but she was certain some of them were Bentleys, Daimlers or maybe even a Rolls-Royce.

'I'll find my own way home, Amanda, I doubt that I will want to stay as long as you do.'

'He's a shocking driver, so I don't blame you. Don't go in thinking you're going to be going home early or you won't enjoy yourself.'

Rodney joined them. 'Come along, sounds like fun in there. We could all do with a bit of that, couldn't we?'

Holding up the skirt of her gown with one hand, whilst using the tiny pinprick of light from her torch to guide her, Ellie set off for the front door leaving the other two to follow behind. The front door was ajar but like everywhere else the blackout curtains had been hung in a semicircle in front so not a smidgen of light could escape into the night.

She slipped through the gap in the curtain not sure what she was expecting. The vast hall had a dozen or so people in it. They glanced in her direction, and seeing she was of no importance, no one they recognised, they continued with their conversations and ignored her.

A year ago she would have retreated, felt out of place and embarrassed. Now things were different. She sailed across the space and walked towards the music. As she got nearer she realised it wasn't a gramophone but a live band – and a very good one at that.

The ballroom had been decorated with balloons and bunting, the band was on a dais at the far end. There was a miscellany of wooden chairs pressed up against the walls and every inch of floor space was packed with gyrating couples.

Most of the women were in evening gowns and most of the men in uniform. She scarcely had time to take it all in before she was surrounded by young men in air force blue eager to dance with her. The three closest to her were clamouring for her attention but a fourth was standing slightly to one side, staring at her through narrowed eyes.

He was a few inches taller than her, broad shouldered and solid looking. His hair was black but his eyes were a strange mix of blue and violet. Ignoring the young men begging her to dance she moved to the black haired pilot.

'Thank you, I should love to dance.'

'I wasn't aware that I had asked you, but if you insist, I'll dance with you.'

She wasn't put off by his reply as his eyes were glimmering with amusement. 'I'm Ellie Simpson, ATA ferry pilot. And you are?'

He took her hand and sort of bowed. 'Hugo Lambourne, Wing Commander, delighted to meet you.'

No wonder he had such an air of authority although he probably wasn't much older than Jack. He led her onto the floor and proceeded to guide her around with assurance. Ballroom dancing wasn't a particularly strong point in her repertoire, but with him she was able to finesse the turns and even reversed without tripping over her skirt. She wasn't sure if she was doing a quickstep, waltz or foxtrot, but whatever it was, she was able to follow his lead.

When the music stopped they clapped politely and she waited to see what he would do. 'You've just arrived.' This wasn't a question, but a statement.

'How observant of you.'

'I am known for my keen eyesight.' He was still holding her hand and she didn't dislike the sensation. 'Although only a blind man could fail to miss the arrival of the most beautiful woman here tonight.'

She couldn't prevent her laugh. 'I enjoy a compliment, Wing Commander, but that was just silly.'

His strange eyes widened and then he too, laughed. 'If I tone it down a bit, will you accept my compliment? If I say I think you're quite stunning – will that be okay?'

'Thank you. You have extraordinary eyes, I don't think I've ever seen any quite the same colour. No doubt that's why you have such keen eyesight.' The band started up again with a lively Glenn Miller number.

His smile was infectious. 'Please call me Hugo. We can't stand here and not dance, we're getting in everybody's way.'

He didn't wait for her reply but swept her away and this time she was almost certain it was a quickstep. It was certainly fast and when it ended she was breathless.

'I really need a drink, not alcohol, something like lemonade.'

'I'm not going to fetch you one as you will be snatched up by someone else if I leave you alone. Come with me to the bar.'

He must have sensed her annoyance at his tone. 'I apologise, let me rephrase that. Would you please come with me to the bar so we can both get a drink?'

'I should like to, but...'

He raised an eyebrow, which made her smile. 'But what? You don't want to be monopolised by me.'

'I came here to celebrate my majority which was last Tuesday. I didn't come here to hook up with a handsome Brylcreem boy.'

'Ouch! In which case, Ellie, we shall get a drink and then I shall introduce you to all the single chaps I know. Safety in numbers.'

The bar was set out in the dining room and not self-service. They were obliged to queue with the others. Fortunately, there was a soft drink for her and beer for him. The thought of being introduced to dozens of men didn't appeal to her.

'Actually, Hugo, I've decided I quite like you after all. There's no need to hand me round like a parcel.'

'In which case, I shall consider myself your designated escort for the evening. Do you live locally?' He grinned and then answered his own question. 'Of course you do, you're based at Hamble, aren't you?'

'I am. Are you fighter or bomber command?'

'Neither. I'm based at Gosport, coastal command.'

The squadrons in this command were tasked with protecting shipping from aerial attack and from German U-boats.

'Then I doubt that I'll be delivering anything to you.'

'We do use Spitfires, I've flown them myself. So it's possible you might come to Gosport.'

With their drinks in hand they moved aside to let others get served. She was surprised he'd not commented on the fact that she'd just reached the grand age of twenty-one. 'How old are you?' She hadn't meant to ask him something so personal, but it was too late to worry about that.

'Twenty-seven, six years older than you. I joined the RAF at eighteen, I'm a career serviceman not a volunteer. Anything else you want to know? I'm single, never been married or engaged. I'm moderately wealthy…'

She choked in her drink. 'Please, stop. I shouldn't have asked you something like that but I'm a bit conscious of age at the moment. I was the youngest in the ATA for a while, but I think there are a couple of others my age who joined recently.'

He had his arm lightly around her waist, nothing intrusive, and guided her to a large room which she thought must be the drawing room. There were various conversation groups of expensively covered chairs and sofas, all but one occupied.

'I don't know about you, but I'm hungry.' He looked at her speculatively. 'I'd be quite happy to wait here for you to fetch some food, or to do the fetching myself. Whichever you want.'

Had she come over as sort of girl who refused to be treated differently? 'I'll save the seats. I should be delighted if you would bring me something to eat.'

He put his glass of beer on the occasional table, nodded, smiled and strolled off. She was almost sure she could hear him humming to himself. He was rather attractive, charming in an authoritative sort of way and whilst she'd been flirting with him she had not thought about either Jack or Greg even once.

She hadn't been sitting long when Amanda and Rodney came over to join her. 'There you are, I was becoming anxious when I couldn't find you anywhere.'

'I've met a Wing Commander Hugo something or other, I forget what, we danced a couple of times and now he's fetching some food. Why don't you join us?'

'If you don't mind, this is the only place with spare seats.' Her friend smiled at her companion. 'Would you mind, sweetheart, finding me some food?'

Rodney nodded and sauntered off.

'Didn't take you long to get paired off with someone, Ellie. Are you inviting him back for the night?'

'Good God! Of course not. I told you, I don't believe in sex before marriage. No, that's not quite true. I would have slept with Greg before we were married because I loved him.'

'I agree, I wouldn't go to bed with anyone I didn't love.'

Ellie didn't want to enquire too closely just how many men Amanda had been in love with. 'I wish Jack had got in touch with me like he said he would. However badly he's been injured, it doesn't matter to me, but not knowing is horrible.'

'Forget about him, at least for tonight and just enjoy yourself. Will you see this Hugo chappie again if he asks?'

'I really don't know, if he asks at the end of the evening I'll decide then. It would be nice to go out occasionally to the pictures or to a theatre in London.'

Hugo arrived with two plates piled high with an assortment of items. He was smiling as he put them down and handed her a napkin and some cutlery. 'God knows what I've got you, it was the strangest buffet I've ever seen. I suppose they just had to put out whatever they could get hold of. The sandwiches are marmite and cress, I've no idea what's in the pasties but they smelt okay.'

The food was palatable and she volunteered to find them something sweet if it was available and also a tea or coffee to wash it down. She discovered slices of apple pie, no custard or cream, but it still looked delicious. To her delight there was real coffee available. There was even a pile of wooden trays so she could take everything through at the same time.

The band had stopped playing whilst the guests had supper. 'I'm going to take the plates and things back to the dining room and then find the ladies' room. I won't be long.'

Amanda smiled, Rodney was too busy eating to answer and Hugo just waved a languid hand. There was a WC in a draughty passageway but there were half a dozen other girls waiting to use it. She decided to investigate upstairs in the hope there might be another one she could use. Eventually she found the lavatory but had now been absent for twenty minutes or more. She half expected to find that her friends and her escort for the evening would have gone.

Hugo was waiting. 'I was going to send out a search party, but was far too lazy. The music's beginning again – do you want to dance or are you happy to sit and talk for a bit?'

'I'm too full to dance at the moment.' She smoothed the silk gown under her bottom and sat. 'I know quite a lot about you, in fact far more than I needed to. It seems only fair that I give you my potted biography – that's if you want me to?'

'Please, go ahead. I'm all agog.' She wasn't sure if he was teasing her or genuinely interested.

'I was engaged and about to be married but my fiancé was killed. That was last September.'

He straightened and leaned across and touched her hand. 'God, how awful for you. Is this the first time you've been out since then?'

'How could you possibly know that?'

'Two things – one, I've not seen you before and two, you looked a bit hesitant when you came in.'

'There's something else you should know just in case you were going to ask me out. I won't sleep with you and I'm not looking for another serious relationship.'

'I had no intention of asking you to, and neither am I. Now we've got that clear would you like to dance? It's one of those American jitterbugs from the sound of it.'

Thirty

As the weeks drifted past Jack became fitter and stronger both mentally and physically. By the middle of November he had even taken the tractor for a spin without too much trouble.

He returned at dusk one evening having been for a run with the dogs at his side to find Fred and Mabel waiting for him in the kitchen.

'What's wrong? Is it Ellie?'

'Not what you're thinking, son, but it is about our Ellie. We thought you ought to know that she's walking out with a Wing Commander. We know you have feelings for her, so if you want to tell her you'd better get a move on.'

This was a definite change of tune from a few weeks ago. I thought you didn't want me to be involved with her.'

'Not when you were still in a state about your arm, you're just tickety-boo now so there's nothing we'd like better than to have you marry our Ellie, but you might have missed your chance.'

'She deserves better than me, I'm not going to interfere.'

'Stuff and nonsense, son, one arm or two, you're better than any other bloke we can think of. You do still love her, don't you?'

'Of course I do, that won't ever change.'

Mabel handed him a mug of tea. 'We didn't like having to lie to our Ellie, she asked after you every time she telephoned.'

'I didn't realise. I'm sorry for putting you in that position. I've been thinking about things myself and have decided to apply to join the ATA. I'm pretty damn sure I could fly a Spit or a Hurry.'

Fred pushed back his chair and leaped to his feet. He snatched up a piece of paper that had been tucked behind a tin on the French dresser. 'We've got the number for White Waltham, Jack, that's the place you want to ring.'

He looked from one to the other and shook his head in disbelief. 'You knew I would come to this decision eventually?' He took the paper and threw his arm around Fred and gave him a hug then did the same for Mabel. 'You're my family. Whatever Ellie says that won't change. If she doesn't want me as a husband then she's stuck with me as a brother.'

He left them smiling and headed for the telephone in the passageway. The operator connected him and the girl answered the phone.

'Squadron Leader Reynolds, I want to speak to the CO.'

Using his rank had the desired effect and a few moments later a man answered. 'What can I do for you, Squadron Leader?'

'It's a courtesy rank now, sir. I was demobbed a couple of months ago. I lost my left arm in Africa, I'm right handed. I'd like to sign up for the ATA if that's possible. I was a fighter pilot.'

'By Jove, that's excellent news.' The CO chuckled. 'Not losing your arm, my boy, but you wanting to join us. How soon can you get here?'

'Tomorrow?'

'Excellent, excellent. I will arrange for a billet, some of the chaps stay at the local hostelry so I'll get you a bed there. Call in at Austin Reed in London and order your uniform – it'll take a couple of months so come in your RAF blue. Do you still have your boots, jacket, et cetera?'

'I do. A friend of mine joined the ATA last year so I know where to go for my uniform. I'll try and get a flip from Hornchurch to White Waltham.'

There was the sound of rustling paper. 'Good show! I'll give them a ring and let them know you're coming. We've got an Anson that could call in and get you if you can be there just after lunch.'

'I'll be there. Thank you, sir.'

'Enough of that sir nonsense. I'm George.'

George disconnected and Jack couldn't stop smiling. After a miserable few weeks he'd got himself sorted and would soon be flying again. Ellie was based at Hamble and he intended to visit the all female ferry pool as soon as he could borrow a kite. There was bound to be a Moth hanging about somewhere he could use.

★

Ellie was waiting in the crew room with the other women for the weather to clear. 'The rain's set in for the day, Amanda, I don't think any of us are going to be working.' She went to the hatch and spoke to the operations clerk. 'What's the Met report? Are you expecting us to fly today?'

'No, typical November weather. Tell the others they don't have to hang about here but to report back if by some miracle the cloud lifts.'

'Thanks, I'll do that.'

Ellie passed the message on and the knitting was put away, cards put back in the box and books closed with a bookmark and put on the shelf for next time.

'Why don't we see if we can catch a lift into Southampton and go to the pictures?'

'I'm going to see if I can get hold of Hugo – he's usually got access to an RAF vehicle and he could take half a dozen of us into the city.'

Amanda grabbed her elbow. 'I don't think you're being fair to him, Ellie. I'm sure he's falling in love with you and you're using him as a taxi driver and escort.'

'I really like him, but I only met him a few weeks ago and we've only been out together three times. Far too soon to be talking about love on either side. He's good fun, intelligent and handsome and that's all I want at the moment. We haven't even kissed.'

Her friend nodded but didn't seem convinced. Whilst Ellie waited her turn to use the public telephone she considered her feelings for Hugo. They got on well together but he was overfond of issuing orders and expecting her to fall in with his wishes. The fact that she was a flyer like him didn't make him view her any differently from a girl who might work in an office for a living.

In the time it took to be connected she thought about Jack. It had been weeks since his accident and he'd not been in touch with Dad or herself. If she didn't hear from him by the end of the month she would start making enquiries. Someone in the War Office must know where he was.

'I was hoping you would call me, Ellie, nothing going on here and I assume it's the same for you at Hamble. I can be there in half an hour – do you want to go into the city?'

'I was hoping you would give a group of us a lift. Then we can do something together. I think there's a good film we could go and see.'

'Hang on a minute.' The receiver clattered down and she heard him talking but couldn't catch what he said. 'Right, I'm going to requisition the lorry and bring some other chaps. I've just been told that there's a tea dance at one of the hotels. We'll do that instead. Be at the gate in forty minutes.'

He disconnected without saying goodbye. She wasn't sure she wanted to be part of a noisy crowd or attend a dance of any sort but he'd not given her an opportunity to say so.

When she announced there was a lorry full of eager RAF officers arriving shortly six other ATA girls asked if they could be included.

'That will make eight of us. It's going to be a jolly day out. Just what we all need,' one of the girls said.

She rang the gate and asked them to keep an eye out for the lorry so they could scamper down there and not keep them waiting. When the call came they were ready with their coats on and umbrellas to hand.

Hugo had said he was bringing a lorry and he hadn't been exaggerating. This was one of the vehicles used to transport pilots backwards and forwards to the dispersal area. He was driving and wound the window down. 'Come round and climb in with me, Ellie, the rest of your friends can go in the back. Won't be that comfortable, but perfectly dry.'

A young man with a ridiculous moustache and slicked back hair was climbing out of the passenger seat as she arrived. He held open the door and she scrambled in.

'Golly, this is fun. I hope you can find somewhere to park, I'm not sure where a lorry can go safely.'

Hugo smiled. 'There's a war on, my dear, I shall leave it wherever's convenient and I can assure you no one will question it.' He expertly double-declutched and the lorry rocked forward. There were squeals and shouts of laughter coming from the back, which must mean not everyone had been safely seated.

This didn't make any difference to him and he laughed and accelerated away. From the merriment in the rear no one was objecting to his behaviour – in fact, the reverse. He glanced across and winked. He really was an attractive man when he was being charming.

They lurched and swerved their way to town and as promised Hugo parked on an empty bit of kerb adjacent o the hotel in question.

'The dance isn't until this afternoon so why are we here now?'

'I rang them and they can do us a decent lunch. Then we can have a bit of sing-song around the piano.'

'That sounds splendid. Does one of your friends play?'

'I do.' He leaned across and opened the door for her. She was perfectly capable of doing this herself. She jumped down and pulled up the collar of her coat. It was tipping t down, the pavement grey and slippery.

'Now, let's get inside and out of the rain.' He grabbed her hand and ran leaving her no option but to race along beside him. They burst into the hotel foyer almost giving he ancient doorman a heart attack.

As she was shaking off the worst of the rain the others arrived and the place was pandemonium for a few minutes. There were seven or possibly eight officers and the eight girls milling about taking off overcoats and shaking them.

There was no sign of Hugo – then she saw him at the reception desk talking to a flustered woman in smart suit and scraped back hair. The woman was pointing at double doors and he nodded.

'The dining room is this way, folks, lunch will be served in half an hour.' He hadn't raised his voice but everyone apparently heard as they obediently started to troop in he direction he'd indicated.

'There seem to be about twenty of us, I hope they can cater for so many at such short notice.'

'I've booked for twenty. We are getting steak and kidney pie, seasonal vegetables – whatever they might be – and apple crumble and custard. Hardly gourmet, but it will be perfectly edible I can assure you.'

'Sounds delicious. It's too long since I had a home cooked meal, if you know what I mean. What I'd really like is coffee. I don't suppose they have any, do they?'

He'd allowed everyone else to go in before him and they were already taking their places at the table, even though the meal wasn't due for a while. The first thing she noticed was the wonderful aroma of freshly brewed coffee. Two large Georgian silver jugs stood in pride of place on the sideboard. There were also porcelain cups and saucers, sugar lumps with silver tongs and two further silver jugs one of milk, the other of cream.

'I take it we help ourselves? I'm not going to wait to be served,' she said and walked briskly to the sideboard. From the noise around the table one would have thought alcohol was involved, but as far as she was aware no one had been drinking. Another loud burst of laughter made her turn her head.

One of the officers was handing round a hip flask. This accounted for the jollity and she didn't blame them. They risked their lives every day they flew and deserved to get tiddly whenever they wanted.

Her oldest brother, Neil, had taught her how to whistle using two fingers in her mouth. She did so now and it had the desired effect. A stunned silence fell and every head turned to stare at her.

'Now I have your attention, ladies and gentlemen, there's real coffee and decent tea here. I'm not waiting on you – you must come and help yourselves.'

Hugo strolled up beside her laughing openly. 'That was magnificent, Ellie, you must show me how to do it, it might well come in useful later on.' He helped himself to coffee and like her, had no cream or sugar.

He nodded towards the grand piano that stood at the far end of the room. 'I'll play something soothing, calm them down a bit before we eat. Do you sing?'

'Not at all, but I'll join in anyway.' She drained a cup and hastily refilled it as the other guests came across to help themselves.

She perched on the windowsill to listen. Hugo played like a concert pianist. Soon the entire room was silent listening to him in appreciation. She wasn't sure what he played, possibly Mozart or Bach, whatever it was, it was quite beautiful.

The food arrived and tasted almost as good as Mabel's cooking. When they were offered second helpings everybody held up their plate. The apple pie was equally delicious and the custard was homemade, not out of a tin.

When someone got out a packet of cigarettes after the meal Hugo intervened. 'In the foyer, Billy old chap, not everyone enjoys the smell of cigarettes.'

The officer he'd addressed nodded, gave a facsimile of a salute, and wandered amiably out of the room. Several others followed suit. She was certain Hugo had done this for her as he knew she didn't like the blue fug that filled the room when there were a lot of people smoking.

The coffee pots had been refilled but not the tea. As she was pouring herself a cup he joined her. 'Do one for me too, my dear, it's the perfect end to an excellent meal.'

'We should have asked before we sat down, but how much is this costing? Are you going to pass the hat around or something?'

He looked shocked. 'You are our guests. No question that any of you ATA girls are paying.'

'In which case you must let us pay for this afternoon's tea dance.' Something flashed in his eyes and she was sure she'd annoyed him. 'Don't look so cross, we earn as much as you do. In fact, I think we are the only profession in which men and women are paid the same amount. Either we split both bills or you let us pay for the tea dance.'

'I don't expect a girl to pay when I invite them out.'

'But you didn't invite us, we invited you. Don't be so stuffy. I'm not going to discuss it any further. Are you going to play something we can sing along to? I'm pretty sure that Pamela can play if you don't want to.'

He nodded and half smiled. 'Thoroughly routed, and I deserved it. We will take care of the meal; you girls pay for the tea.'

'Do you know how much it costs per head?'

'Five shillings – that includes afternoon tea as well as the dancing. It's a pity you are wearing your uniform trousers instead of your skirts. I do love to see a pretty pair of legs whirling around the dance floor.'

'Shall I suggest that we roll them up to the knees? We wouldn't want to disappoint the boys in blue.'

He raised his cup in salute and strolled off to the piano. The dance didn't start until three o'clock – another hour at least. This would mean they would be driving back in the blackout, in the rain, in the winter. For some reason she really didn't care. This was the most enjoyable day she'd had since Greg had died and she wanted it to last as long as possible.

Thirty-One

Jack called in at Austin Reed to be measured for his new uniform. 'I understand it will take several weeks to complete.'

'No, sir, you're in luck. We've just had a delivery of material and can get it done immediately. If you don't require a second fitting we can have it sent to you at the end of next week wherever you're going to be based.'

'White Waltham, as far as I know. Yes, please parcel it up and send it to me there.'

The assistant took all the usual measurements and then stopped. 'I would suggest, Squadron Leader Reynolds, that you have the arm of your left sleeve made shorter. I think you would find that easier to manage.'

'Good idea, I hadn't thought of that. Can you do the same with the shirts?'

'It will be done. I remember that you came in here with your young lady when she joined the ATA a while ago. It's a pleasure to be taking care of you now, sir.'

Jack didn't correct the assumption that he was Ellie's young man – he hoped he would be when he eventually aw her again. He would wait until he had his uniform as t was going to be done so speedily.

He left the shop feeling better than he had since God knows when. He was going to be doing something useful again, not spend the remainder of the war on the scrapheap like some other poor sods he knew.

When he arrived at the gate at Hornchurch he was waved past, didn't even have to identify himself. His empty sleeve was quite visible, but he was still in the uniform and the insignia of his rank was quite clear.

He reported to the adjutant and was greeted like an old friend even though he'd never been there before. 'You're in luck, there are a couple of ATA girls waiting for the Anson to drop in and collect them. It's going to Hamble first and then onto White Waltham.'

'Bit of a detour from here to Southampton and then back to Oxford.'

'Piece of cake for these chaps. The Anson is wanted at Waltham tomorrow so makes sense to do it that way.'

'Great, where should I wait?' Was it possible one of the girls could be Ellie? This wasn't how he'd intended their first meeting to be, but half of him hoped it was her and the other half that it wasn't.

'In the Officers' Mess. They wait in there.'

'You don't happen to know their names, do you? I know some of the ATA pilots.'

'I'm hopeless with names, but one is a petite blonde and the other a redhead. Does that help?'

'It does, thank you, neither of them sounds familiar.'

He decided it might be wiser not to mix with them as they might mention they had spent time with a red headed, one armed, squadron leader who was joining the ATA himself. Ellie would immediately recognise the description and he would rather see her face to face so he could gauge her reaction to his disability.

He wandered outside and the first thing he saw was the red, white and blue bicycle Ellie had painted for Greg the Christmas before last. He had one, painted red and black that he'd abandoned at Kenley.

Having a bicycle would make life so much easier and he decided to bring Neil's with him when he went. He was amazed the bike was still there and functioning. He hefted it up with his one hand, and then swung his leg over the crossbar.

Cycling with a kitbag across your back was precarious but after wobbling dangerously for a few yards he got the hang of it. He pedalled around the apron until he spotted the Anson coming into land. These kites were used as taxis to take the ATA pilots back and forth and save them having to endure the horrors of the trains.

An erk lifted the cycle into the aircraft for him. He could have done it himself, but the ground engineer was eager to help and he didn't like to stop him. This meant he was safely installed at the rear of the plane when the two girls scrambled in.

They stopped to collect another girl and two blokes and then flew directly to Hamble. The two guys remained where they were.

'What's the next stop?' He yelled over the engine noise

'Waltham.'

'Great. That's where I'm going.'

This time the two middle aged ATA men manhandled his bicycle out of the Anson. They waited for him to join them on the tarmac. 'Are you joining us here? Simon Billings, and this is Frank Rhodes.'

'Jack Reynolds. This bicycle belonged to a good friend of mine who went for a Burton last year. I'm going to be billeted at the pub and thought this might be handy for getting backwards and forwards.'

'Like bloody gold dust, old man, but at least no one can claim it as theirs.'

Frank wheeled the bike for him and on the walk to the office he gave them a potted version of his flying history up until that point.

'Ah! That explains why you sound a bit like a Yank,' Simon said. 'A colourful history, but I think there are one or two chaps who can outdo that.'

They left him to find his own way into the administration block. He'd learned they were both married and lived locally. Whether this was fortuitous, or they'd moved their families here for convenience, he'd no idea.

After filling in a dozen or so forms he was officially a member of the ATA. He was told to report at eight o'clock the following morning. The ATA now ran an excellent training programme at this pool and he was going to be put through his paces.

He thought he would just be flying fighters, but they thought he might eventually be able to manage a Mosquito, an Anson, and possibly one of the smaller bombers like a

Beaufighter or a Blenheim. Unless he had someone with him he wouldn't be able to do that one handed. He was to return for further instruction after he proved himself delivering Hurricanes and Spitfires. He was so pleased with his progress that he began to believe he could fly anything, even a four engine kite as long as he had a flight engineer with him to raise and lower the undercarriage and put the flaps down when needed.

The two days he spent doing circuits and bumps proved he was more than capable of ferrying whatever aircraft was put his way. He was added to the roster. He had had a flight suit issued to him but had his own jacket, helmet, goggles and boots.

He had been studying the handling notes every ATA pilot was issued with, making sure he knew as much as he could about any of the kites he was going to be asked to ferry. He'd been assured there would be someone with him if needed, but not necessarily an engineer, it could possibly be an air cadet. He was fine with that. Initially he would remain at White Waltham, but could possibly be moved elsewhere at a later date.

Not only would he have to collect aircraft from factories, he would also have to take them to the maintenance units, known as Mus, where they would be fitted out with the armaments, radios or have other fine adjustments.

His billet at the pub was adequate, not as good as his quarters at Kenley, but a damn sight better than living in a tent in the desert. He didn't have an orderly to take care of his laundry – something he could no longer do for himself even if he wanted to.

There were three other guys living where he was and they were more interested in the beer than they were in the comfort of their rooms. He managed to waylay the landlady.

'Mrs Dawson, would it be possible for me to pay extra to have my laundry taken care of?'

'Go along with you, Jack, it'll not cost you a penny. The least I can do for a brave boy who's lost his arm protecting us.'

'Thank you, but I don't want to be treated any differently. Please add it to my bar bill and I'll settle up at the end of every week.'

'Right you are, just leave it in the hamper by your door. Will you be getting the navy blue uniform?'

'Hopefully, by the end of next week. I enjoyed the spam fritters tonight, very tasty.'

She beamed and he left her polishing the glasses and joined the men he would be working with in future in a noisy game of darts. One of the blokes was deaf in one ear, the other two wore glasses so hadn't been A1 and therefore not suitable to join the RAF. They had all been civilian pilots and were about his age.

He was first down to breakfast the next day and Mrs D's daughter, a pretty little girl of about ten or eleven, giggled when he came in.

'Good morning, Mr Reynolds, you're ever so early so you'll get hot toast and fresh tea. It's porridge today – do you want any?'

'No, toast and tea will be fine, thank you.' The Daily Express was neatly folded in the centre of the breakfast table. He would be able to read it first today.

He was shocked to see it was a Saturday, and the last one in November. He'd wondered why the child was there this morning as he'd not seen her before. The headlines were about the Battle of Moscow. German Panzers were on the outskirts of the city. He was pleased to see that the last of the Italian Armed Forces in East Africa had surrendered.

It seemed as if the war was nothing to do with him now, that it was up to the serving members of the Armed Forces to save the United Kingdom from extinction. The army that had been evacuated from Dunkirk was still based in camps all over the country and would only be called into action if Hitler changed his mind and decided to invade. The Royal Navy was protecting the seas and the RAF the sky.

He didn't want to make small talk this morning, he was unexpectedly nervous about his first ferrying job. The three blokes walked the two miles every morning, but he had Neil's cycle.

With his greatcoat flapping, a scarf tied around his face and his gloves on, he pedalled slowly to White Waltham pool. He was ridiculously early and only the cleaners were there.

'Morning, sir, we'll be out of your way in a minute,' one of the ladies called out cheerily.

He busied himself filling the tea urn, washing up the dirty mugs and tidying the crew room. He could do most things for himself but preferred not to be watched whilst he did them. The admin staff arrived first and were delighted to be offered a cuppa.

The telephone rang stridently at half past seven. He'd visited the gents' several times and was relieved when the others began to arrive. The chalkboard appeared and he saw his name three from the top. He was collecting a Hurricane and delivering it to Kenley. This would be easy enough as he knew the route and the base.

He collected the paperwork and was about to head out when George called him into the office. 'You're going to be busy today, Jack. You'll collect a badly damaged Hurricane and take it to be repaired. It could be an exciting flight. I've no idea exactly what doesn't work on the kite.'

'Sounds good to me. I can't wait to get going.'

'You'll be given the paperwork for your third delivery – I'm not sure exactly where you'll be taking the aircraft. It could be anywhere in the country so remember to take your overnight bag.'

'Sod it. I'll remember next time.'

'Good luck, my boy, not that you need it. From what I heard from your instructors you're a natural, one arm or two will make no difference to your efficiency. It's your fitness we're testing not your flying ability. It was only a few weeks ago you lost your arm and we don't want to overtax you.'

He stiffened. 'I don't want special treatment...'

'You're not getting it. We've had several injured RAF pilots join us and this is standard procedure. Complete your thirteen days without mishap and I'll consider sending you back to get the hang of the twin engine aircraft.'

'Fair enough.' There wasn't anything else to say and Jack strode off to get himself suitably dressed. Getting in and out of a flight suit with only one hand had proved tricky initially, but he'd discovered he could use his other arm like a lever or a hook which made things simpler.

He didn't linger at Kenley, didn't want to see anyone he knew, he just signed the paperwork and climbed into the damaged Hurry.

The engine was fine, there were just large holes in the fuselage and one wing. He'd flown with worse and arrived safely at the Mus. His next ferrying job was to Debden in Suffolk. He was going to be away overnight and didn't even have his shaving kit with him. He was going to look like a vagrant tomorrow morning as his beard grew ferociously. Being a redhead also didn't help.

The days literally flew past and he was loving every minute of it. He'd thought he would miss the excitement of sorties, scrambles and dogfights but just being in the air was enough. He slotted into the routine with ease and no one offered to help him do anything any more; they all understood he was quite capable of doing things for himself.

On Monday, 8th December he reported early as usual. There was a large parcel waiting for him in the crew room – his uniform had arrived ahead of time. He snatched it up and took it into the locker room and changed. The cut and cloth were superb, he felt a million dollars. His discarded RAF blue was rammed into his locker and then he headed back to the crew room.

The room was packed but silent. George had been speaking to them. From his face, he'd been giving them grave news. Jack waited quietly until the CO left and then turned to the man standing next to him. 'What's happened? What have I missed?'

'The Japs have bombed the Yanks at Pearl Harbour. No warning, just attacked and thousands of sailors have been killed and most of the fleet destroyed. The US has declared war on Japan. They'll be fighting beside us soon. About bloody time, is all I can say.'

There was a murmur of agreement around the room. Britain had been fighting the war on her own for too long. Whatever the reason, he would be glad the Yanks were finally joining in. With the might of the US Army, Navy and Air Force alongside, Germany could be defeated.

Thirty-Two

'Have you heard the news?' Amanda asked Ellie as she sat down to eat a leisurely breakfast on her second rest day.

'No, I couldn't hear the wireless upstairs. What's happened? You look shocked.'

'The Japanese attacked the Americans at Pearl Harbour two days ago. They didn't give any warning. Those poor sailors – thousands of them have been killed and half the American fleet destroyed.'

'How absolutely dreadful. Although, to be honest, I'm not surprised. From what I've been reading things have been on the brink in the Pacific for months. I suppose this means that the President will finally agree to help us fight the Germans. It shouldn't have taken him so long to come to our aid.'

'They have been sending us armaments and so on and the government doesn't have to pay until the end of the war. I expect we'll be overrun with Yanks in the New Year.'

'You say that as if you don't like them. I've met quite a few American girls who have joined the ATA. They seem very nice. My friend Jack spent four years out there with a flying circus and he really liked the country and the people, so they can't be all bad.'

Ellie scraped a little butter onto the toast and added a thin layer of marmalade. This had come from Glebe Farm the last time she'd visited. 'Are you going home for Christmas or are you spending it with Rodney? I worked last year, but this year my days off are Christmas Day and Boxing Day, which is a bit of luck.'

'I'm going to spend it with his parents. They're having a bit of a house party so it should be very jolly and I'll get a chance to wear pretty frocks for a change. I shall also be able to hunt.'

'Mabel said in her last letter that there's nothing in the shops, no toys for the kiddies, no decorations or cards, and precious little extras for the Christmas table. It must be so hard for families.'

'Imagine if you'd been bombed out and lost everything. Doesn't bear thinking of – we're the lucky ones.' Amanda poured them both a second cup of tea. 'I thought you and Hugo got on really well the other day in Southampton. Why haven't you seen him again?'

'Because he hasn't asked me to. I let him kiss me and I think now he thinks I'm a bit cheap. He's certainly not been in touch since then.'

'Are you disappointed or relieved? He is absolutely gorgeous, you know, most of the single girls would be only too happy to take your place.'

'I'm not altogether sure how I feel about him at all. I enjoyed kissing him, as you say, he is very attractive, but he's a bit bossy. I've got used to making my own decisions, running my own life, and I'm not prepared to become someone's stay-at-home wife which is what he wants, I think.'

Amanda slopped her tea onto the tablecloth. 'Good God! I didn't know you'd got around to talking about marriage. I'm sleeping with Rodney and we carefully avoid mentioning the subject at all.'

'We haven't talked about it. It's just something I've picked up from things he said and the way he treats me. He's rather old fashioned and thinks all women should be protected, cared for and guided by their husbands.'

'In which case, he's not the man for you. You're not the sort of girl to go to bed with him if you're not engaged, so what's the point of carrying on the relationship?'

'There's more to going out with someone than sex. Not that I'm an expert on the subject, as you are.'

Her friend laughed at the dig. 'I'm afraid you're right. We upper crust girls take a more relaxed attitude than you do. Remember how casual Elizabeth was with her favours?'

'I sometimes regret what you did...'

'Don't, she married the father of the child. He is not as rich as Greg was, but she'll not go hungry and neither will the baby. It's a pity she didn't...' Amanda turned an unbecoming shade of beetroot. 'I'm sorry, that was tactless of me. But whilst we're on the subject there's something I've been wanting to ask you. Have you decided what you're going to do with your inheritance?'

'I'm sure I told you I intend to set up a scholarship of some sort in Greg's name when the war's over.'

'Yes, you did, but I was hoping you might have reconsidered. He wanted you to have his money not some strangers. Don't make any rash decisions.'

There was the sound of someone crunching up the path. There'd been a heavy frost last night and everywhere was silvered which made the visitor's footsteps more audible than usual. There was a loud bang on the door.

Neither of them was dressed. She was in her scruffy dressing gown, winceyette pyjamas and her hair was hanging in a tangle of curls halfway down her back. Amanda didn't go in for such utilitarian nightwear so at least she was looking pretty in an expensive matching nightgown and robe. As she had short hair she looked fairly presentable.

'You'd better see who it is. I'm going to make myself scarce.'

The kitchen was at the back of the cottage on the left, on the right was the scullery, larder and laundry room. A narrow passageway divided the house and there was a little used front parlour on the right and a more comfortable sitting room on the left. Unfortunately, she would have to go past the front door in order to go upstairs.

'Hide in the sitting room and I'll bring whoever it is into the kitchen. Then you can nip up and get dressed.'

Amanda waited until Ellie was safely hidden before pulling back the bolt and opening the door.

'Hi there, I'm not sure if you remember me...'

Ellie forgot she was inappropriately dressed and flew from the sitting room into Jack's embrace. 'Where have you been? I've been so worried about you. Come in, don't stand on the doorstep.' Only then did she notice he only had one arm. His other was around her waist. 'Have you been hiding from me because of this? I thought you must be horribly disfigured, mutilated or something, not just lost half an arm.'

She was pulled closer. His mouth closed over hers in a kiss that said everything it should. He was her Jack, he was back and she wasn't going to let him go again.

There was something very familiar about the coat she had been pressed against. She looked down and couldn' restrain her shout of excitement.

'You've joined the ATA. So that's why you waited until now to come and find me.'

They were alone in the icy passageway and she took his arm and bundled him into the sitting room, always warm as they lit a fire every evening.

'You look as beautiful as ever, Ellie. I love your hair long, it really suits you.'

'You're a lot thinner than when I saw you last, but not as bad as I thought you might be. How long have you been with us?'

He shrugged off his coat and draped it over the back of the chair before answering. 'Several weeks, I stayed at Glebe Farm to recuperate and then applied to join you. I've just completed my first thirteen days.'

The overwhelming joy she'd experienced when she'd first seen him was trickling away. Why hadn't her parents told her he was staying there?

He sensed her change of mood. 'Sweetheart, it's not their fault. I asked them not to tell you. Don't let's spoil today with recriminations.'

'You're right. Go into the kitchen and get yourself something to eat and drink whilst I go and get dressed. I've got to be back at work tomorrow, but I've got the rest of today. I can't tell you how happy I am to see you after all this time.'

He returned her smile. But it wasn't only his left hand he'd lost, he'd lost the sparkle from his eyes. She'd known immediately when he kissed her that things would be different between them now. They'd both changed. She didn't think of him like a brother any more, and if his kiss was anything to go by he certainly didn't view her as a sister.

As she clattered up the uncarpeted staircase to her bedroom she fleetingly thought of Hugo. She scarcely knew him, had made no commitments. As far as she was concerned, she was free to pursue whatever happened between her and Jack.

Hello from Aria

We hope you enjoyed this book! Let us know, we'd love to hear from you.

We are Aria, a dynamic digital-first fiction imprint from award-winning independent publishers Head of Zeus. At heart, we're avid readers committed to publishing exactly the kind of books we love to read – from romance and sagas to crime, thrillers and historical adventures. Visit us online and discover a community of like-minded fiction fans!

We're also on the look out for tomorrow's superstar authors. So, if you're a budding writer looking for a publisher, we'd love to hear from you. You can submit your book online at ariafiction.com/we-want-read-your-book

You can find us at:
Email: aria@headofzeus.com
Website: www.ariafiction.com
Submissions: www.ariafiction.com/we-want-read-your-book
Facebook: @ariafiction
Twitter: @Aria_Fiction
Instagram: @ariafiction

Printed in Great Britain
by Amazon